Annie Emma A. Challice

Heroes, Philosophers, and Courtiers of the time of Louis 16

In two volumes. Vol. 1

SALZWASSER VERLAG

Annie Emma A. Challice

Heroes, Philosophers, and Courtiers of the time of Louis 16

In two volumes. Vol. 1

Reprint of the original, first published in 1863.

1st Edition 2022 | ISBN: 978-3-37500-715-7

Verlag (Publisher): Salzwasser Verlag GmbH, Zeilweg 44, 60439 Frankfurt, Deutschland
Vertretungsberechtigt (Authorized to represent): E. Roepke, Zeilweg 44, 60439 Frankfurt, Deutschland
Druck (Print): Books on Demand GmbH, In de Tarpen 42, 22848 Norderstedt, Deutschland

HEROES,

PHILOSOPHERS, AND COURTIERS.

VOL. I.

HEROES,

PHILOSOPHERS, AND COURTIERS

OF

THE TIME OF LOUIS XVI.

BY

THE AUTHOR OF

THE SECRET HISTORY OF THE COURT OF FRANCE
UNDER LOUIS XV.

IN TWO VOLUMES.

VOL. I.

LONDON

1863.

PREFACE.

"HISTORY," said M. Rollin, "is the book of Kings." It ought not less to be the book of Peoples. The history of the American Rebellion against the Crown of England,—of the contest of Right against Might in the New World, and of the time when young Democracy was about to spring from corrupt Feudalism in the Old World,—is peculiarly the book of Kings and Peoples too. It is the history of a war between France and England, and of facts which drew together, in grotesque contrast, the most distant and different members of the human family,—the courtiers of

Versailles, and the savage tribes of North America.

A complete narrative of the intervention of France in the American Rebellion has never yet been written from French contemporary sources. Little has been remembered, little is generally known, but the names of some of those brave Frenchmen by whose aid it was that America achieved her liberty. France herself, too soon interested and absorbed in the events of her own momentous Revolution —which was precipitated by French sympathy with American Rebellion—appears well-nigh to have forgotten these men. It was no part of England's duty to immortalize the actions of her too successful enemies. America was too much occupied in her cities and fields, repairing the wastes of the recent war, to analyze the sources of French sympathy to which she mainly owed her independence.

A part, therefore, of the object of the

present work is to supply, in some measure, an admitted deficiency. It has been, moreover, the endeavour of the Author to place some of the last century records of France, and England, and America, within the reach of all in any of those countries whose leisure demands amusement rather than laborious research; whilst, by permitting each man to speak for himself—hero, philosopher, courtier, statesman, or savage, it is hoped, at least, that the imputation of partiality may be avoided.

In tracing the course of events which led to French intervention in the affairs of America, the earlier period of the reign of Louis XVI. and of Marie Antoinette is necessarily enlarged upon. Those in the confidence and constant society of this ill-fated King and Queen, may show, in this narrative, how, even in the first years of their reign, they were the tools of party and the victims of necessity, in an age of transition from old things to new.

The American question was the touchstone by which Voltaire's and Rousseau's doctrines were tested in France. It is, therefore, as the leaders of French opinion that Voltaire and Rousseau find a large place in this narrative.

During the twenty years which had elapsed since France lost Canada,* the pens of these men had assailed abuses in Church and State, and had exposed the iniquity of Might when opposed to Right. The people of France, deeply imbued with the doctrines of Voltaire and Rousseau, were eager to embrace the cause of Liberty in America.

The Cabinet of France was prompted to espouse that cause by the hope of thereby

* During the Seven Years' War, when England was allied with Prussia, in which country the people now (in 1863) propose to celebrate the Hundredth Anniversary of the Peace which concluded that war.

redeeming Canada, or at all events of retaliating the past policy of William Pitt (which had robbed France of Canada), by depriving the Crown of England of its dependencies in North America.

By a curious coincidence, Voltaire, Rousseau, and Pitt (first Lord Chatham), died within three months of each other in the same year that France had openly declared her alliance with America.

The account herein contained of Pitt's acquaintance with Dr. Benjamin Franklin, and the narratives of the last days and deaths of Voltaire and Rousseau, are derived entirely from French contemporary sources. Nor, whilst Philosophers are admitted, are Charlatans excluded from these volumes. Cagliostro himself may therein help to show how, as reverence for religion slowly decreased, credulity and superstition rapidly increased in France during the last century.

It is hoped that this work, though not presuming to usurp the place of existing histories of the period it embraces, may not be unwelcome, as linking together some circumstances which, though important in their results, seem to have been overlooked by professed historians, who have also told but little of the private lives, and characters, and motives of some personages who find a place in these pages.

The Author does not presume to determine who were right and who were wrong in the conflict of countries, creeds, and opinions, to which the American question of the last century gave rise. That question has yet to be determined; but its history from the French point of view, if possibly throwing light on the present aspect of affairs in England, France, and America, may be not only of local but of European interest; and, at all events, it naturally suggests that the Liberty which the best and the bravest men of France helped America to win, ought not to be wasted, as now, in civil strife and bloodshed.

Such was the reflection of America herself in the eighteenth century ;—witness two popular toasts of George Washington's soldiers:

"May our love of Liberty be shown in the virtuous use of it!"

"Peace, Liberty, and Happiness to the whole world!"

HEROES,

PHILOSOPHERS, AND COURTIERS

OF THE TIME OF

LOUIS XVI.

CHAPTER I.

Louis XV. on his death-bed—The King's Confession—Madame du Barry—The King's Monologue—Marie Antoinette, the Dauphiness—The Dauphin's Aunts—Political Alliance between France and Austria—Position of the Dauphiness at Versailles—Letter of the Queen-Empress, Maria Theresa, to the Dauphin on his marriage—The Dauphin's brothers—The Dauphin's charity—Political disunion in the Royal Family of France—"Vive le Roy!" The new King and the new Queen—General aspect of affairs in France, A.D. 1774—The dawn of Revolutions—Contemporary chronicles of Madame du Barry, of the Duc d'Aiguillon, of Chancellor Maupeou, and of the Abbé Terray—The Princess Louise (Nun of St. Denis)—Letter of Pope Clement XIV. to her—Burial of Louis XV.—The new and the old nobility of France in 1774—Court Portraits of that time—The f [illegible] Louis XVI.—

The first act of Queen Marie Antoinette—Madame du Barry "at home"—The Abbé Terray, Finance Comptroller of Louis XV.—Turgot, Finance Comptroller of Louis XVI.—Malesherbes—The Church in France, 1774-5—The Queen of France, 1774-5—Courtiers' debts in France, 1774-5—Pamphlets in France, 1774-5—Coronation of King Louis XVI.—Voltaire in 1774-5—Mirabeau in 1774-5—Biographical sketch of Mirabeau—Royal Allegories of 1774-5—Recall of the Duc de Choiseul to Court—Position of William Pitt (Lord Chatham) in 1774-5—Growing signs of Rebellion in America, 1774-5—Contemporary Chronicles of Political Parties at Versailles, 1775—Recall of the Ancient Parliament to Paris—Popularity of Louis XVI. and of Marie Antoinette—Aspect of affairs in America, 1775—John St. John's Address to the House of Commons on behalf of the Crown—Parliamentary promises in England, 1775.

In the month of May, 1774, Louis XV. lay dying of the small-pox at Versailles. In the month of May, thirty years before, almost to a day, Louis XV. had ridden forth to the war against England and Austria—the "well-beloved" hero of his people.

The statue in the centre of the Place Louis XV., in Paris, represented the King as he was in those days; it was called the *chef d'œuvre* of love and art, for it had been designed by Madame de Pompadour and executed by Pigalle the sculptor; but it bore no resemblance to the man who now, worn out with sinful self-indulgence, lay dying at Versailles.

All the courtiers were in consternation. They dreaded to approach the King, for fear of their lives and beauty, but they dared not fly from the infected atmosphere, lest, should his majesty recover, they might be leaving all hope of future favour behind them.

The King confessed to the Cardinal de la Roche Aymon: "I am sorry to have caused scandal to my subjects. To God alone have I to render an account of my conduct; but, if I live, I will live henceforth for the welfare of my people, and as an example to them of pure faith and practical religion."*

Madame du Barry, the King's favourite, would fain have nursed him in his illness; but (as in the case of Madame de Châteauroux, just thirty years before) the priests demanded that she should absent herself from his majesty before he was confessed and absolved.

Madame du Barry, therefore, withdrew to the

* Discours du Cardinal de la Roche. Aymon. Paris, 1780.

estate of the Duc d'Aiguillon,* her friend, and the King's chief Minister of State; and the courtiers at Versailles were still further perplexed by her absence; for she required constant news of the monarch's health, and those about him, not knowing whether he was going to live or to die, feared either to give or to withhold that news. By attention to Madame du Barry they compromised themselves with the Dauphiness, (Marie Antoinette) who now any hour might be Queen; and by neglect of Madame du Barry they compromised themselves with the first Minister, the Duc d'Aiguillon, and with the favourite herself, who, in the event of the King's recovery, would certainly be recalled, as Madame de Pompadour had been in 1757, after having been dismissed in that year, when his majesty was supposed to be dying from the wound inflicted on him by Damiens, the would-be regicide.†

Louis XV. was prematurely infirm. Naturally of a gloomy disposition, he had, for the last

* The Duc d'Aiguillon who, in 1770, had succeeded the Duc de Choiseul in the ministry, and who, in 1758, had commanded the troops of Brittany against the English.

† Secret History of the Court of France under Louis XV. Vol. ii. p. 161. London, 1861.

thirty-five years, sought a refuge from ennui in pleasure. Pleasure had degenerated into debauchery, and debauchery had produced satiety.

Louis XV. was weary of life, but he dreaded death. To one in the daily confidence of the Duc d'Aumont (first gentleman of his Chamber) we are indebted for the following picture of Louis XV. in his later years; a picture taken of him when he thought that no human eye beheld him: for the narrator was invisible, having lain down to rest on a sofa, and covered himself with his cloak, at night-time, in an ante-room of the Duc d'Aumont's apartments at Versailles.—"I was awakened by the noise of a door opening. I raised my head and saw Louis XV. At first he looked round the ante-chamber, here and there. The lights in the chandeliers were burning low. 'There is nobody here,' said the King; and then he began to walk up and down, sighing and murmuring, in the tone of a man who has drunk himself sad. Presently he paused before a large mirror, and, after having considered himself a long time in it, he pressed his hands on his forehead, his cheeks, his chin, and thus apostrophized himself: 'Miserable wretch that thou art! Murderer of thine own soul and body!' Then his pacing up and down, his groans, his sad monologue recommenced. At last he stopped again before the glass. 'Thou wilt not die old,' said he to his own image reflected there; 'not threescore years and ten!—And hell!—hell!' Five minutes passed whilst he stood looking at himself with horror. And then he muttered, 'France! How is she governed?' Afterwards: 'But this supper to-night they say will be delicious—though all is weary—weary! Why cannot they give me something new?'"

Marie Antoinette, the Dauphiness, was tenderly regarded by Louis XV.; her youth and freshness, from the moment of her first appearance at the French Court, had attracted and amused him.

She, therefore, was an object of jealousy to his mistress, Madame du Barry, to whom this daughter of Maria Theresa gave additional offence soon after her arrival in France, by openly manifesting her indignation at being compelled, by French custom then prevalent at Versailles, to endure the presence and to submit to the society of the courtisane who reigned there.

The aunts of the Dauphin, who as unblushingly

exhibited their sanctity as Madame du Barry did her sin, were also violently opposed to Marie Antoinette.

Austria was an object of traditional abhorrence to these French Princesses. The union of blood between France and Austria, in 1770, by the Dauphin's marriage, was the consequence of the political alliance between those countries in 1756, when, after more than 200 years of sanguinary discord, they combined against England and Prussia. France attributes the Seven Years' War, which then began, to England's transatlantic aggression on French boundaries: be that as it may, certain it is, that in the course of that war France lost, and England won, Canada. Since that time the burthen of taxation in France had much increased. At the period of the Dauphin's marriage the people were still groaning beneath the consequences of the Seven Years' War, and the bride, an Austrian Princess, was not welcome to them.

But the Dauphin's aunts had special, not to say spiritual, reasons for regarding this marriage with aversion.

The political alliance between France and Austria, in 1755-6, had been achieved by the Duc de Choiseul, Minister of France, and by Madame de Pompadour, who then held the reins of government; and therefore the Queen of France and her son (both since dead), and these, the King's daughters, regarded that alliance with aversion, as the work of the man and the woman—the one a "philosopher" and the other a "parvenue," who had succeeded in crushing the temporal power of the Jesuits, to whom they, French Princesses born, were spiritually affiliated.

In the person of the Dauphiness, Marie Antoinette, they beheld the living representative of the political alliance which had long been hateful to them.

Besides, by this marriage their own hopes of power over the Dauphin, their nephew, the future King of France, were shaken; and they took every means to prevent the ascendancy of the young wife over the young husband. Thus, women at Versailles, the chief saints and the chief sinner, were combined together against the daughter of Maria Theresa.

From the period of her marriage,* four years before the time when Louis XV. lay dying of the

* Appendix A.

small-pox at Versailles, the Dauphiness had found herself involved in machinations, of which she was too young and innocent to guess the secret springs. Although then scarcely more than a child in years, a malignant destiny already overshadowed her.

The Abbé de Vermond, her tutor, who had accompanied her from Austria to France, was not a good adviser to the Dauphiness. His experience in courts was too recent for such a trust, especially in the court of Versailles, traditionally opposed to the court of Vienna, which had raised him from obscurity, and to which he was exclusively devoted. In the early days of her marriage, Marie Antoinette's letters to Vienna passed through the hands of the Abbé. She was by nature frank, and by maternal education fearless; by youth fond of pleasure, and impatient of old régime French court restraints. The Abbé de Vermond derided the etiquette of the House of Bourbon. This was an offence to the Duc de la Vauguyon, the Dauphin's tutor, and the protégé of the Dauphin's aunts. The Abbé de Vermond was suspected by them of playing politically into the hands of Austria; and his pupil, the future Queen of France, who openly expressed her antipathy to some old French customs, was suspected of correspondence treasonable to the country of her adoption. At least, the Dauphin's aunts and the Dauphin's tutor endeavoured to instil this suspicion into the Dauphin's mind. And, seemingly, with effect; for during the first four years of his married life, the future Louis XVI. manifested an indifference, amounting to aversion, towards the Austrian Princess who was, in after times, the Queen of his idolatry.

He was only sixteen years of age at the period of his marriage with Marie Antoinette, and she was a year younger than himself. His father and mother, who had both died young, were notorious for the sanctity of their lives. From them he inherited an extreme reverence for the authority of the Church, and this reverence was fostered by the teaching of his tutor, the Duc de la Vauguyon, to whom his dying father had solemnly entrusted his education.

Marie Antoinette, who, from her infancy, had been educated at Vienna, with a view to her future position at Versailles, regarded her marriage, which had long been premeditated between the two courts, as her destiny; she was prepared to look with tender regard upon the boy husband who had been chosen for her; but the first years of her wedded life were not happy.

An evil omen had marked her birth. She was born upon the day of the Lisbon earthquake (November 2nd, 1755.) An evil omen had marked her marriage. That event, which was celebrated with great magnificence at Versailles, was also the occasion of splendid fêtes in Paris; and it was during those fêtes, that, through the carelessness of the city authorities, in not having properly tested the safety of the ground, innumerable sight-seers perished in the Place Louis XV., near the statue already mentioned of the King.

Her mother, the Queen Empress Maria Theresa, wrote the following letter * to the Dauphin, when his bride had set forth on her

* Réflexions sur mes entretiens avec M. le Duc de la Vauguyon. Par Louis Auguste, Dauphin (Louis XVI.). Précédées d'une Introduction par M. de Falloux, Représentant du Peuple, Ancien Ministre de l'Instruction Publique. P. 21. Paris, 1851.

journey to France, after the marriage by proxy, at Vienna:*—

"Your wife, my dear Dauphin, has just parted from me. She was the delight of my life, and I hope that she will be the joy of yours. In this hope have I reared her, because I have long foreseen that she would share your destiny. I have inspired her with the love of her duties towards you, with a tender and personal regard for you, and with the intention of considering and obeying your wishes.

"I have recommended to her a constant devotion to the King of kings, being persuaded that rulers cannot realize the welfare of the people confided to them, when they themselves are wanting in service to Him, who hath power to break sceptres and to overthrow thrones. Love, then, your duties towards God. I say this to you, my dear Dauphin; I say this to my daughter. Love the welfare of the people over whom, in any case, you will reign too soon . . . . My daughter will love you, I am sure, because I know her; but the more I can answer for her love and for her care to please you, the

* Appendix A.

more I recommend you faithfully to keep your vows to her. Adieu, my dear Dauphin. Be happy. I am bathed in tears.

"MARIA THERESA."

But even this letter, although congenial to the pious tone of his mind, did not stimulate the Dauphin to a sense of his responsibilities, as husband.

The Dauphin's brothers, especially the gay young Count d'Artois, (afterwards Charles X.,) were more agreeable companions to the Dauphiness in those early days, than was her own gloomy and abstracted husband; and when, in course of time, through a fear that the Dauphin would have no offspring, his two brothers were made to marry the two daughters of the King of Sardinia, the Dauphiness joyfully welcomed these princesses of her own age at Versailles, and was only ambitious of being Queen of the revels, in which (a young court within an old court) they innocently indulged amongst themselves.

In the course of time the Countess d'Artois had

hopes of being a mother. Marie Antoinette warmly sympathized in her rival's expectation of bringing forth an heir to the throne of France; and, when that expectation was fulfilled, merely said of herself, that she had "the politest husband in all the world, for he never even troubled her with his presence."*

The Duc de la Vauguyon, however, records in his Mémoires,† that the Dauphin's presence withdrawn from his wife, was as that of an angel to the poor and afflicted.

Charity seems to have sharpened the Dauphin's wits; for, by the same authority we are told, that one day he was met by some of his pages coming out of a hovel near Versailles, where he had been to carry relief both to the bodies and souls of its inhabitants. Naturally bashful, the heir to the throne was ashamed at being caught in the fact of his charity; but, quickly rallying, he cried: "Gentlemen! Have mercy on me. You, all of you, are free to enjoy your little adventures; but I, from my rank, cannot indulge

* Mems. de la Famille Royale de France. Vol. i. p. 65. Paris, 1826.

† Pub. Paris, 1851.

in mine, without being exposed to observation!"

The royal family of France was politically divided against itself when Marie Antoinette, the Dauphiness, first appeared at Versailles.* The different places of residence adopted by the heads of either party denoted opposition. The Orleans branch of the royal family had established itself at the Palais Royal, situated in the midst of the city of Paris, of the Parliament, and in the heart of popular sympathies. The King had withdrawn himself from his capital to Versailles. The people went on great occasions—at the Dauphin's marriage fêtes, for example—to look at the King at Versailles; but that was not the same thing as having a monarch in the midst of them. The magnificence of Versailles, although for the moment it flattered their national vanity to gaze at, yet, on reflection, it oppressed them with the memory of heavy taxes. Since the attempt on his life by Damiens, in 1757, Louis XV., once the "well-beloved" of his kingdom, had grown suspicious and fearful. After that event he no longer rode through the midst of the people,

* Appendix B.

bareheaded, as when he went forth to the war in 1744,* (to the war against England and Austria,) which had given temporary glory to France, and which, having drained her of much money, was concluded by a peace, disadvantageous to her. Then all the people cried, "God bless the King!" Now French loyalty was dumb, and Louis XV. lay dying at Versailles.

The Dauphin was not allowed to approach his majesty for fear of infection; but his tutor, the Duc de la Vauguyon, tells us that that Prince gave alms, and offered to pay the poor out of his pension (of 6,000 livres a month) to pray for the King's recovery.

One May day, the courtiers in the antechamber whispered together, for it was not etiquette to say aloud, "The King is dead." But that all might know when to go and worship the rising sun, a candle had been placed in a window, which everyone could see; and when this candle was snuffed out, it was understood as a preconcerted signal that the time had come to cry: "Vive le Roy!" The King never dies.

* Secret Hist. of the Court of France under Louis XV. Vol. i. p. 1. (Narrative.)

When Monseigneur the Dauphin, that "big, lubberly boy," as Madame du Barry had called him, first heard the sound of "Vive le Roy," that May day, and was hailed by all around as King of France, he cried out: "Oh! my God! What a misfortune for me!"

The big lubberly boy was a prophet.

When courtiers at the same time came flocking round Madame the Dauphiness, and bowed down before her, as Queen, she cried, "We are too young to reign;" then, covered her face with her handkerchief, and wept bitterly.

Marie Antoinette, the new Queen of France, had sighed for liberty rather than a throne, although she had naturally objected to Cardinal de Rohan's scheme of supplanting her upon the throne by marrying her sister to Louis XV., as at one time had been proposed by that wily politician.*

The snuffing out of a candle changed, in a moment, the fate of Marie Antoinette. Yesterday, she was comparatively neglected by the court, where Madame du Barry reigned supreme. Unfruitful to the future hope of France, she,

* Appendix C.

the wedded maid, had been a mark for the court's uncharitable satire. To-day she was worshipped as Queen.

With the exception of exclusive favourites, courtiers at Versailles had sighed for a change, each one hoping to be the elect of fortune and of new favour.

To the people, both Parisian and provincial, Louis XVI. was "the desired." Not that his young majesty had then done much to make himself so, but the compliment to him was, as compliments in this world generally are, a censure on another.

The once "Well Beloved" now lay dead and deserted. Why watch any longer by a King who had nothing now but the small-pox to confer on his faithful subjects?

But, Louis the "Well Beloved," had left work for "Louis the Desired" to do. French provinces were destitute and starving. Paris tradespeople were murmuring bitterly against their court patrons at Versailles for bad debts.*

"The people's misery, and the despotism that

* Appendix D.

gives rise to it," says a contemporary chronicler,* seem to have arrived at the highest pitch that it is possible for human patience to bear, or for tyranny to exercise. A famine, occasioned by the monoply of corn, has desolated the provinces. The capital and other great towns are so overrun with spies, that there is no either writing or speaking on any subject that has the most remote relation to the present state of affairs. . . . No regular administration of justice in any part of the kingdom. . . . The vanity, avarice, and weakness of the Princes,—the miseries of the lower class! . . . There seem to be a number of circumstances concurring to bring the monarchy to its dissolution, or at least to bring about a revolution."

King Louis XV. died, but not before he had seen the dawn of revolutions in the Old and the New World. In the summer of 1771, the revolution of Sweden had taken place.† In

* Memoirs of the French Court. MSS. unpublished. Mus. Brit. Date—Paris, 1771-1775.

† Gustavus III., King of Sweden, at first (in 1771) professed to govern a free and independent people, according to the laws of the country; but, having thus gained the love of his people, he quickly effected a revolution. He surrounded the Diet with

1772, the partition of Poland had been agreed upon, between Catharine of Russia, Frederick the Great of Prussia, and Joseph II. of Austria, the brother of Marie Antoinette.* In 1774, although the first blow was not yet struck, the rebellion of America, against the Crown of England, had begun, and the oppressed people of France were inclined to sympathize in the transatlantic struggle for liberty. At Versailles, during the last years of the reign of Louis XV., "ministerial and court intrigue," declares one who was there at the time, "are the only things worth mentioning."†

armed men, and offered to it a new form of government, in which he made himself absolute. The members, alarmed, and unable, being thus taken by surprise, to help themselves, signed away their liberties. The King of Sweden thus became the most absolute monarch in Europe.

* "Sire," said somebody one day to Frederick of Prussia, "your century is one of revolutions." "And little passions cause them," answered the philosopher king. "God only can count their numberless chains of circumstance. Just as music" (King Frederick had his flute in his hand at the moment), "just as music revolves on seven tones, so does the harmonious system of causes and consequences, in human economy, revolve upon seven or eight passions, which we see too thoroughly diversified for the human intellect thoroughly to trace or to sift out."—*Les Conseils du Trone.* Paris, 1828.

† Of these last years we are told—"In the present Admi-

Madame du Barry trafficked in Government appointments; and at the universal discontent against Government, says the same chronicler, "the King seemed not at all concerned, except

nistration the only persons of consequence are d'Aiguillon (Minister and Secretary of State for Foreign Affairs), the Abbé Terray (Comptroller-General of the Finances), and Maupeou (Chancellor). The other members of the Cabinet are the tools or the creatures of these three. But even these would attempt nothing without being supported by Madame du Barry, and the influence of each of them is proportioned to the degree of favour in which he stands with her. In this the Duc d'Aiguillon holds decidedly the highest place. He was intimate with her before she was taken into keeping by the King. . . . . The King never liked him, he was forced on him by Madame du Barry. But," continues the same authority, "Maupeou hated d'Aiguillon and Terray, especially the latter, and he determined to turn them, or, at all events Terray, out of the Ministry." [This was in 1771, during the insurrections in the provinces on account of the monopoly of corn.] "So he (the Chancellor) sent a trusty person to Languedoc, whom he ordered to prepare a piece of bread of the worst sort that could be found in the country, and to make it still worse by mixing sand, and such materials, with it. This he had packed up in a close box, sealed, and directed to the King, together with a memoir relating the wretched state of the people, and mentioning the causes to which it was owing. . . . . These were put into another box, likewise sealed, which was directed to Madame du Barry at Versailles. This double package was sent and delivered as directed. The King was surprised, and determined to dismiss and to exile the Comptroller, Abbé Terray. Madame du Barry, who knew nothing of the Chancellor's scheme, opposed this, because she feared if Terray were turned out of office before the Farmers-General had rewhen Madame Louise, the Nun of St. Denis, his daughter, remonstrated with him on the disorder and licentiousness of his life." From a scandalous

newed their leases of the revenues, she should lose a considerable sum which that company gave, according to custom, as a *pot-de-vin* to the Comptroller who signed the lease; and which, by an agreement with Terray, she was to have. By this opposition of Madame du Barry to Chancellor Maupeou's scheme, Terray got over his impending disgrace for the present. . . . . Terray, incensed at the endeavours of Maupeou to inflame Madame du Barry against him, prevailed on the King to double her appointments, which had hitherto only been £2,000 sterling a month. Also, on the death of the Comte de Clermont (by which an annuity devolved to the crown), the King gave her a third of it and left the remainder to be disposed of as she thought proper.* But Terray and d'Aiguillon, who had been so closely united against the Chancellor, quarrelled with each other about this time. Terray determined to become a Cardinal. He solicited a long time at Rome, but there the Duc d'Aiguillon privately opposed him; because if he were Cardinal and Minister at the same time, he would take the lead in the Cabinet of all the other ministers. Terray, seeing that nothing could be done at Rome, applied to the Pretender, who has, in his turn, the nomination of a Cardinal. For this Terray offered the Pretender 40,000 pounds sterling down, and an annuity of 5,000 pounds; but these offers the Pretender† thought proper to refuse."‡

* This remainder Madame du Barry employed in the following manner:—To the Duc d'Aiguillon, 50,000 livres; to the Chancellor, 50,000 livres; to the Abbé Terray, 50,000 livres; and the same sum to the Comte de la Marche (the only son of the Prince de Conti).

† Appendix G.

‡ Memoirs of the French Court. Mus. Brit. MS.

court, this Princess had, voluntarily, sought a refuge in the sanctity of a cloister. She was much attached to her father, and, to the last, the King would often go to her convent, there to spend hours in her society, which, despite her remonstrances just alluded to, he preferred to that of her sisters, who were intriguing at Versailles against the Dauphiness.*

The Pope (Clement XIV.) wrote letters of congratulation to the King, and to the Princess Louise, on her taking the veil. "To the very Christian King, who must rejoice that his daughter in the flesh, has had grace given her, to choose the better part"; and "to our very dear daughter in Jesus Christ, Louise Marie, Princess of France, exhorting her to courage and perseverance, and not to forget, that her rare example of religion and virtue may excite in others the desire of imitating it, and so not a little assist in advancing the cause of Religion, and in stimulating a zeal for true holiness."†

* Appendix E.

† In another letter of this liberal and wise Pope he says, writing to Cardinal Cavalchini, "I suppose" (for the sake of argument) "Rome the aim of all crowns. How will she sustain herself in the midst of storms? We are not yet in heaven; and if God

Years since, when quite a child, the Princess Louise, gave evidences of the warmest love for her father. When she heard him coming down the long galleries of Versailles, says Madame Campan, who was her companion, to pay his daily visit to her and her sisters, she being small and ill made, had difficulty in running to meet him, as fast as her wishes would carry her. "Her soul," continues the same informant, "was elevated; she loved great things. . . . She could but perform one transcendant action:—to quit a palace for a cell, to exchange rich vestments for a robe of serge. She has done it!"

And when all the courtiers fled from the corpse of Louis XV., she alone, watched over it. For fear of infection, the royal body was not even enbalmed. The first lord of the bed-chamber told the first surgeon of the King, that his neglect of this duty was high treason. "Very well," answered the surgeon, to the lord of the bed-chamber, "if it be my duty to open the body, and to embalm it, your duty is to

preserve His church to the end of ages, it will be by His inspiring her rulers with prudence relative to times and places, as also with a love of peace."

hold it while I do so." After that nothing more was said upon the subject, and the once "Well Beloved" of his people was thrust down into the vaults of the Abbey of St. Denis, where he was left with none but his pious daughter, the Nun Louise, to weep and to pray over him.

Money began at this time to make itself peculiarly felt in France. Many of the Farmers-General had amassed enormous fortunes, which enabled them to buy up the estates of such of the old noblesse as had beggared themselves, and (in default of heirs-male in the rightful line) to assume their names by right of purchase. These lords of the Bourgeoisie aped the habits and feudal customs of the rank which, by the power of gold, they thus usurped.

The Church felt the innovation, but was obliged to succumb to it. The *nouveau riche* was probably a "philosopher" in theory. He sneered at old creeds, and time-honoured customs, but he practically adopted them, as part and parcel of the rank he had bought.

The venerable Curé of the parish was transferred with it from one owner to the other; he was compelled to bless the meat upon the rich man's table, for the sake of the poor tenantry, between whom and the landowner he, the Curé, was the appointed medium. The young aristocrat Abbé was hired by the *Bourgeois Gentilhomme*, as tutor to children who knew not their own grandfather.

Many of the old nobility, and especially some of those about the court of Louis XV., in his later years, had not only beggared, but disgraced themselves. To the last, the Duc de Richelieu was the King's greatest favourite.

"The Duc de Richelieu," says one who knew him at this period, "was in his youth the handsomest, wittiest, most agreeable, and most gallant man in the kingdom; and even at this day, now that he is above eighty years old, he is the most polite, and well-bred man I ever saw. But his moral character is as detestable, as his social character is agreeable and amiable. He has been guilty of the most infamous actions that ever disgraced a man; and, at this very time, he has a suit pending in the Parliament of Paris, for notes of hand, which at one time he acknowledged to have signed, and afterwards denied. He was raised to the highest dignities in France, and to some in Spain, Germany, and Italy, not by any superior abilities, but by art, intrigue, and good fortune; for certainly though no great general, he was almost always surprisingly successful in all his military expeditions." *

The same observer declares, that another court favourite, "the Duc de Biron, is an honest gentleman: *i. e.*, he is not remarkable for fraud or profligacy. He has great personal bravery, and this raised him to be Marshal of France, and Colonel of the French Guards. He is exceedingly ignorant, and vain, bombastic and turgid in his manner of acting and thinking; but he is very good-humoured, and not deficient in generosity."

"Bouret, the Farmer-General," another favourite, "raised himself from poverty and obscurity, to great wealth and credit at court. His first rise in the world was so singular, that it deserves to be mentioned. He was a clerk at a small salary, in one of the offices of M. de Machault, then Comptroller-General, and after-

* De Richelieu, in 1746, had had golden statues erected to him at Genoa, as the "Liberator of Italian Liberty;" in 1756 he was the conqueror of Minorca.—Secret Hist. of the Court of France under Louis XV. Vol. i. p. 190, vol. ii. p. 180.

wards keeper of the seals. Machault had a favourite spaniel, of which he was extravagantly fond; but, unfortunately, having had him for some years, he inadvertently, in playing with him, let him fall off a balcony, by which he was killed. The minister was inconsolable for the loss of his dog, but M. Bouret thought that, by getting another dog resembling him, and training him up to the same manners and character, he would assuage the minister's grief. In this he was so fortunate as to succeed. Machault became fond of the new dog, and was so well pleased with Bouret, that he made him his confidential secretary, and obtained for him immediately a pension of 10,000 livres." He afterwards was made a Farmer-General, and presented to the King, with whom he became a favourite.

"The Noailles family," declares the same authority, "are all well at court . . . They are the vainest, most haughty, and ignorant family in the kingdom." *

The Countess de Noailles (appointed first lady of honour to Marie Antoinette, upon the mar-

* MS. Mems. of the French Court. Mus. Brit.

riage of the latter) had hoped to rule the mind and manners of the future Queen of France; but the Dauphiness disregarded her injunctions, and gave her the *sobriquet* of *Madame l'Etiquette.*

The Countess kept her appointment, but never forgave her nickname. Henceforth, she united with the Dauphin's aunts in condemning the conduct and costume of the Dauphiness, which were more consistent with the simplicity of girlhood than with the dignity of court conventions. The young Marquis de Lafayette, of republican sympathies, was about to be married to a daughter of the de Noailles family; and hence it came to pass, that the word "Liberty" was already breathed in the midst of the family the most bigoted in France to exclusive prejudices.

In all classes, reverence for rank was dying out, and society was already in a state of transition, when Louis XVI. and Marie Antoinette ascended the throne of France.

The first act of the young king, upon hi accession, was to recall the old Count de Maurepas from exile, to be his minister. Count de Maurepas, formerly first Minister of Marine had been exiled from the court and cabinet twenty years before, for making ribald rhymes upon Louis XV., and Madame de Pompadour.* Horace Walpole had, in the meantime, paid a visit to the ex-Minister of Marine, at Portchartrain, his estate, where he found him still gay, except when politics were named, when he became gloomy and restless. Portchartrain was not far from Versailles; de Maurepas therefore could understand the torments of a lost spirit shut out beyond the gates of Paradise, but still permitted to look within.

But, by the late King's daughters, (the present King's aunts) de Maurepas was regarded as a martyr to their father's mistress, who had promoted the political Austrian alliance with France, in 1756; and it was by the advice of Madame Adelaide, the young King's most revered aunt and godmother, that he recalled the Count de Maurepas to guide his inexperience in council.

"I am King," wrote Louis the Desired, to the exiled minister—"I am King, and that title conveys all my responsibilities. But I am only twenty years of age. And I am ignorant

* Secret Hist. of the Court of France under Louis XV. Vol. i. p. 314.

of all that I ought to know. Moreover, I can see no minister, as all have been with the late King in his last infectious illness. The conviction that I entertain of your honesty, and of your profound knowledge of business, induces me to beg you to aid me with your advice. Come to me as soon as possible." *

The first act of Queen Marie Antoinette, on her accession to the throne of France, was to banish Madame du Barry from Versailles. The Duc d'Aiguillon was too intimately connected with Madame du Barry not to share her disgrace, and her wealth; for although forbidden to re-appear at court, she was permitted to keep her pensions.

Henceforth she installed herself at St. Brin, her estate, from whence, contemporary gossip tells us, "she wrote to all the Seigneurs in her neighbourhood, informing them, that she was

* "When the present King ascended the throne .... the Count de Maurepas was, by the intrigues of Madame Adelaïde, recalled from exile, and, without being nominally, became in reality prime-minister. The first revolution was that of changing the old ministry and recalling the parliaments."—Memorial on the Affairs of France. Contemp. MS. Ex. Dono. Coxe. Unpublished—Mus. Brit.

now "at home," and that every day beneath her roof there was a table prepared for twenty-five guests, and a ready welcome."

The provincial Seigneurs, and subsequently some who were not well received at Versailles, were not slow in availing themselves of this hospitable hint.*

The Abbé Terray, who, as we have seen, had politically intrigued with Madame du Barry,† was dismissed. He, (the Comptroller-General of Finance,) had been bitterly pasquinaded by the people of Paris, although upheld by the late King's mistress in the cabinet of Versailles.

The Farmers-General of State Finance had long been murmured against by the people, but they had still been permitted to retain certain privileges with impunity; yet so unpopular was Terray, that, when he sought to reform this body, his motives were instantly suspected, and a caricature appeared in Paris, in which the Abbé was represented as a leech sucking blood, with the motto:—"*Non missura cutem nisi plena cruoris.*"

* Appendix F.

† See foot-note to page 22 of this chapter.

One day, in a popular assembly, Terray was recognized, and asked by the mob, "Who puts our money into his pockets?" But Terray only answered, "My friends, I really do not know where better I could put it;" which retort amused the mobile Parisians, and therefore restored them to good humour for the moment, although some rhymes soon afterwards appeared, which were anything but flattering to Terray and his colleagues.*

Turgot, a severe master of the new school of political economy, was made Comptroller-General of Finance, in Terray's stead. Turgot was a philosopher, but the young King, notwithstanding his educational prejudices against philosophy, (which was then too often another name for atheism) soon found out that Turgot was an honest man, and respected him accordingly, although it is more than probable that he (Turgot)

* "Ami, connaissez vous l'enseigne ridicule
Qu'un peintre de St. Luc fait pour des parfumeurs?
Il met en un flacon, en forme de pillule
Boysnes, Maupeou, Terray, sous leurs propres couleurs,
Il y joint d'Aiguillon, et puis il l'intitule
'Vinaigre des quatre voleurs.'"

The people of Paris excused themselves for rhyming and caricaturing upon all occasions, by declaring that they were not allowed any liberty of speech but what their own wits afforded them.

was the author, or at least the instigator, of an anonymous pamphlet, which appeared in Paris soon after his majesty's marriage, (1770,) and protested strongly against the expenditure of the Fêtes at Versailles on that occasion.*

"Instead of amusing the lazy inhabitants of court and capital," says that pamphlet, "by vain and momentary diversions, it would have been wiser to have applied the twenty millions which those diversions cost, to the cultivation of the earth, or in easing the people's burthen of taxation."†

This burthen was a heavy one, especially, as before said, since the time of the Seven Years War; but Louis XVI., above all things, desired the love of his people, and soon he declared, "No one loves the people, but Turgot and myself."

Malesherbes, the colleague of Turgot, affirmed of him, "He has the head of Bacon, and the heart of l'Hôpital."‡

* For description of these fêtes see Appendix A.

† *Idée Singulière d'un ben Citoyen.* Paris, 1770.

‡ Christian William de Lamoignon Malesherbes. Born in Paris, 1721. Became President of the Court of Aids, and Superintendent of the Press. In 1771, when the legal constitution was abolished, was banished to his country seat. Wrote

But the "very Christian" young King soon began to be uneasy; for Turgot, his honest minister, never went to mass. His majesty consulted old Count de Maurepas, who had been recommended to him by his godmother, about this: "Sire," said the resuscitated courtier— "Sire, I beg to remind you, that M. the Abbé Terray was public in his devotions, but his frauds were patent also."*

The Church looked forward with much hope and joy to the coronation of the King, who was devoted in his allegiance to her; but political economists, with Turgot at their head, censured the idea of a coronation, when Frenchmen in the provinces were starving for want of bread. The Church regarded the coronation as a holy rite. Philosophy derided it as a superstitious and costly ceremony.

The King therefore, "only twenty years old,"

an "Essay on Rural Economy," and "Memoirs on the State of France." In 1774-5 made Minister of State. Soon resigned, and went into Switzerland. In 1786 was again consulted on the affairs of the nation; considered them irretrievable. In 1792 voluntarily issued from his safe retirement to plead the cause of the King. Was condemned to death for his loyalty. Died on the scaffold with his daughter in April, 1794.

* Journal d'un Observateur. Paris, 1774.

soon began to feel the want of unity amongst his most trusted advisers in Church and State. But he was accustomed to obey the former, and in this matter the Church triumphed. The aged Archbishop of Rheims declared: "I baptized the King, I administered his first Communion to him; I married the King, and when I have crowned him, I shall have nothing left to wish for, but to sing 'Nunc Dimittis.'"

The Church and the Archbishop prevailed; the young monarch submitted to their guidance, and grand preparations were made for the coronation in the ancient city of Rheims.

Meanwhile, the Queen was happy. Louis "the Desired," so long insensible to her charms, had lately began to manifest the most tender affection towards her. He awoke, at the same moment, to his duties as man, monarch, and husband. Marie Antoinette was beloved, and love beautified her. It made her anxious, too, for her own adornment. As Dauphiness, she had openly expressed her scorn for the outward trappings of her rank. As Queen, as wife, she soon gave orders concerning her coronation diamonds, which were minute, to judge from the note (subjoined) which was addressed by her majesty's chevalier d'honneur.

"To the Master of the Ceremonies, and Keeper of the Privy Purse, at Rheims," * to ensure suitable accommodation there for the privileged being who was present daily at the Queen's toilet.

Marie Antoinette in her childhood had been a pupil of Gluck, but, until she sent for him to France, as we shall see, she had, by her marriage, been too soon removed from the tuition of that great master, at Vienna, to achieve excellence from it. Music, however, was her favourite accomplishment; as Dauphiness she still pursued it, although, conscious of her deficency, she would permit no audience, declaring that "a Dauphiness of France should never cast discredit on an Archduchess of Austria." Lately,

* "Versailles, Sunday, May 28, 1775.

"The Queen having given orders to the Sieur Loire (whom she has commissioned to mount her diamonds) to go to Rheims, it is necessary that you seriously consider how to accommodate him with apartments. .... The Sieur Loire, being upon his mission concerning the Crown diamonds, you see that it is indispensable that he be suitably lodged, as he is daily employed at the Queen's toilette. Therefore, I recommend him specially to you. You know, sir, the estimation in which you are held by me,—Le Comte de Lacaultz."

animated by fresh life, she appears, by another letter, from her chevalier d'honneur, to have resumed her studies with vigour, as she could not even travel to Rheims without her music masters.*

Just before the coronation, 1775, there was printed and sold in Paris, "A Detail of the Rich Treasure of the Abbey of St. Denis, which is to be used at the Coronation of his most Christian Majesty Louis XVI. This Treasure consists in the Crown of the Emperor Charlemagne, his sceptre, sword, and hand of Justice; his Spurs, and the Clasp to fasten the Royal Mantle; with the Book containing the Prayers to be used at the Coronation Ceremony."

A dazzling account was also given to the public, by the Paris press, of the furniture to be used on this occasion, which was "to be brought

* "Compiègne.

"The Queen, Monsieur, has ordered two musicians, Sieurs Cardon and Zimmer, to follow her here and to Rheims; fortunately, two apartments were found vacant for them here. I hope that this letter may reach you before our arrival at Rheims, that you may have time to lodge these musicians suitably; the one being her majesty's harp master, and the other her accompanist. . . . . We shall start from here at six o'clock P.M., and arrive at one o'clock A.M.,—after midnight.

"To the Master of the Ceremonies, &c., at Rheims."

MSS. Eg. Coll. Mus. Brit.

forth from the Chapel of Gold; some presented to the Crown by Cardinal de Richelieu, in 1636, and some made by order of Francis I., and reserved for the Coronation of Kings of France. Also, of Embroidery and Pictures kept specially for that service. And of the Crown Diamonds, which his most Christian Majesty wears all the day of his Coronation."

It was expected that programmes of kingly magnificence and saintly reliques would have drawn large crowds from all parts of France to Rheims, there to witness the coronation of Louis XVI. Warned by the disaster in the Place Louis XV., on the occasion of the marriage of the present monarch,* the civic authorities at Rheims had taken every precaution to prevent accident. The young King and Queen both ardently desired the love of their subjects. The King, when asked if it were his pleasure that the streets of Rheims should be hung with tapestry, answered, "No, my chief wish is to see my subjects, and to be seen by them."

But there were not so many people gathered together at Rheims as had been expected. The

* Appendix A.

cries of "Vive le Roi!" were more rare, and less rapturous upon this occasion than had been anticipated from the impulsive and sight-loving people of France.

Political economy was gaining ground. The Church had triumphed for the moment, in having the King crowned; but Turgot was now in office, and Voltaire and Rousseau had long since shaken the faith of the people in their ancient creeds, and in their reverence for ancient customs.

A pamphlet which Voltaire wrote at this time, on the "Free Commerce of Corn in the kingdom of France," attracted, to say the least, almost as much attention in Paris as did the accounts of the coronation splendour, which were printed and published by court authority.

It was now more than twenty years since Voltaire had been exiled from the court and capital of France. Louis XV. had never pardoned that philosopher, (who had been made, by the intercession of Madame de Pompadour, historiographer of France, and court poet at Versailles) the transfer of his allegiance to Frederick of Prussia, the enemy of France, and the reviler of Madame de Pompadour. From the time when Voltaire (in 1750-3) took up his abode at the court of that King of Protestants and philosophers, he was regarded at Versailles as a traitor to his country, and an apostate to her faith.*

Louis XVI. had been taught, from his cradle, to abhor the name of Voltaire, as the enemy of religion; but the people of Paris regarded it as the watch-word of their rights and liberties. They looked upon his continued exile as an act of oppression towards themselves.

His writings, (which often appeared by stealth, and were suppressed by government) were eagerly read in Paris, and every chance detail of the daily life of the philosopher at Ferney, (his retreat in Le Pays de Gex) was caught up eagerly in the capital of France, and repeated there with enthusiasm.

Pilgrims often journeyed now, not from Paris to Rome, but from Paris to Ferney, there to worship the Patriarch of Philosophers and the Chief of Reformers.

The people, generally, are naturally idolatrous;

* Secret Hist. of the Court of France under Louis XV. Vol. ii. p. 1.

if turned from one shrine, they will only prostrate themselves with the more enthusiasm before another.

Mirabeau, also, excited the sympathies of Paris at this time, for he was now incarcerated, by paternal tyranny, in the fortress of St. Joux.* His father had written a pamph-

* Old Marquis Mirabeau, author of "*l'Ami des Hommes,*" a family tyrant. Has one son, Count Mirabeau (born 1749). Young Count serves in Corsica as volunteer, but is married by family command, in 1771. Soon afterwards challenges the Baron de Villeneuve for insulting his sister. Villeneuve refuses to fight. Mirabeau inflicts coward's stripes upon him. Old Mirabeau procures a *lettre de câchet* and imprisons his son in the Château d'If. Prison governor intercedes for him, whereupon his father transfers him from Château d'If to Fort St. Joux, near Portarlier. His wife refuses to join him there. New prison governor pities Mirabeau, and takes him into society with him at Portarlier, where Mirabeau falls in love with a married lady, Madame de Monnier, to whom prison governor is also attached. Governor and prisoner, rivals. Governor writes to prisoner's father, and denounces him to lady's husband. New *lettre de câchet* from prisoner's father, and criminal process from lady's husband. Young Mirabeau escapes into Switzerland, where he is joined by Madame de Monnier. They fly together into Holland. Mirabeau lives by his pen; writes from six o'clock in the morning till nine o'clock at night. Amongst many other things writes scandalous memoirs of his own father. Afraid of consequences, Mirabeau is about to embark for America with Madame de Monnier. His father gets a *lettre de câchet* whereby he can arrest his son in a foreign country. Instead of going to America, therefore, young Mirabeau is conducted to the

let called "The Friend of Mankind;" but paternal philanthropy did not begin at home. Charity, legislation, and benevolence, seldom do; and even if they did, they might not be appreci-

château of Vincennes, and Madame de Monnier, *enceinte*, is conducted to a convent. They contrive a correspondence. Mirabeau also writes books by stealth. He is allowed books to read but no paper to write them on, so he tears bits of the margins out of the printed books;—a leaf here, a scrap there—were not likely to be missed; and having written over these scraps, hides them in the lining of his coat, and at last manages, by help of his jailer, to get these scraps into the hands of a bookseller. These fragmentary MSS. are published, and turn out to be Mirabeau's famous work against *lettres de câchet* and state prisons. The work is eagerly read. Its eloquent denunciations against despotism and the abuses of arbitrary power are enthusiastically echoed. Government is afraid of being any longer the instrument of old Mirabeau's paternal tyranny in keeping his son a prisoner, and young Mirabeau is set at liberty. Immediately he flies to Portarlier, there to overthrow the sentence against him for the abduction of Madame de Monnier. With a lock of her hair upon his breast, and a phial of poison in his pocket, he pleads his own cause, with such energy and eloquence that his judges weep. The sentence against him and Madame de Monnier is revoked; Madame de Monnier is set at liberty, and her fortune is secured to her. Encouraged by this success, Mirabeau, by an odd paradox, now lays claim to his own wife, notwithstanding his notorious passion for Madame de Monnier. His wife refuses to return to him. The Parliament of Paris protects her, and a separation is decreed in 1783. England and Prussia are the next abodes of Mirabeau; but Mirabeau scandalizes the hospitality which shelters him by his "Secret History of the Court of Berlin." Prince Henry, brother of King Frederick the Great,

ated there as the world appreciates them. Since the days of Socrates a philosopher has not been a philosopher in his own house.

But Mirabeau the younger, though imprisoned, represented a third section in the Coronation question.

This future hero of the Revolution did something at this time to stimulate French loyalty in favour of the Crown, by issuing a pamphlet entitled, "The Coronation, or the Rights of the French Nation recognized and confirmed by this ceremony." In the elaborately illustrated frontispiece of this pamphlet, the motto, "Vox Populi, Vox Dei," issues from the clouds—a trite motto enough, but full of a new signifi-

is in Paris when this book appears. The Parliament of Paris fears the offence the publication will give to Prussia; and, to conciliate that power, condemns both the book and its author. Mirabeau now goes into Provence, seeking rest. The noblesse of Provence refuse to receive him into their assembly. Mirabeau, disgusted by the despotism of his own class, openly flings himself into the arms of the people. He rents a shop at Marseilles, and sets up there as a cloth merchant. Versailles scoffs at "the plebeian count." The Governor of Provence threatens to transport the plebeian count to the Indies. Mirabeau scorns court scoffs, and defies the Provence Governor's threats. The grand drama of the States-general is preparing. Mirabeau presents himself before the Assembly, which soon becomes the theatre of his glory. Madame de Monnier commits suicide.

cance for Louis XVI., if he had only known how to read it.

In this pamphlet the argument of Mirabeau was, that "the greatest of all events for the people, is, doubtless, the Coronation of their King; it is then that Heaven consecrates our monarchs to our service, and imposes upon them the bonds which bind them to us."

In old feudal France the King was, henceforth, but the servant of his people. But young Louis XVI., the child of tradition, an "angel of sincerity," (as his tutor the Duc de la Vauguyon calls him) in his own private conduct, believed not only in the divine right of Kings, but in the divine impulse of his own good intentions. He celebrated his own coronation by an allegory of Virtue, pregnant with the promise of good things. His Rights were Righteousness to him. A drama was performed at Rheims, in which all the vices surrounding a throne, (Luxury, Despotism, Voluptuousness, and Flattery,) were personified as hideous, and all the virtues that can support a throne were pourtrayed as beauteous.

An engraving was also issued of "Le Sacre

de Louis XVI.," in which the King is represented crowned by Religion, protected by Justice, and encircled by Virtue, Zeal, Happiness, and Glory.

But in both the allegorical drama, and the emblematic engraving, the people beheld as much a satire on the reign just past as a promise in the reign just began.

Louis XVI. was "the Desired," only in proportion to the latter-day worthlessness of Louis XV., who now lay unembalmed and buried, in the abbey of St. Denis, from whence came all the rich "treasure" displayed at the coronation of his successor at Rheims, and which was once a grand sight at his own.

One circumstance, however, roused popular attention at Rheims, and more especially, because it showed, too, the sudden ascendancy which the Queen had gained over the King—the Duc de Choiseul, the ex-minister who had been banished from court during the latter end of the reign of Louis XV., was not only present at the coronation, but was, after the ceremony, closeted with their majesties for more than half-an-hour.

Previously to this, the Duc de Choiseul had been to do homage to Louis XVI. (on his accession) at Compiègne, but he had been badly received there by the King, for the ex-minister was a friend of Voltaire.

With Marie Antoinette, the Duc de Choiseul was naturally a favourite. He had been ambassador at Vienna, during her infancy; it was he, as before said, who had achieved the alliance between the country of her birth and the country of her adoption, before the Seven Years' War. Her mother, from whom she had now been five years separated, but for whom she entertained the highest respect and the warmest affection, had spoken to her of him in terms of approbation.

It was the Duc de Choiseul, also, who had opposed the policy of William Pitt, (Lord Chatham,) in the last war against England.

Twenty years had sufficed to change the aspect of affairs in England, and the position of the man who was once her greatest minister. During the Seven Years' War, Lord Chatham had been the most mighty foe in the cabinet of England to the power of France, across the seas; and he was still alive to see the consequences of his enmity, in the reign that in France was now just dawning.

"It was William Pitt," as says Macaulay, "who in the late war had inflamed every soldier who dragged the cannon up the heights of Quebec, and every sailor who boarded the French ships among the rocks of Brittany, *Then* (twenty years before) "England was drunk with joy and pride at the victory over the French in Canada. . . . The English Church was drowsy and indulgent. . . . The great civil and religious conflict which began at the Reformation, seemed to have terminated in universal repose. . . . A new generation of country Squires and Rectors had arisen which knew not the Stuarts." *Now*, the Church, State, and Senate, of England were divided against themselves on the American question. Dissent rose up in favour of American insurgents. Stormy sermons were preached in English pulpits, for and against the American cause. Stormy speeches were made in the English Senate on either side of American politics. *Then* (twenty years before,) William Pitt's "name had acted like a spell at Versailles, and at St. Ildefonso; and even after the Seven Years' War was over, and a change had taken place in the English Ministry, English travellers on the Continent had remarked that nothing more was necessary to silence a whole room of boasting Frenchmen, than to hint that William Pitt would return to power." *Now*, William Pitt,—no longer the great Commoner of twenty-years before, when he was blessed by the English people, and feared by France,—was the unpopular new Peer, with nerves relaxed by a cruel and mysterious malady, from which his intellect only awoke from time to time, in its old force, "as from a sickly and gloomy dream."

France, now, had nothing to fear from Lord Chatham, who had been her greatest foe, and who, in his moments of spasmodic energy, disagreed with King George III. in his majesty's conduct towards the American colonies; for the King called him (his faithful subject, who had made England so great) a "trumpet of sedition."

William Pitt was out of favour with the King of England; the Duc de Choiseul, the former opponent of that minister during the war, in which England won, and France lost Canada, was suddenly taken into favour by the King of France. France yearned to repossess herself of Canada, and America was disaffected towards the Crown of England.

In all this there lay cause for speculation.

It was with peculiar interest that both the Government and the people of France regarded the growing signs of rebellion in America against the power of Great Britain. The sympathies of the French people were in favour of the American struggle for Liberty, as none knew better than they did how to estimate the evils of unjust taxation, complained of in the New World.

Besides, many families in France had near relatives in Canada, who, by the treaty of peace by which the Seven Years' War was concluded, had been transferred, as British subjects, to the crown of England. But the faith, the language, the blood, of these Canadians were French.

The sentiment of loyalty to France was still popular amongst her late subjects in Canada. Canadian cities, roads, and rivers, were still called by the names of old French rulers.

The peace which had concluded the Seven Years' War had been declared by the Duc de Choiseul, then first minister of France, to be "but a truce!" The return, therefore, of de Choiseul at this time to the court of Versailles was significant, although that ex-minister was not re-admitted into the Cabinet.*

Those appointed to succeed the d'Aiguillon and du Barry ministry, were all, more or less,

* The Duc de Choiseul had been happier and more honourable in his exile than he could have been as the head of a corrupt ministry under Madame du Barry, to whose machinations he originally owed his dismissal from the cabinet of Louis XV. Madame du Deffand (of whom we shall see more hereafter) was in the habit of visiting the Duc and Duchesse de Choiseul in their retirement at their estate at Chanteloup, and she thus describes (to Horace Walpole) the life of the ex-minister there: "Would that you had a magic glass in which to see what passes here! . . . In every discourse, in every action, and certainly in the soul, peace reigns here. Everybody here is harmonious; each one does as he likes, and says what he thinks, and yet there is perfect unity. . . . . 'Grandpapa' (her *sobriquet* for the Duc de Choiseul) 'surprises me. Within himself he has found resources which leave no void even to a mind that has been occupied with affairs of state. He seems as though he had never studied aught but how to turn his estate to profit. He builds farms; he grubs up the ground; he buys flocks that he may sell them again after they have manured his land and he has sold their wool. . . . . . I am quite persuaded that he regrets nothing, and that he is perfectly happy."—Lettres de Madame du Deffand, tome ii. pp. 351, 352.

friends of old Count de Maurepas. As the diary of an Englishman, resident at that time in France, declares: * "The Count de Maurepas seems to have the same influence over the councils of the beginning of this reign, as Madame du Barry had over the latter part of that of Louis XV.; and his character becomes the study of all those who desire to succeed in important negotiation. It was soon seen that his plan was to leave foreign matters much in the same situation as they had been in at his coming into the ministry. To preserve peace abroad, and to re-establish tranquillity and confidence in the government at home, which it was hoped would effectually have been done, by restoring the old Parliaments, by destroying the monopoly of corn, and by introducing such regulations in the management of the finances, and in the levying of taxes, as would, in some degree, alleviate the misery in which the oppressive measures of the late reign have involved the people.

"The designs of the Queen's party are, to have Choiseul at the head of the ministry,

* MS. Mus. Brit. unpublished.

and to have Maurepas disgraced; to have the Count d'Estaing at the head of the Admiralty, in the place of de Sartine.*

"Some means are devised by this party of paying off the whole of the national debt—or, in case that should be impossible, to make bankruptcy; of abolishing the Farmers-General, and of diminishing the taxes to one-fourth. As to foreign affairs, to connect themselves closer than ever with Spain and Sweden, and to bring the King of Sardinia into the family compact.†

"Above all, the Queen's party desire to undermine the British power in America. To this party belong most of the Princes of the blood, and the whole family and connections of the house of Lorraine.

"The other party consists of the King's aunts, M. de Maurepas, (and all his connections,)

* Admiral Count d'Estaing, of whom we shall see much more hereafter in America.

† The Family Compact, or the Alliance of all the enthroned members of the House of Bourbon. This alliance was achieved by the Duc de Choiseul in 1762-3. The daughters of the King of Sardinia, it will be remembered, were now married to the brothers of Louis XVI.

de Sartine, and Miromesnil, keeper of the seals. Their measures are entirely pacific. They are for countenancing the dissensions which reign in the British colonies, but not for so interfering with them, as to endanger a rupture between France and England.

"Parties thus render the councils of the court of Versailles negligent and fluctuating, on every point which is not in some way connected with the private interests of the heads of them.

"However averse the leaders of the present ministry may be to a war, they are obliged by the King to set both the military and naval establishments on a better footing than they have been heretofore. Considerable augmentations have been made in the last six months, and M. de Sartine, (the present head of the Admiralty,) has himself visited the docks at Brest and Rochefort, to hasten and direct the works there. The Governor of St. Domingo has brought over with him a re-inforcement of troops, with considerable quantities of arms and ammunition; *and private persons are secretly encouraged to supply the American agents with such commodities as they shall seem to want.*

"All these particulars may show what the spirit of the court of Versailles is, and what the parties of it are; and they account for its measures, and the fluctuation of its measures, during this last year."

But although the councils of Versailles were fluctuating, the young King Louis XVI. was, for the moment, popular.

So, likewise, was his financial comptroller, Turgot, the conscientious successor of the unscrupulous Abbé Terray.

With Turgot and Malesherbes, philosophy had entered the cabinet of Versailles.

The young King, of unhesitating rectitude in his own private conduct, sought rather than gave advice, politically. His position was not enviable. He was perplexed on four sides by a *parti-carré*.

Turgot, the comptroller of his finance, was opposed to the priests, the comptrollers of his conscience; and the King's aunts allied with his minister de Maurepas, were opposed to his Queen, and her political adviser, de Choiseul.

Louis XVI. had neither age, nor experience, nor energy, enough to control others. His new duties, as King, were opposed to his favourite scientific pursuits, in which he still sought a refuge, when the cares of state allowed him.

But the love of his people, which he earnestly desired, he had for the moment; because (in 1774) he had recalled the ancient Parliament.

Subsequently, at his coronation, he had issued an edict, that the sentence of prisoners then condemned to death should be commuted to working on the public roads.* But even this measure, though a pledge of a reign of mercy, was not so welcome to the people as was the recall of the Parliament, upon which they traditionally believed that their rights depended.

As Dauphin, the King was known to have looked with indignation on the conduct of the Parliaments; but (our English resident informs us)†

* Hitherto it had been found difficult, from the imperfection of communications through France, to bring hands from any distance to assist in making or mending public roads; but Turgot introduced a beneficial innovation, by employing contractors to make the roads, and assessing the whole district with the cost. By this means, not only roads were made, but waste lands were cultivated; hands were in request; labour was well paid; and vagrants, who had hitherto lived on alms, and had infested the hospitals of France, were converted into profitable servants of the state.

† MS. Ex Dono Coxe, Mus. Brit.

"de Maurepas prevailed on him to recall them, only by representing to him that this step would acquire him popularity, and establish a confidence in his government; and that the Parliaments were so weary of their exile, as to accept any terms that might be offered to them; and that their accepting anything derogatory of their former pretensions would at once destroy that popularity which they had hitherto enjoyed, and which had enabled them to oppose, with such unrelenting obstinacy, the will of the late King."

In the long run, as everybody knows, Louis XVI. by no means found the Parliamants so obsequious as he had been thus led by the crafty de Maurepas to suppose; but at the beginning of his reign, the reign which was destined to end so tragically, the entrance of that monarch into the capital, accompanied by his young and lovely Queen, attended by all the Princes of the blood, and followed by the members of the old Parliament, who, during the last reign, had been banished, and were now proceeding, with all magnificence, to their restoration, filled the hearts of the people with joy.

There was no lack of enthusiasm upon that day. Cries of "Vive le Roi!" "Vive la Reine!" made Paris echo. And when the cry arose of "Long live the Parliaments!" the King and the Queen were compelled, in assent, to bow their heads to the people.

The streets, lined with guards, were filled with vast crowds. The houses, adorned with flags and banners, seemed alive, even to the roofs, with human beings. There was joy in Paris on that day—there was triumph even as of a great victory.

The King declared, upon this occasion, that it was his will to consign all past grievances to oblivion; he recommended the magistrates to limit their attention to the discharge of their respective duties, and to co-operate with his wishes, which were altogether for the happiness of the people entrusted by Heaven to his charge.

Just as all this was going on in France, and the people there, for the moment, were blessing and praising their King, the government of Great Britain was harassed and tormented by the continued resistance of her American colonies to her system of taxation. The people of America, the reader will remember, had not only denied the right of the Parliament of Great Britain to tax the colonies, but blamed certain appointments made by the Crown in various departments of the colonial administration. This resistance had already so far ripened into rebellion, as to leave the King of England with nothing, as regarded America, "but a barren sceptre in his hand." Unless the Parliament of Great Britain was prepared to concede the claims of America, there was no other course now open to the Americans but an appeal to arms. *

* It is scarcely needful to remind the reader that the first tax imposed by Great Britain on America was in 1764, on stamps. The colonists petitioned against this tax, and pleaded the royal charters granted to them; by which charters all the privileges of British subjects were conferred upon them, although they—the colonists—were not represented in the British House of Commons. The Stamp Act was attempted to be enforced by the Government of Great Britain, and the people of Boston broke out into insurrection against it. Bells tolled, Government houses and officers were assailed and attacked. In 1767 the British parliament repealed the stamp tax, but brought in a bill for granting duties in the British Colonies on glass, painters' colours, and tea. The people then determined to use no tea which had paid duty; they emptied newly-arrived tea chests into the water, and, sheltering themselves under "non-importation agreements," sent back some cargoes to Great Britain. The government at

In England a new Parliament met for the first time on the 24th November, 1774. King George III. then declared in his speech, that he had resolved to resist every attempt to weaken or to impair the supreme authority of the legislature over all the dominions of the Crown. But "in December 1774, such was the short-sighted policy of government, that the navy estimates

home, determined to resist upon this point, repealed the other newly made taxes, but continued to enforce that on tea, so that the Americans refused to drink it, or supplied themselves with it through smugglers. The colonists also murmured loudly against a board of commissioners in Boston, and against armed vessels being stationed in the harbour, &c. &c. In 1774 was the repeal of the charter of Massachusetts. A committee was then appointed by the general congress at Philadelphia for arming Massachusetts. The command of the province was given to Jedediah Pribble, Artemus Ward, and Seth Pomeroy. The names and the spirit of the times recalled the republican and religious tone of Puritanism. A committee of supply was empowered to disburse 15,000 pounds sterling for the service of the forces. Delegates raised a force of 12,000 men, and afterwards were stimulated to increase them to 20,000. "When the Boston Port Act was to come into operation, the House of Burgesses of Virginia set apart a day (the 1st of June) for fasting, humiliation, and prayer, to implore the Divine interposition for averting the heavy calamity which threatened destruction to their civil liberties, and to give them one heart and one mind firmly to oppose, by all just and proper means, every injury to American rights." Amongst those who fasted and who prayed in church upon that day was George Washington, the future hero of the American rebellion. When,

for the year showed a reduction of 4,000 men. This force was augmented by 2,000 in the following February, but the whole naval force for the year 1775 amounted only to 18,000 men. The land forces voted for North America and the West Indies did not exceed 34,000 men. Such were the armies and navies by which a great continent and three millions of the British race were to be subdued." *

The King's generals in America were, at one time, inclined to flatter his Britannic majesty and themselves that the continued resistance of the people of Boston to the Crown was unpopular to the colonies at large.†

In 1774, upon receipt of these too favourable advices from America, John St. John ad-

eventually, it was proposed by the English Ministry to levy a fine on the town of Boston, by way of compensation for the tea destroyed, and to deprive the port of its privileges, until the Crown should be pleased to restore them; and, also, when it was decreed by the parliament of Great Britain that "if any person in the province of Massachusetts were indited for murder or any capital offence, such person or persons should be sent by the governor to some other colony or to Great Britain for trial," the rebellion in America became inevitable.

* Life of Charles James Fox, by Lord John Russell, vol. i. p. 103.

† Appendix H.

dressed the House of Commons in behalf of the Crown. John St. John's speech (even judging from the original short-hand notes of it),* is a singular specimen of the logic whereby King George III. deluded himself into the belief that his cause against America was a righteous cause.

"England," cries St. John, in the course of this speech, "England might say to America, who has been called her daughter, 'Daughter! thou art my flesh, my blood, my daughter!' Or, rather, 'Thou art a disease that's in my flesh which I must needs call mine. . . .' But the query now is: How are we to treat this thankless and ungrateful child? . . . What have we to fear? 'Tis said America will be exasperated. Will she then take arms? 'Tis not yet, thank God, the strength of America which we dread when put in competition with this country. She has neither armies, navy, money, nor men, though she doubles every twenty-five years, and has increased from 4,000, in the reign of James I., to two millions at this day.

* These notes were for many years preserved in the private library of his Majesty George III., and are now amongst the Cavendish MSS.—Bibl. Egerton, Mus. Brit.

". . . Shall we fear the destruction of our trade? Believe it not; while it is her interest to trade with us, so long she will, in spite of her resentment. . . .

"Will she give herself up to other European Powers? 'Tis an absurd supposition. . . . Let us, therefore, go on; not violently and weakly, as has been said, but with temper and resolution, in the completion of the system which we have so happily begun. . . ."

The Government of Great Britain did "go on." A message was sent to the two Houses of Parliament; and both houses, in 1775, "readily promised to assist the Crown in providing for the due execution of the laws, and in securing the dependence of the colonies upon the Crown and Parliament of Great Britain."

CHAPTER II.

War Chants in America—Thomas Paine ("Common Sense") in America—Pensylvanian "Cato"—George Washington, his early life and daily habits—Model slave estate of the 18th century—George Washington in Congress, and in command of the Army—Dr. Benjamin Franklin, his early life, &c.—Dr. Franklin's own account of his own condemnation—Dr. Franklin before the Privy-Council—His vow—Horace Walpole on American affairs in 1774—Autograph (unpublished) letters from Dr. Franklin to his son—Lord Chatham (William Pitt) —Dr. Franklin's own account of his acquaintance with Lord Chatham—interviews between Dr. Franklin and Lord Chatham—Dr. Franklin in the House of Lords—Lord Chatham's motion, Lord Chatham's speech—Sunday visit of Lord Chatham to Dr. Franklin—Attack of Lord Sandwich on Dr. Franklin in the House of Peers—Dr. Franklin's return to America (1775)—The first blow struck in America—Dr. Franklin's letter to Mr. Strahan, M.P.—Dr. Samuel Johnson upon American affairs—Dr. Franklin and Dr. Johnson—Rumours in Paris of Voltaire at Ferney—John St. John again—Foreign mercenaries and Frederick the Great—Statue of the King in Philadelphia—Dr. Franklin at the ruins of Scoon—Irish and Scotch American emigrants—Original (unpublished) "Memorial from an American Royalist and Colonist"—Old Feudalism the hot-bed of young Democracy.

War chants were now sung in America. Lord Chatham had once declared, that if he were left to write the patriotic songs for any country, he cared not who made the laws.

(Lord Chatham at this time—1774-5—was in seclusion at Hayes, but the war chants of America were about to find an echo even in his retreat, and to draw his lordship forth from thence, as we shall see, in strange company.)

America wrote and sang her own patriotic songs. She studied laws, too; and Voltaire had declared, "When once a people begin to study laws, their rulers are no longer safe."

In the year 1774, Thomas Paine* went to

* Thomas Paine, born in Norfolk, 1737, son of a Quaker staymaker. Went to America, because he had been dismissed as an exciseman at Lewes for selling contraband tobacco. Became editor and pamphleteer there. In later years was famous for his share in the French Revolution. Thomas Paine was the *bête noire*

America, and became editor of the "Pennsylvania Magazine," in which periodical, under the signature of "Common Sense," he declares, that for their sins a king had been given to the Jews. The Pennsylvanians believed both in the Bible and in common sense; but not in their own sins. The "Pennsylvania Gazette," therefore, in an article signed "Cato," quotes Locke and Montesquieu to show why America should not have a king, although resisting the imputation that one had been inflicted on the Pennsylvanians, (the elect people, who had originally taken possession of their portion of the New World by right of their saintship,) for any such reason as "Common Sense," just arrived from the profane old world, presumes to suppose.

The law by which the followers of William Penn established their right to the land now called Pennsylvania, was, as is well known, simple and primitive enough. "The earth is the

of our grandfathers, and of Mrs. Hannah More; but his works have their good as well as their bad qualities. His "Manifesto" (published in his Political Works) at the time of the American rebellion, is declared by those of this century whose judgment is sound and impartial, to be a splendid specimen of declamatory manly eloquence.

Lord's. The saints shall inherit the earth. We are the saints. Therefore, this earth is ours." This was in 1681; but even then the saints could not establish their rights to the earth, or such part of it as they looked upon as their divine inheritance, without a grant from the greatest sinner (Charles II.) who ever sat upon the throne of England. Perhaps this paradox originally led these primitive settlers to test the virtue of human laws. Be that as it may, at the end of nearly two hundred years the Pennsylvanian "Cato" brandishes the weapons of the old world lawgivers, French and English, to prove that "the union of the three powers, the legislative, the executive, and the judicial, in one man, or in any number of men, is not liberty, but tyranny comp*leat*." *

When Pennsylvania had in most things adopted "Common Sense," and had brought forth such a "Cato" as this, was the King of England, according to Voltaire's maxim, just quoted, any longer safe?

George Washington was now forty-two years of

* Original American newspaper, "Pennsylvania Gazette," April 10, 1776.

age.* At the age of twenty, after a boyhood in which he was distinguished by his frank, generous spirit, and for excellence in all athletic exercises, he was made Major in the Colonial Militia. That was during the Seven Years' War, when France and England were fighting against each other both in Europe and America.

George Washington then fought by the side of Englishmen against Frenchmen. The time had yet to come in which he was destined to fight by the side of Frenchmen against Englishmen. When General Braddock fell, in the late war, Washington conducted the retreat under so heavy a fire, that the Indians had ever since believed that he bore a charmed life.

The intervening years of his life he had passed at his estate called "Mount Vernon," from his wife's maiden name.

This estate in Virginia might be instanced as a model of what a slave estate ought to be; for George Washington, the elected champion of American Liberty, was a slave-owner.

"A large Virginian estate in those days was a

* George Washington was descended from Sir Henry Washington, who defended Worcester against the forces of Cromwell.

little empire. . . . In his mansion the planter reigned supreme; his steward or overseer was his prime-minister. . . . He had a legion of house negroes for domestic service, and his host of field negroes for the culture of tobacco, Indian corn, and other crops, and for other out-door labour. . . . Their quarter formed a kind of hamlet apart, composed of various huts, with little gardens, and poultry-yards, all well stocked, and swarms of little negroes gambolling in the sunshine. . . . Among the slaves were artificers of all kinds. . . . so that a plantation produced everything within itself for ordinary use."*

The precision and energy with which Washington applied himself to whatever was his duty to do at the moment, may be guessed from a glimpse at his MS. Agricultural Common-place Book.†

* "Life of Washington," by Washington Irving, vol. i. p. 222. London, 1855.

† MS. Mus. Brit.—"Autographs and original Agricultural Memoranda of General George Washington," (presented by Professor Tucker, through Sir Robert Inglis).

"Barley.—A rich loam (but not too much mixed with sand) is good for it."

"Oats will grow on any kind of soil, the richer the greater the produce, and the stiffer the more it should be worked." So on with turnips, potatoes, cabbages, &c.

George Washington is as scrupulous in the manner and matter of what he writes, when noting down the best way of growing cabbages and potatoes; and his handwriting is as clear, exact, and masculine, in such memoranda, as in his autograph War Despatches. Whatever his hand found to do, he did it with his might. Duty is not less dignified in the plough-field than in the battle-field.

When Washington was, in 1774, called upon to leave the peaceful retirement which was congenial to him, his colony of black and white dependents, who equally adored him, and his wife to whom he was tenderly attached, he did not hesitate to comply with the desire of his countrymen, although he knew the path they had chosen for him was full of difficulties.

Washington had to begin his part in the war without money, without ammunition, without stores. He had to direct a great and courageous nation, but unpractised in war; and the impulse of whose newly-awakened enthusiasm was more likely to lead it into errors, than to insure the success due to zeal when combined with discretion.

The energy of Washington sustained the enthusiasm of his countrymen; his calm and well-trained mind directed it. His courage and determination, combined with the strong will of other men like himself, defeated the logic by which the mother-country tried to persuade herself that the American Rebellion would soon be calmed or crushed like the passion of a turbulent child.

In 1774, a fresh impulse had been given to the indignation of America against England by the condemnation of Dr. Benjamin Franklin, the Postmaster for the Colonies, by the Privy-Council in London.*

* Dr. Benjamin Franklin, born at Boston in 1706. The son of a tallow-chandler. In youth a printer at Philadelphia. Early, a great reader and ardent thinker. Sir William Keith, governor, observed the young journeyman printer's diligence at his trade and in his studies, and sent him to England to buy a press on his own account. (This was in 1724, when Benjamin Franklin was nearly nineteen years of age.) Franklin stayed in London two years, still working as journeyman printer and book-keeper to a merchant, and picking up scraps of new knowledge in the Old World. He then returned to America, and was employed as compositor at Philadelphia. In 1728, he became partner in a printing firm, and set up a newspaper, half full of his own "Moral Essays." He opened a book shop and married a widow, who, as maiden, had been his first love. Franklin then formed a literary club and reading society, and in 1732 began his "Poor

Dr. Benjamin Franklin was now sixty-eight years of age. He was one of the fathers of the American Press. For many years of his earlier life a printer himself, he had conducted the second newspaper that had been established in America. His countrymen were deservedly proud of him. His name was not only associated with all their great movements, political, social, and philan-

Richard's Almanack," and "The Way to Wealth." In 1736 he was made clerk to the Assembly of Pennsylvania, and was afterwards chosen a representative for Philadelphia. In 1737 he became postmaster of that city, and formed a Fire Insurance Company. In 1755, at the first beginning of the Seven Years' War between France and England, he was elected colonel of the Philadelphia regiment, but at first declined the honour. He applied himself to philosophical pursuits. The results of his electric experiments are well known, and gained him a gold medal from the Royal Society in London. Schools in Philadelphia were opened on a plan proposed by Franklin. The Pennsylvanian Hospital also. Appointed Postmaster in 1753 for all the Colonies, he brought forward a plan for the consolidation of the provinces by the adoption of a general government, which plan was rejected by the Administration at home. When Braddock was defeated in 1755, Franklin was made colonel, and, although he had formerly refused that appointment, conducted himself bravely. In 1757 he was sent to England with a petition to the king and council against the proprietaries who refused to pay their share in the public expenses. Whilst in England, Franklin, by his writings, stimulated the British Government in the conquest of Canada, and in 1762 he was dubbed Doctor of Laws at Oxford, when he returned to America. The remainder of Dr. Franklin's life will be told in the course of this narrative.

thropic, but it was connected with scientific discoveries of world-wide reputation.

Dr. Franklin, "the Philadelphian philosopher," had been the architect of his own fortunes; his strength had been acquired by a struggle against difficulties. He was possessed of the self-confidence inspired by self-elevation. Of obscure birth and humble parentage, he had by natural abilities, earnest study, integrity of conduct, and favourable opportunities, raised himself to honour and renown both in the Old and the New World.

But when America was in a state of insurrection against Great Britain, a man so remarkable as Dr. Franklin, who was known as a leader of public opinion in America, naturally became an object of suspicion to the parent Government. "Yet, on the contrary," says he of himself, "in America I was said to be too much of an Englishman, although in England I was condemned for being too much of an American."

Dr. Franklin was not opposed to the Crown of England until after his condemnation. How that came to pass, he shall tell us now in his own words:*

* "Recit du Procès contre moi-même, au sujet des Lettres

"Mr. Hutchinson, the governor of Massachusetts, and his secretary, Mr. Oliver, had written various letters to England; in which letters 'American leaders of sedition' were held up to scorn, and the most active and powerful enemies of the English government were recommended 'to be taken off!' On the occasion of the Stamp Act, years before, I had minutely examined the nature of the union of England with her colonies, and I was then convinced that the link of that union was the king, and not the parliament.... If the latter, our Puritan forefathers, in transporting themselves to the New World, would have renounced the Old World in vain, with all its vexations of acts, taxes, and inhuman laws, of civil and ecclesiastical courts of injustice.... Nevertheless, I regarded the supreme power of the King over all the colonies as of the greatest importance to them ... as a last resource for the settlement of their disputes; as a means of maintaining peace amongst them; as a centre of reunion for com-

d'Hutchinson et Oliver." This "Récit," from which the above extracts are translated, was written in France, and published there long after Franklin had adopted that country and language as his own.

mon strength against a common enemy. . . . I had opposed the stamp act and other measures —infringements on colonial rights—by which Great Britain hurt herself. . . . (She might have reckoned upon larger subsidies from our own free-will.) . . . I was grieved to see armed troops sent out to Boston. . . . I feared the fatal result of an armed English force placed over Americans. . . . I lamented the loss of love and trust, on the part of the mother country, towards us. . . . But what was my surprise, when (in England) I heard an Englishman of credit and distinction declare, that these vexatious proceedings on the part of the English government did not originate in the English government itself, *but that they had been projected, proposed to the administration, and obtained, by some Americans holding high offices, as essential to the welfare of their country!*

"I could not believe this. To convince me, my informant came to see me a few days afterwards in London, and produced the original letters of Lieutenant-Governor Hutchinson, of Secretary Oliver, and of some others.

"I was painfully surprised, but convinced. I

felt it my duty to apprise my fellow-citizens of the fact. I hoped that by so doing, by exposing the real origin of the grievance, my offended countrymen might still be reconciled to the British Crown. . . . But my informant would not permit me to take copies of the letters; and even had I done so, how could I convey evidence of their authenticity, which it would be to the interest of others to deny? It was useless, simply, to assert that I had seen such letters.

"At last, with difficulty, I obtained permission to send the original letters themselves over to America, under protest that they should not be printed, that no copy of them should be made, and that they should only be shown to a small number of specified persons at the head of government. . . . (I must here observe, that I never knew to whom these letters were addessed in England, as, before they were shown to me, their addresses had been removed.)

"It was afterwards declared that I sent these letters to a *cabal of my own private correspondents*, instead of to the committee of the assembly, which, in my quality of postmaster-general, I was bound to do, and which I did."

In America the perusal of, and the report of the existence of these letters, naturally excited violent indignation. A petition was instantly sent to the King, for the removal of Hutchinson and Oliver from the government of Massachusetts.

This petition was transmitted from America to Dr. Franklin; and Dr. Franklin, in the regular course of things, forwarded it to Lord Dartmouth, the Colonial Secretary, for presentation to his majesty. Under cover with this petition, Dr. Franklin wrote a letter to his lordship, declaring his belief, that America still desired the maintenance of peace with the mother country. In answer to this letter, Lord Dartmouth declared, in one to Dr. Franklin, that he was glad to hear "this good account of the general disposition of the American people, and that soon, he hoped, all cause of discontent would be removed, and that order and happiness would be re-established in America."

A day was appointed for hearing the petition. Dr. Franklin was summoned to appear before the Privy-Council, to support the petition in person, on Saturday morning, the 29th January,

1774. Thirty-five peers sat at the council-board.

The Solicitor-general, (Wedderburne) appeared on behalf of Governor Hutchinson. Franklin was supported by two counsel. The room was filled. Everybody who could gain admittance was in that crowd. Amongst the rest, Edmund Burke, and Dr. Franklin's friend, Dr. Priestly. *

Dr. Franklin stood calmly before the Privy-Council; although, as he afterwards declared, he knew himself to be hated by Englishmen. He was dressed in a "suit of Manchester velvet." (This suit, as we shall presently see, became famous in history.) His hair was straight and unpowdered; his whole appearance that of quaker-like simplicity. But Dr. Franklin was not a quaker. He solemnly affirmed the truth of the facts as already alleged. His statement was calm and consistent. But the judges were his enemies, and the sentence was a foregone conclusion. He was submitted to a complex examination; in the course of which, his early life was brought up before him. He was accused of

* See "Life and Times of Edmund Burke," Thomas Macknight, vol. ii., p. 45.

having printed Hutchinson's and Oliver's letters, and of having effaced their addresses. Franklin bore all this without any exhibition of anger. He defended himself by the calm statement of facts, which we already know.

Wedderburne, the Solicitor-general, had prepared one of the most elaborate and bitter invectives against Franklin which had ever been uttered by man to man.

Franklin still stood, outwardly unmoved, beneath this scorching torrent of words, which seared his reputation.

He was accused of falsehood and treachery. The petition was declared to be scandalous and vexatious. Dr. Franklin was dismissed from his office of Postmaster-General.

Even then he showed no sign of emotion. But the sense of insult, injury, and injustice, was, though smothered, deep and abiding.

In condemning Dr. Franklin, England had pronounced the decree against herself, as regards America. Franklin turned to quit the Privy-Council Chamber. Upon its threshold he met Dr. Priestly, and then and there declared to him: "I will never again put on the clothes I now wear, until I have had satisfaction for this day's work."*

"It was now," says Franklin, "*bon ton* to insult me in all English societies and in all English newspapers. . . . It was also signified to me that the petition praying for the recall of Hutchinson and Oliver should be rejected and the assembly censured. I myself was deprived of office. . . . And this is what is called 'Government!'"

But Government was not to be envied. Just at this time Horace Walpole wrote to General Conway:†

"The long-expected sloop is arrived from America at last, and turns out to be indeed a *man of war*. The General Congress have voted: Non-importation — Non-Exportation — Non-Consumption.

"Well, I believe you don't regret being neither in Parliament nor in Administration. Yet, if you have any inspiration about you, I assure you it will be of great service. . . . We are at our wit's end, which is no long journey. . . .

* Nine years afterwards, Franklin re-appeared in this suit of clothes when he went to sign the treaty of Paris, which for ever cut off the United States of America from the Crown of England.

† Walpole Correspondence. Year 1774.

Oh! you conclude Lord Chatham's crutch will be supposed a wand, and be sent for. . . . They might as well send for my crutch, and they should not have it. . . . The stile is too high to help them over. His lordship is fitter for raising a storm than for laying one, and of late seems to have lost both virtues."

Three days after the scene in the Privy-Council Chamber, Dr. Franklin wrote the following letter to his son, William Franklin, who was governor of New Jersey.* (The handwriting of this letter is clear, but rather cramped).

"London, Feb. 2nd, 1774.

"DEAR SON,

"This line is just to acquaint you that I am well, and that my office of Deputy-Postmaster is taken from me. As there is no prospect of your being ever promoted to a better Government, and that you hold has never defrayed its expenses, I wish you were well settled in your farm. 'Tis an honester and more honour-

* Original autograph.—Mus. Brit. Ex Dono. E. Wilmot. Red Seal. Folded in square. Addressed: 'To his Excellency William Franklin, Governor of New Jersey, Burlington. Via N. York packet." Postmark, "New York."

able, because a more independent employment. You will hear from others the treatment I have received. I leave you to your own reflections and determinations upon it, and remain ever, your affectionate father,

"B. FRANKLIN."

The next letter in the same collection from Dr. Franklin to his son is dated—

"Feb. 18th, 1774.

"Some tell me that it is determined to displace you likewise, but I do not know it for certain. . . . Perhaps they may expect that your resentment of their treatment of me may induce you to resign, and spare them the shame of depriving you whom they ought to promote. But this I would not advise you to do. Let them take your place if they want it, tho' in truth I think it scarce worth your keeping, since it has not afforded you sufficient to prevent you running every year behind-hand with me. But one may make something of an injury, nothing of a resignation."

"7th May, 1775.*

"I don't understand it as any favour, either to

* From the same to the same. Aut.

me or to you, the being continued in your office, by which, with all your prudence, you cannot avoid running behind-hand, if you live suitably to your station. While you are in it, I know that you will execute it with fidelity to your master; but I think independence more honourable than any service; and that in the state of American affairs, which, from the present arbitrary measures, is likely soon to take place, you will find yourself in no comfortable situation, and perhaps wish you had sooner disengaged yourself."

In the next letter in the same collection Dr. Franklin tells his son that he is staying with Lord Le Despencer for a little country air and exercise. This letter is dated "August 1st, 1774." In the course of it the writer reflects: "Posts and places are precarious; I would have my grandson a Free Man."

Very soon after Dr. Franklin wrote that letter, Lord Chatham, (who Horace Walpole has just declared "is fitter for raising a storm than for laying one") expressed a desire for an interview with him.

He was, as already declared, the determined foe of the Bourbons, whose name for years had made France tremble, whose policy during the last war had defeated allied France and Austria, who had then wrenched Canada from France and planted that gem of France in the colonial diadem of Great Britain, was now in opposition to the Crown on the subject of American taxation.

King George III. did not love Lord Chatham. The king was absolute on the American question. Lord North was, as Horace Walpole called him, "the ostensible minister;" but his majesty's obstinacy in pursuing the course so irritating to his colonial subjects, would suffer no opposition.

In the last war, Lord Chatham, as before said, was in the full vigour of his intellect, in the plenitude of his power, at the height of popular favour. His elevation to the peerage had been an offence to the people. His intellect, now mysteriously obscured for long intervals together, only revealed itself from time to time. At such times its splendour was the more dazzling, in contrast to the heavy clouds from which it emerged. At such times, when the clouds were rolled back, when (what

Lord Camden calls) the promethean fire of his eloquence returned to him, Lord Chatham's insight into truth was an inspiration; his politics were prophecies.

The House of Lords was an uncongenial atmosphere to the once popular minister. Ideas and language which would have electrified the lower house, and have stimulated hearers there to enthusiastic applause, were out of place in the more august assembly, which, as a rule, repudiated all outward demonstration.

It may be that the injustice of which, even he (Lord Chatham) in later life had been the victim—the obstinate opposition of the king to his views, the ingratitude of the people for his past services, the want of sympathy in the senate,—may have insensibly imbued him with feeling for American wrongs. However great the statesman or the philosopher, self is the centre of each man's system.

Lord Chatham believed himself to be an injured man. Dr. Franklin believed himself to be an injured man. These two men were, by country, custom, creed, and class, originally as wide apart as one hemisphere from another.

"When I went to England, in 1757," says Franklin, "I made several attempts to see William Pitt, but failed in doing so.* He was then first minister of the Crown. From that time I regarded that statesman as inaccessible.

"At the end of the autumn of 1774, I went, according to promise, to visit my friend, Mr. Sargent, at his estate in Kent. He told me that he had promised Lord Stanhope, who lives near, to take me to see him whenever I arrived. We went that evening. Lord Stanhope informed me that Lord Chatham wished to see me, and proposed that we should journey together the next day to Hayes. Which we did.

"Lord Chatham, that truly great man, rereceived me in the kindest way possible.... He questioned me closely on the affairs of

* The following account by Dr. Franklin of his intercourse with Lord Chatham, during the latest phase of that great statesman's life, was published in French, Paris, 1828, with other MSS. in possession of the family of M. le Veillard, an intimate friend of Dr. Franklin during his long residence in France. The above abbreviated extracts are translated from the *Récit des Négociations entre l'Amérique et l'Angleterre*, p. 106 to 167 inclusive.

America. He spoke with feeling of the latest measures taken against the province of Massachusetts. He testified much esteem and interest for the inhabitants of America. He told me that 'he hoped that they would continue firm and united in defending, by all legal and pacific measures, their constitutional rights.'

"I told him, in reply, that I did not doubt of their doing so. I told him, that if his lordship, and other great and wise Englishmen would unite, it might still be time to save America from the hands of an ignorant ministry which desired to tear her to pieces . . . . still time to re-establish between Great Britain and her colonies that union and harmony so essential to their mutual well-being.

"Lord Chatham replied, with great politeness, that my views were sound, and worthy of a benevolent mind. Also that he still hoped that the different fractions of opposition would unite, so as to work in concert, in re-establishing concord between the Old World and the New.

"I took advantage of this opportunity to remark, that the fall of great empires had always begun at their extremities, because the men appointed to rule distant colonies hoped that the people's complaints against them would be stifled by time and distance. I further declared, that, having eaten, drank, and talked with Americans, of every class, in their own country, I did not believe that any sane or sober man there desired a separation from the mother country, if their rights and liberties could be secured without such a stroke; but that Americans would die sooner than forfeit their rights and liberties."

At a later date, in the same diary, in the same year, Dr. Franklin continues:—"Having promised to send Lord Chatham news of Congress, when it reached me, I did so. About a month afterwards, on the 26th December, I went to him. His lordship received me with affectionate regard. . . . But his opinion of the Congress was still more welcome to me than his courtesy. 'They have acted,' said he, 'with calmness, wisdom, and moderation. I do not think that a more respectable assembly could be found since the finest times of the Greeks and Romans.'

"The 19th of January, 1775, I received a note from Lord Stanhope, stating that Lord

Chatham intended to bring a motion, relative to the affairs of America, before the House of Lords, the next day; that Lord Chatham strongly desired my presence in the house, and that, therefore, he, Lord Stanhope, would endeavour to secure my entry. The next morning, (the 20th,) came another note from Lord Stanhope, informing me that Lord Chatham would be in the entrance hall of the House of Peers at two o'clock, and would himself undertake my introduction.

"I went. . . . Certainly you are right in coming here,' said Lord Chatham to me; 'your presence at this day's debate will be more useful to America than mine,' and, taking me by the arm, his lordship conducted me to the entrance near the throne; but one of the door-keepers reminded him that this entrance was reserved for the eldest sons and brothers of peers. He then went with me to the door near the bar, where many persons were waiting for their friends, who had promised to get them admitted.

"In the midst of this crowd Lord Chatham presented me to the door-keepers, crying out with a loud voice, 'Here is Dr. Franklin! I desire that he may enter the house.' And the door flew open to me.

"The public knew nothing of any acquaintance subsisting between Lord Chatham and myself. His words, therefore, as I perceived, caused much astonishment.

"Lord Chatham entered the house. Something of importance was always expected, or apprehended, whenever this great man was seen in the senate, from which his infirmities too often caused his absence for a long time together. As he now appeared, a thrill of agitation seemed to pass through the assembly. Messengers were hastily despatched from all sides, doubtless to fetch in the friends of the ministry.

"Lord Chatham rose and spoke. With pleasure I listened, the more so, as in his motion I recognized the result of our recent conversation.

"'I move,' said his lordship, 'that an address be presented to his Majesty, humbly praying, and advising him to open the way for a pacification of the dangerous troubles of America, by beginning to moderate fermentation, and to allay animosity there. To prevent, at the same time, a fatal and sudden catastrophe at Boston, now a prey to daily irritation, caused by the presence of armed troops, may it please his Majesty graciously to cause immediate orders to be despatched to General Gage, for the withdrawal of his Majesty's forces from Boston, as soon as the rigour of the season, and other circumstances indispensable to the safety of the troops may permit.' *

"I was enchanted," continues Dr. Franklin, "with the speech by which Lord Chatham supported his motion. 'The spirit,' said he, 'which now resists your taxation in America, is the same which formerly opposed loans, benevolences, and ship-money in England, and, by the Bill of Rights, vindicated the English constitution. . . . This glorious spirit of Whiggism, ani-

* Most Englishmen are familiar with Lord Chatham's immortal speech which followed, but perhaps few have considered it as spoken in presence of Dr. Franklin, who instigated it. Lord John Russell, in his Life of C. J. Fox, (vol. i., p. 73,) makes Lard Chatham antedate his "conversing in a friendly confidence" with Franklin by "some years ago;" but Franklin declares that until the autumn of 1774 no personal communication had ever taken place between them. *Récit des Négociations*, as contained in *Mems. sur la Vie de B. Franklin, écrits par Lui-Même*, tome 2, pp. 106, 109, 110. Paris, 1828.

mates three millions of people in America, who prefer poverty with liberty to gilded chains and sordid affluence, and who will die in defence of their rights as freemen! . . . You may destroy their towns, and cut them off from the superfluities, perhaps the conveniences of life; but they are prepared to despise your power, and would not lament their loss, whilst they have—what, my lord?—their woods and their liberty. . . . Every motive of justice, or of prudence, of policy, or of dignity, urges you to allay the ferment in America, by a removal of your troops from Boston, by a repeal of your acts of parliament, and by a demonstration of amicable dispositions towards your colonies. On the contrary, every danger, every hazard, impend to deter you from perseverance in your present ruinous measures. . . . Foreign war hanging over your heads, by a slight and brittle thread. . . . France and Spain watching your conduct, and waiting for the maturity of your errors, with a vigilant eye to America, and the temper of your colonies, more than to our concerns, be they what they may. . . . As an American, I would recognize in England her supreme right of commerce and navigation; as an Englishman, by birth and principle, I recognize in the Americans their supreme inalienable right in their property—a right which they are justified in defending to the last extremity. . . . To maintain this principle is the common cause of the Whigs, on the other side of the Atlantic and on this. . . . ''Tis liberty to liberty engaged,' that they will defend themselves, their families, their country. . . . In this great cause they are immoveably allied. It is the alliance of God and nature, . . . immutable, eternal, fixed as the firmament of heaven! . . . With a dignity becoming your exalted situation, make the first advances to concord, to peace, to happiness; for that is your true dignity, to act with prudence and justice. . . ."

"The motion," says Dr. Franklin, "was rejected. Sixteen Scotch peers, and twenty-four bishops, linked to all the lords who hold or who expect places, form, when they agree amongst themselves, (as they generally do, in support of ministerial measures,) an overwhelming majority, which render all debates ridiculous, the result being a foregone conclusion." *

"On Sunday, the 29th January," continues Dr. Franklin, "Lord Chatham came to London, and to my home in Craven Street. He brought me his plan in full, in the form of an Act of Parliament. He asked me to read it. . . . He called himself the watch, and me the regulator. . . . He said, in the course of our conversation, that he feared, on account of his precarious health, to defer measures on behalf of America. Finally, he resolved to lay his plan before the house on the following Wednesday. . . . He remained with me two hours, his equipage standing at my door. People, coming out of church, saw it; and as everything concerning so great a man is interesting to the people, and their attention was eagerly alive to American affairs, Lord Chatham's visit to me was observed, which not a little flattered my vanity—the honour yielding me the more pleasure, when

* A copy of Lord Chatham's motion was sent by Lord Stanhope to Dr. Franklin, then resident in Craven Street. Dr. Franklin transmitted the said copy to America. Complimentary letters passed between Lord Chatham, Lord Stanhope, and Dr. Franklin.

I remembered the insult I had received in the Privy-Council Chamber exactly one year before.

" . . . . On Wednesday, Lord Stanhope, at the request of Lord Chatham, conducted me to the House of Peers, which was soon full. Lord Chatham, in an excellent and eloquent speech, proposed, developed, and defended his project in favour of America.

"When he was seated, Lord Dartmouth rose, and said, agreeably enough, 'that the subject before the house was of such weight, and of such dimensions, that it necessitated the most mature reflection. . . . that he hoped, therefore, that the noble lord did not intend to ask the house immediately to vote upon his proposition.'

"Lord Chatham replied, that he 'desired nothing better than mature reflection.'

"Lord Sandwich then rose, and, in a petulant harangue, voted that Lord Chatham's proposition should be instantly rejected, with the contempt it deserves.' . . . 'Nay,' continued Lord Sandwich, 'I cannot believe that this is the work of an English peer. . . . It seems to me rather to be the production of some American.'

"I," says Dr. Franklin, "was leaning on the

bar of the house; Lord Sandwich turned himself towards me 'I think,' said he, after a pause, 'I think that I have before my eyes, at this moment, the person who has originated this production,—*one of the most bitter and pernicious enemies that this country has ever had.*'

"This sally," says Dr. Franklin, "fixed upon me the looks of a great number of lords. But, as I did not choose to take it to myself, I did not change countenance, any more than if my features had been made of wood. . . . . Many other lords were for rejection of Lord Chatham's 'production.' (It was rejected by 61 to 32.)

"Hereditary legislators!" groaned I to myself; "better would it be to have, as in a certain German university, hereditary professors of mathematics!"

"But," Dr. Franklin afterwards confesses, "this reflection was the result of momentary ill-humour; for, on consideration, what better is the elected House of Commons? What better can it ever be, as long as electors receive bribes for their votes, and give money to the ministry, wherewith to corrupt the representatives which they have chosen?" *

Soon afterwards, in the ensuing spring of 1775, Dr. Franklin bade farewell to Lord Chatham for ever.

Dr. Franklin appeared before his countrymen, in Congress assembled, primed with the latest information from the mother country, and stung into antagonism against her, by the personal wrongs she had inflicted on him.

All hope of reconciliation between Great Britain and her American colonies was now at an end.

The first blow was struck.

On the night of the 18th April, 1775, a detachment of the Royal forces was sent from Boston to seize some military stores which the insurgents had collected at Concord, for the purpose,

* On the next day, Feb. 2nd, Lord North moved an address: "We consider it our indispensable duty humbly to beseech his Majesty that he will take the most effectual measures to enforce due obedience to the laws of the supreme legislature; and we beg leave, in the most solemn manner, to assure his Majesty that it is our fixed resolution, at the hazard of our lives and properties, to stand by his Majesty, against all rebellious attempts, in the maintenance of the just rights of his Majesty and the two Houses of Parliament." Which motion of "the ostensible minister" was carried by a majority of 199.

it was suspected, of destroying or harassing the royal troops. A small body of the insurgents determined to oppose the military, and to prevent their seizure of these stores. The insurgents were defeated and the King's soldiers destroyed all the stores at Concord which they could find there.

The alarm spread like wild-fire. The militia quickly assembled, and furiously assailed the royal troops upon their return to Boston. Every house, every tree, every wall, every hedge, seemed alive with fury. The military were shot down; sixty-five were killed, one hundred and eighty were wounded, twenty-eight were taken prisoners; and it was only by the aid of a regiment sent from Boston, under command of Lord Percy, that the remainder of the detachment was saved.

The triumph of the insurgents was small, but it brought volunteers from far and near to their standard. The fortresses of Ticonderago and Crown Point were surprised by a body of militia, and the Americans thus obtained one hundred pieces of cannon, and a large quantity of ammunition, of which they stood in need.

Boston was blockaded. Towns and villages were garrisoned. General Gage, whom Lord Chatham had, in January, implored the King to withdraw from Boston with his troops, was reinforced by Generals Howe, Burgoyne, and Clinton. General Gage proclaimed pardon to all Americans who would lay down their arms. But the insurgents now laughed the King's general to scorn.

Merchants gave up trade. Farmers forsook their tillage. Mechanics left their work, to take up arms against Great Britain.

George Washington, lately called from the plough, and from his peaceful estate in Virginia, and now placed in command of the American forces, exclaimed: "Unhappy it is to reflect that a brother's sword has been sheathed in a brother's breast, and that the once happy and peaceful plains of America are to be either drenched with blood, or inhabited by slaves!"

Dr. Franklin wrote from America to an old friend of his in England:

"Philadelphia, July 5th, 1775.

"Mr. Strahan,

"You are a member of Parliament, and one of that majority which has doomed my country to destruction. You have begun to burn our towns, and murder our people. Look upon your hands! You and I were long friends. You are now my enemy and I am your's.

"B. FRANKLIN."*

Dr. Franklin having washed his hands of England and English friends, now turned his eyes across the Atlantic towards France.

France was a weak government, torn and tossed by cabinet contention, as we have seen, and "gyrating like a weather-cock with every wind that blows."

England was a strong government; but, as says Earl Russell, "a strong government which overleaps wisdom, and violates justice, is one of the worst evils which can befall a country."

* A facsimile of this letter is exhibited in the Life of Dr. Franklin, by his son. It disproves a statement made in Nichols' Literary Anecdotes of the 18th Century, (p. 392, vol. iii.) that, notwithstanding the difference of political opinion between Dr. Franklin and Mr. Strahan, "there was never anything acrimonious in their letters." Mr. Strahan was the king's printer, In 1775 he became M.P. for Malmesbury in Wiltshire. In sobriety of demeanour, former pursuits, and fondness for science and literature, Mr. Strahan and Dr. Franklin much resembled each other.

Yet Englishmen, whose common honesty was a common proverb, defended the violation of English justice in America, as the maintenance of right. Even that great moralist, Dr. Samuel Johnson, essayed to prove taxation no tyranny!

"Since the Americans" says Dr. Johnson, "have made it necessary to subdue them, may they be subdued with the least injury possible! . . . When they are reduced to obedience, may that obedience be secured by stricter laws and stronger obligations! There are some who start at the thoughts of England free and America in chains. Children fly from their own shadow, and rhetoricians are frighted at the sound of their own voices. *Chains* is undoubtedly a dreadful word, but perhaps the masters of civil wisdom may discover some gradations between chains and anarchy. . . . The contest may end in the softer phrase of English superiority and American obedience."

Dr. Franklin insinuates that Dr. Johnson's motives in thus defending the cause of government were not altogether disinterested. "One of my friends," says Franklin, "William Strahan, the king's printer, came to my house" (in London, in 1774). "He had just been to the treasury, and showed me what he called 'a pretty thing' for one of his friends. It was an order to pay Dr. Samuel Johnson £150 for his half year's salary. . . . ." *

But Londoners, and people, generally, under the strong government of England, did not care half so much for Dr. Johnson's essay on Taxation, as the people of Paris, under the weak government of Versailles, cared for all that was written, done, or said by Voltaire, the exile at Ferney, and the friend of Frederick the Great, king of Prussia.

Every rumour concerning the patriarch of philosophy was eagerly caught up and echoed:

"M. de Voltaire has rendered the country from Gex to Ferney free . . . He has enfranchised it from statute work, and from Farmers-General, and from jobbery. . . . Seventy-two commissioners have retired from that country. . . . External commerce is achieved with Geneva and all Switzerland. . . . Savoy is about to become perfectly free.† . . . M. de Voltaire builds a great many houses. . . . Madame St. Julien, the wife of the

* Mémoires sur la Vie de B. Franklin, ecrits par lui-même, tome ii., p. 103. Paris, 1828.

† Mercure de France, 1775.

Receiver-General for the Clergy, has taken one of M. de Voltaire's houses."*

And M. de Voltaire, the philanthropist, was under the ban of the Church and State of France. He had built a tomb for himself at Gex, half inside and half outside the church walls there; which tomb he showed to pilgrims who went to do homage to him. . . . saying, that the position of this tomb was significant of his intermediate future state, or of that which the Church would assign to him; and above the little chapel at Gex flamed in letters of gold, "*Deo Erexit Voltaire.*"

Meanwhile, the King of England made treaties with Hesse and with Brunswick, by which 12,000 Hessians and 5,000 other German troops were engaged to fight in North America for English money. Frederick of Prussia made these troops pay the cattle toll on their passage through his states, saying, "they have been hired as such."

But a great part of King Frederick's own army in the last war was composed of foreign mercenaries. These had helped to beat the French at Rosbach and at Leuthen.†

* Journal d'un Observateur, 1775.

† Les Conseils du Trone, vol. i., p. 162. Paris, 1828.

The attempt to establish despotism in America, by the hands of these foreign troops, cut asunder there the last remaining links of attachment towards the mother country.

Nothing now but war was talked of in the American Congress and in the English Parliament.

The strong government of the King had prevailed against the remonstrances, the entreaties, the unrivalled eloquence of statesmen opposed on other points, but united in favour of American reconciliation.

Burke spoke. Fox spoke. Chatham spoke. The Ministry were enraged by opposition almost to madness. But rival statesmen had united together, and spoken in vain. The will of the King was absolute.

"Let us be careful," had said John St. John, "how we permit ourselves to be drawn aside by mistaken ideas of lenity. . . . I thank God for the spirit of the people of England, who, before the revolt becomes general, while discrimination is still possible, are resolved to vindicate and to rescue the authority of the British Legislature."*

* Cavendish MSS., Egerton Collection, Mus. Brit.

John St. John had said this in 1774. In 1775 blood was flowing in America.

There was more wisdom in Lord Chatham's entreaties to, than in John St. John's defence of, the Crown. Eloquence, for once, was sounder than logic.

In Philadelphia, a statue of the King was smelted and made into a clock for the dome of the Town-hall there. Upon the clock's face was inscribed: "Announce Liberty, as you strike, to this city and its inhabitants."*

The people of England were taught to regard the "Philosopher of Philadelphia" as the firebrand of anarchy and the root of rebellion. An inimical account of Dr. Franklin's early life was published in London in the *Political Magazine* (1780); and amongst other things it is declared in this article, that Franklin had (before his return to America, in 1775) visited the ruins of Scoon, the ancient palace of the Kings of Scotland, in company with a gentleman of learning and character; and that when standing upon the ruins, he had declared, with all the solemnity of prediction: "We are now treading on the ruins

* Franklin's MS. Common Place Book, Mus. Brit.

of ancient palaces. Our descendants may do the same in future days, and say, 'Here formerly stood the abode of the King.'"

Scotland and Ireland had lately been drained of a large portion of their peasantry, who were driven, by the rapacity of their landlords, to emigrate to America. The Irish were favourably inclined, by the mutual faith of Rome, to France. France had formerly been the refuge of Scotch Jacobites. The love for, and memory of the Stuarts, had not yet died out in Scotland. Irish and Scotch emigrants were hardy adherents of Transatlantic discontent. Hardy in body; trained to endure; with everything to gain, and nothing to lose by rebellion; animated, in the cause against England, by the memory of their own past grievances against the motherland, which had not afforded them a sufficient shelter; full of resentment against the 'German mercenaries' who arrived with the troops sent out to quell their resistance of Old World evils in the New World, where they had hoped for freedom.

As for the determination of the descendants of old settlers in America to defend and to die for "their woods and their liberties," it was, as a Transatlantic loyalist secretly affirmed to his Majesty's Government (through General Haldimand):*

"No other than that ancient, republican, independent spirit, which the first emigrants to America brought out with them. . . . This is the seed which, planted together with the colonies, early took deep root, and being nourished by the beams of civil and ecclesiastical government, though at some seasons it hath appeared withered and almost dead, yet accidental causes, like showers on the natural world, have from time to time revived and given it fresh growth, but never before with that luxuriance with which we now see it spread." And after this flower of speech the "American Colonist and Royalist" declares, "The immediate causes which brought it to its present enormity lie obvious to every observing eye here. . . . They originated in the disappointed ambition of one man of great influence, and of no private or public virtue" (Dr. Franklin.) "The

* Memorial—"From an American Colonist and Loyalist to Major-General Haldimand, Brigadier-General to the Southern District of North America." Dated "Boston, 30th May, 1775." MS. Mus. Brit. Haldimand Collection.

occasion did not escape those watchful, turbulent spirits which are ever to be found in all governments partaking of democracy. By the help of the single word "liberty," they conjured up the most horrid phantoms in the minds of the common people, an easy prey to such specious betrayers."

If, by the word "liberty," Dr. Franklin conjured up the most horrid phantoms in the New World, he used it as a spell whereby to call up the most delightful visions in the Old World. Already we have said that Dr. Franklin, when returning to his own country, in 1775, had turned his eyes across the Atlantic towards France. How young Democracy sprang from old Feudalism in France, must here be told by the Marquis de Lafayette, one of the future heroes of the American rebellion and of the French Revolution.

CHAPTER III.

M. le Marquis de Lafayette. (His own account of his early life and flight to America)—M. le Comte de Ségur. (His own account of himself when forced to remain at the court of Versailles)—Queen Marie Antoinette—The Princesse de Lamballe. (Her own account of how the friendship began between the Queen and herself)—The King's sister—Christopher Glück, the composer—Music, the Drama, and Court politics in France—Beaumarchais and the Barber of Seville—New Philosophy in Paris and at Versailles—The Emperor Joseph II. in France—The Emperor's arrival at Versailles, his conversation there—The Queen's rebuke to the Emperor—Public toilettes—Horace Walpole—Picture of the toilette of a French belle of the 18th century—Turgot, Minister of Finançe at Versailles—Turgot's early life—Lent in 1775—The people clamour for bread at Versailles—The King's placard—Resignation of Turgot and Malesherbes—Curious MS. (Bibliothèque Impériale) concerning Protestants—James Necker, the Protestant—James Necker's previous life—James Necker, Director-General of Finance at Versailles.

"It would be too tiresome to enumerate all the details of my birth," says M. de Lafayette, "which followed close upon the death of my father, at Minden. . . . too tedious to dwell upon my childhood at Auvergne. . . . or on my translation to a college in Paris, at eleven years of age, when I soon lost my virtuous mother, and when the death of her father made me rich, poor though I was born.*

"Nor must I tell too much of some scholastic successes, animated by the love of glory, and troubled by that of liberty; . . . nor of my enrolment in the corps of Black Musketeers, which took me from the school-room on review days; . . . nor of my marriage, when I was sixteen years old; this event having been preceded by my sojourn at the academy of Versailles.

"You ask me the epoch of my first sighs for liberty and for glory. . . . I can recall nothing in my life anterior to my enthusiasm for glorious anecdotes, nor to my projects of run-

* The above abbreviated extracts are translated from Mémoires de ma Main. (MSS. de Général Lafayette, publiés par sa Famille. Bruxelles, 1837.) Lafayette's father was Colonel of the Grenadiers of France and Chevalier of St. Louis. He was killed at the battle of Minden when 24 years of age.

ning through the world in search of reputation. At eight years of age, my heart throbbed with the hope of encountering, in the course of our school walks, a certain hyena which did some harm, and made still more noise in our neighbourhood. . . . At college, my only dislike to study was its restraint. Republican narratives charmed me; and when my wife's relations contrived to procure a place at Court for me, I did not hesitate to displease them, that I might retain my independence.*

"In such a disposition did I first hear speak of American troubles. These were not notorious in Europe until the year 1776. America's ever memorable 'Declaration of Independence' reached Europe at the end of that same year.

"England, being covered with laurels, and enriched by conquests, having domineered over all seas, and insulted all nations, turned her pride against her own colonies. For some time past North America had given umbrage to her; she

* Lafayette, the future republican hero, was, as before said, married to a daughter of the Noailles family, already described as the haughtiest, most exclusive family of the old French noblesse, and the most bigoted to old French customs and conventions.

desired to link on new vexations to former shackles, and to invade the most sacred privileges.

"Never had so fine a cause claimed the attention of mankind. It was the last combat for liberty, and liberty, if now overcome, had no hope, and no refuge in the future. Oppressors and oppressed, all were about to receive a lesson. Either this great work must complete itself, or would be buried beneath its ruins. . . . At the first news of this combat, my heart was enrolled in it, and I dreamed but of fighting under the banner of liberty.

"Silas Deane" (American envoy to crave the aid of France against England) "was in Paris. But Paris was afraid to see Silas Deane, and his voice was drowned in the vociferations of Lord Stormont" (English Ambassador at Versailles).

"I presented myself to Silas Deane; my face was only nineteen years old, and spoke like my tongue, more of my zeal, than of my experience. But I made Silas Deane feel the value of my proposed departure for America, and he signed arrangements for it. My project was well received, but money was wanted wherewith, secretly, to buy, and to arm a ship, in which I might set sail for America. . . . I said to Silas Deane: 'I will purchase a ship, which will carry your officers. It is in danger that I love to share your fortunes."

"All was promptly executed. . . . The secrecy of my preparations was truly miraculous. Family, friends, ministers, French spies, English spies—all were blinded.

"In the meanwhile, I was engaged to visit England with the Prince de Poix. . . . When I reached that country, I first paid my respects to the American Bancroft, and afterwards to his Britannic Majesty. . . . At nineteen years of age it is not unpleasant to cajole the King one is about to fight, and to dance at my Lord Germain's (minister for the American colonies) in company with my Lord Rawdon, newly arrived from New York, and to meet at the Opera that same Clinton, who would be found again at the Battle of Monmouth.

"But, though I kept my intentions a secret, I made no secret of my sentiments. . . . I declined to be a witness of the English seaport embarkations against the 'Rebels.'

"At the end of three weeks I refused to accompany my uncle, the ambassador, to the court of Versailles.* I excused myself, by saying that I had a fancy for a little run to Paris. It came into his head to account for my absence on the plea of illness. . . . I should not have suggested that plea, but I did not oppose it."

Lafayette reached Bordeaux, where he learnt that his flight was known at Versailles, and that an order for his arrest was issued. He then feigned to go to Marseilles, where he was ordered by the Court to join his father-in-law, who was about to travel into Italy. At some leagues from Bordeaux, Lafayette disguised himself as his own courier, and rode before the post-chaise, which he had hired, taking the Bayonne road. At Bayonne there was a halt. Lafayette lay down upon the straw in the stable. The postmaster's daughter came in and quickly discovered that the young marquis was no courier. But she pledged herself to aid his flight, and by her adroit fidelity afterwards turned others off from the right road in pursuit of him.

* The Marquis de Noailles, brother of the Duc d'Ayen, and uncle of Lafayette's wife.

Thus, M. de Lafayette joined his ship, on the 26th of April, 1777, and set sail for America the same day, leaving his wife, his "*femme chérie*" as he calls her, *enceinte* with their first child, and his family, and the Court of Versailles outraged by his departure.

When Lafayette arrived in America,—at Philadelphia,—he sent this note to the assembly:

"I have earned by my sacrifices the right to ask two favours: the one is to serve as a volunteer; the other is, to serve at my own expense."

The Congress unanimously appointed Lafayette Major-General in the American army.

George Washington, the Generalissimo of the forces, was then with his troops near Philadelphia. Washington and Lafayette met. From that hour dated a life-long friendship between these two men.*

The young Count de Ségur, at Versailles, had been the friend and confidant of Lafayette, De Ségur had shared Lafayette's enthusiasm for liberty, but was too much shackled by authority and circumstances to share his flight.†

* Nouvelle Biographie Générale. Paris, 1831.

† The young Count de Ségur was the son of Philippe Henri

Of the young nobility at Versailles at this time de Ségur tells us:

"We passed the winter in games, in balls, and in pleasures. Frenchmen then resembled those young Neapolitans, who laugh, sing, and sleep without fear, upon the lava-sides of a volcano. . . . We had a young King who was virtuous, beneficent; and whose first thought was for the happiness of his subjects; who desired no other authority but that of justice; and who, by his example, gave a new impulse to all generous and philanthropic ideas.*

"Old custom excluded the youth of France from public business. To associate one's-self with politics and legislation it was essential to have attained a mature age, which does not always

de Ségur, who distinguished himself at the battle of Lawfield (before the peace of Aix-la-Chapelle). His (Philippe Henry's) arm was there fractured, but he rallied his men, forced the intrenchments, and did not quit his post until after the victory was gained. Louis XV. on the field of battle turned to the Lawfield hero's father (who was also present at that engagement), and exclaimed, "Men like your son deserve to be invulnerable as they are invincible."—Siècle de Voltaire.

* Mémoires, &c., par M. le Comte de Ségur, abridged Extracts translated from. (Vol. i. p. 93 to 108 inclusive.) Paris et Londres, 1825.

bring wisdom with it, although it is supposed to do so. . . . . . . The ministry of Louis XV. had allowed the shameful partition of Poland, by Russia, Prussia, and Austria. . . . . . . a fatal partition, whereby France was reduced from the first to the second rank of monarchies. . . . which augmented considerably the three already formidable powers of Europe, and which, by dismembering an innocent power, without pretext, threw open the door to the violation of all rights, all properties, and all engagements. *

". . . Liberty, drowsy in the Old World during so many ages, awoke in another hemisphere, and wrestled gloriously against an armed and antiquated domination, of most formidable strength. . . . A whole nation which wills to be free, is with difficulty conquered.

"The courage of these new republicans attracted the esteem of all Europe, and the good wishes

* Joseph II., surnamed "The Amiable," was then Emperor of Austria; but, unfortunately for him (as Lord Brougham considers it), "his mother Maria Theresa, the Empress-Queen, was resolved that her son, even when clothed by the election of the German diet with the imperial titles, should exercise none of its prerogatives during her life. Long after he had arrived at man's estate, he was held in a kind of tutelage by that bold and politic princess!"

of the friends of justice and humanity. The youth of Europe, especially, reared in the bosom of old monarchies, but familiar with the great writers and heroes of Greece and Rome, were, by a strange contrast, enthusiasts in the cause of the American insurrection.

"The first three Frenchmen distinguished by their rank at Court, who offered the aid of their swords to the Americans, were—the Marquis de Lafayette, the Vicomte de Noailles, and myself. We three had long been united by the ties of friendship, and still more by conformity of sentiment. Soon, also, by ties of blood. * ... We three vowed secrecy to each other, in our arrangements with the American commissioners. The conformity, however, of our sentiments, our opinions, and our desires, did not just then, unfortunately, exist in our fortunes. The Vicomte de Noailles and myself were de-

* Lafayette and the Vicomte de Noailles were married to two daughters of the Duc de Noailles (then d'Ayen). Their mother (the Duchesse de Noailles) was daughter of the first marriage of Chancellor d'Aguesseau's son. De Ségur, in the spring of 1777, married a daughter of the second marriage of Chancellor d'Aguesseau's son, and thus became uncle of his two friends' wives.

pendant on our relatives, and only enjoyed the pension which they allowed us. The Marquis de Lafayette, on the contrary, although younger and less advanced in military rank than we were, found himself, by a singular chance, at nineteen years of age, master of his wealth, of his person, and of an income of 100,000 livres. . . Lafayette was at all times, especially when young, of a cold and grave demeanour, which made him appear, very falsely, timid and embarrassed. This cold exterior, and his slowness of speech, were in singular contrast to the petulance, the levity, and talkativeness of people of his age; but this exterior, so frigid in appearance, concealed the most active mind, the firmest character, and the most burning soul. . . . I could not help laughing to myself, when listening to Marshal Noailles, and others of his family, begging and praying me to warm his coldness, to rouse him from his indolence, and to impart a little fire into his character. . . . Judge, then, what must have been their astonishment, when they suddenly found that this young sage of nineteen years old, so icy, so indifferent, was carried away by the passion for glory, and its perils; that he had set sail, arrived without accident in America, and was there received with the welcome due to his noble and generous audacity!

"The French Government, desiring to undermine the English power, secretly gave, or permitted to be given, aid in arms, ammunition, and money to the Americans; but, through weakness, dared not proclaim itself openly—affecting, on the contrary, an impartial neutrality, and blinding itself to the point of believing, that its secret measures would not be suspected, and that it would ruin its enemy without incurring the danger of measuring its strength with that enemy.

"Such an illusion could not last. The Cabinet of England was too clear-sighted to let the Cabinet of France thus reap the advantages of war without incurring its risks."*

* The American press, encouraged by this secret assistance, buoyed up the hopes of the Insurrectionists as to French intentions, and kept alive the animosity against England by such notices as the following, from *The Pennsylvania Evening Post*, (published every Tuesday, Thursday, and Saturday evenings. —Intelligence from England by way of France.)

"Saturday, Feb. 8, 1777.

"LONDON, OCTOBER 21.

"The public may be assured that the French consider a war with England as inevitable, and that the same will take place

Young French nobles, shut out, as one of them has just told us, from politics and legislation, and forbidden for a time to cross the Atlantic in search of glory, formed a brilliant staff around the person of Marie Antoinette, Queen of France. And surely no Queen was ever more formed by nature to rule over the hearts of a brave and impulsive nation than was she!

In the years since her marriage, the Queen had gained in beauty, grace, and dignity.

Englishmen, whilst France was still open to them, were glad, at times, to fly from stormy debates on the American question, and from the strong Government at home, for momentary relaxation at the Court of France. Amongst these, Edmund Burke. Years afterwards, he says:—

immediately. Lord George Germaine has received positive intelligence, which he laid before the King, that the American Congress, before they published their Declaration of American Independency, received a positive assurance from France and Spain . . . . . they requested it sooner, but were answered it was impossible, as the preparations of France were not in sufficient readiness. The King has declared repeatedly that he will persist in the American war, were it to be at the hazard of his crown; and will next summer have a force there sufficient to finish the dispute in one campaign more. His Majesty is much encouraged by the *bloody junto*."

"I saw the Queen of France at Versailles, and surely never lighted on this orb, which she scarcely seemed to touch, a more delightful vision! I saw her just above the horizon, cheering and decorating the elevated sphere she just began to move in, glittering like the morning star, full of hope, and splendour, and joy."

Those who knew her best, who lived in hourly intercourse with this lovely daughter of Maria Theresa, declare that her gentleness and affability were equal to her majesty and grace. The King, so long indifferent, was now devoted to her. Mesdames, the Princesses, his aunts, might scowl as they chose, at this "supremacy of the Austrian," but it was now established beyond the power of their evil interference. A new life, a fresh inspiration, had accrued to the Queen with her new position. The attachment between herself and Louis XVI. was mutual.

The Princesse de Lamballe, the Queen's most intimate friend and confidante at this time, lays great stress on the happiness of domestic life at Versailles and at Trianon, of which she was the witness—a mournful witness; for the Princesse de

Lamballe was the widow of a man whom she had passionately loved.*

As her fate is so intimately and tragically associated with that of Queen Marie Antoinette, we must pause a moment to contemplate her, and to consider what she has to tell us of herself.

From the portrait which has survived the Revolution, the Princesse de Lamballe looks down upon the beholder with mingled sweetness and sorrow, challenging sympathy, yet, at the same time, by her dignity, rebuking vulgar curiosity. The long, luxuriant hair, destined to be wound round a ruffian's arm, is carried back, so as to display a brow on which truth is nobly revealed; truth dearer to her than life.†

* Marie Thérèse Louise de Carignan, Princess of Savoy, born in 1749. (She had three sisters, one married to Prince Colonna, another to the Prince Doria Pamphila, and the third, at Vienna, to Prince Lobkowitz, the patron of the immortal Haydn. Her brother was the Prince de Carignan.) She married, when scarcely more than a child, the Prince de Lamballe, son of the Duc de Penthièvre, whose daughter (the Prince de Lamballe's sister) married the Duc de Chartres, afterwards Duc d'Orléans, grandfather of the present Orléans family, now exiled in England.

† In the Revolution she was led dying to the terrible wicket. "Who are you?" asked the executioners in scarfs. "Louisa of Savoy, Princesse de Lamballe." "What part do you take at Court? Are you acquainted with any plot?" "I never was ac-

The soft eyes rest mournfully on you, but they are gazing at something beyond you, far away either in the Past or the Future. The lips are parted in a smile, betokening rather amiable endurance than any vivid interest in the present. She is tall and slender, richly apparelled, as when she stood near the Queen at Versailles, in the midst of the Court; but the costly lace upon her fair bosom seems to heave with a sigh from the heart which is desolate beneath.

"I was married when a child," says she; "I was a widow without being a mother; my days are passed in mourning the memory of the time when I was a wife."

quainted with any plot." "Swear to love liberty and equality; swear to hate the king, the queen, and royalty." "I will take the first oath—the second I cannot take; it is not in my heart." "Swear, however," said one of the bystanders. But the unfortunate lady could no longer see nor hear. "Let Madame be set at liberty," said the chief of the wicket. . . . . At the door, however, she was received by some wretches eager after carnage. At the first stroke of a sabre on the back of her head, the blood gushed forth. She still advanced, supported by two men, who perhaps meant to save her; but a few paces further, she fell from the effect of a second blow. Her beautiful form was torn in pieces. It was even mangled and mutilated by the murderers, who divided the fragments among them. Her head, her heart, and other parts of her body were borne through Paris on the points of pikes!—Thiers' French Revolution, vol. ii. pp. 42, 43.

Until lately, when we find her at Versailles, she had lived the life of a recluse with her husband's father, the Duc de Penthièvre.

"Shut up with my sorrow," she tells us, "retired from the world, alone with my dear and venerable father-in-law, trying to compensate to him for the loss of his son, and for his regret at not seeing himself (as my marriage was childless) re-produced in his son's posterity, we sought to console ourselves by works of charity. . . . In the midst of this mournful existence, a new star suddenly shone on me through the clouds. . . . Marie Antoinette, the Queen, young and beautiful, came to me as a messenger from heaven, and, in the softest language of compassion, offered the balm of consolation to heal my wounds. . . . She ceased not to visit me. She never wearied of soothing the affliction of an old man, and a sorrow-stricken woman, whom she found sinking beneath the weight of grief. From that first day when she came to us, I loved the Queen. . . . It was during that hard winter, when so many of the people were perishing for want of fuel and bread. The Queen asked me to assist her in mitigating the misery of others. Sledges were just introduced in France. These German conveyances suited our purpose. The Queen, the Duchesse d'Orléans, the Duc de Penthièvre, and myself, adopted this mode of travelling."*

"We visited poor families, who were starving.

"'The King,' said the Queen to me, during one of these expeditions, 'is out hunting now; not the stag, but wood for the poor. He will not return to Trianon until he has sent his prey to Paris.'

"That same day the Queen invited the Duc, my father-in-law, and myself to dine with her at Trianon. The Duc begged to be excused, but I, at the hour agreed upon, went alone, and had the honour of dining with the Queen *tête-à-tête.* I was sad, as usual.

"After dinner the Queen said to me, 'the King and his dear sister Elizabeth, desire, as I do, that you, Princesse, should come and live with us at Versailles. What say you, Madame?'

"I thanked her majesty, the King, and the Princesse Elizabeth, for their goodness towards

* Madame Campan tells us that in these sledges ladies of the eighteenth century travelled masked. Therefore the Queen was *incógnita.* Afterwards, when calumny attacked her Majesty the mask was declared to be convenient for intrigue. The Queen then relinquished both sledge and mask, but her good works of charity were impeded thereby.

me, but I said that the state of my health and spirits rendered it impossible for me to respond, worthily, to the favour with which they honoured me. As I spoke, my tears flowed. The Queen, with that benevolence peculiar to her, took my hand, and gently dried my eyes with her handkerchief.

"'I am about,' said she, 'to re-establish a long-suppressed office in my household. The one who holds it must be near my person . . . I hope that this appointment may contribute to the happiness of some estimable individual.'

"I replied, that her majesty could not fail in attaining her wish, as none could be otherwise than happy near one so generous and benevolent as herself.

"The Queen then merely said, affably, 'If, indeed, you think as you say, my hope will be realized.'

"Three or four days afterwards, I again had the honour of dining with her majesty. The Princesse Elizabeth was present. After dinner, the Queen asked me 'if I were still of the same opinion concerning the person she was desirous of adding to her household?' Having forgotten the subject of our conversation, I knew not what to answer.

"The Princesse Elizabeth began to laugh.

"'The Queen, my dear Princesse,' said she to me, 'has appointed you Superintendent of her Household, and that with the glad consent of the King.'

"'Yes,' added the Queen, advancing towards me, 'it is the truth;' and she condescended to embrace me.

"I remained silent from astonishment.

"'I thought,' continued the Queen, 'that I should surprise you, but I believe that Versailles is a more suitable abode for you than the gloomy Château of the Duc de Penthièvre. From this day,' she added, 'let us confirm the friendship which unites us, and may it contribute to our mutual happiness!'

"The Queen then took me by the hand, to which the Princesse Elizabeth joined hers, saying to the Queen: 'Oh! my dear sister, you must let me form a trio in this concert of friendship.'"*

* The above are abbreviated extracts, translated from Mémoires relatifs à la Famille Royale de France, containing fragmentary Mémoires de la Princesse de Lamballe, edited by an

Between the Queen and the Princesse de Lambelle there was another bond; that of language. The Queen having been, in early youth and childhood, the pupil of Metastasio, (who was the protegé and court poet of Maria Theresa) was accustomed to speak Italian, which was the native tongue of the Princesse de Lamballe.

The Queen clung with affectionate tenacity to all that pertained to the memory of her childhood. We have seen this in the case of her partiality for the ex-minister of France, the Duc de Choiseul. This characteristic was also apparent in her patronage of Gluck, her earliest instructor in music.

This patronage of Gluck affected the politics of France, and helped to show how society amused

English lady, who, as a child, was placed by her guardian, the Duke of Norfolk, in the Irish convent Faubourg St. Germain, and was afterwards adopted as secretary by the Princesse de Lamballe. Published, in French, Strasbourg, 1810. The Princesse de Lamballe, as beforesaid, was the sister-in-law, by marriage, to the Duchesse de Chartres. Court scandal declares that the Duc de Chartres (afterwards Duc d'Orléans) entertained a violent and unholy passion for the Princesse de Lamballe. Be that as it may, she evinced as much abhorrence of him, through life, as she showed love and commiseration towards his wife, which state of feeling, on the part of the Queen's confidante, did not help to draw the interests of the King's party and the Orléans party (of Versailles and the Palais Royal) nearer together.

itself there with musical discords under the old *régime.*

When Marie Antoinette first came to France, she found that, under the parvenue, Madame du Barry, nothing but trifling *ariettes* and petty *refrains* were in operatic vogue there, although more serious works were produced at Versailles in honour of the Dauphin's marriage, as befitted the advent of the daughter of Maria Theresa. Marie Antoinette was in those days no great musician herself; but Gluck, having cultivated her ear, she openly expressed her distaste for French follies in music, and thereby gave additional offence to Madame du Barry.

Marie Antoinette declared that the German Gluck could alone show of what fine harmonies French poems and tragedies were formed, and invited her old instructor to Paris. He came, bringing with him his "Iphigénie," composed at the express request of the Dauphiness.*

* Christopher Gluck, (whose works are now performed in London,) was born 1716, on the frontiers of Bohemia. He studied at Prague and in Italy, but was unsuccessful in England, 1745. In 1764 Glück produced his celebrated "Orféo." His summons to Paris by the Dauphiness was the more distasteful to Madame du Barry, because her predecessor, the Pompadour, was one of the first to discover and to patronize his genius.

Madame du Barry, in opposition to the Dauphiness, at the same time imported the gay and seductive music of Italy into France. The brilliant strains and gay tones of Italy were generally more agreeable to Paris than the dreamy compositions of Gluck and Germany—especially so to Louis XV., who, in these his last days, was seeking how to drown thought and how to stifle conscience. The Court was thus divided into Gluckistes and Piccinistes—the former in favour of the Dauphiness, and the latter in favour of Madame du Barry, when the celebrated Beaumarchais stepped upon the scene with his libretto of "The Barber of Seville."* But the "Barber of Seville" was not produced in full force until after the King, for whose amusement it was professedly written, was dead and buried at St. Denis, and Madame du Barry

* Peter Augustin, Caron de Beaumarchais, born in Paris, 1732. His father was a watchmaker. The son was bred to his father's business, but took more to music and play writing. He excelled upon the harp, and was made harp-master to the Princesses, the daughters of Louis XV. He speculated. Lost two wives, and gained three lawsuits. Was afterwards unfortunate in commercial affairs. Was secretly employed by Government for exportation and importation of arms, wood, and military stores, at the time when France began to traffic (secretly) with America.

was banished from Versailles. Queen Marie Antoinette, however, in 1775 could afford to be generous, and she wished to be popular; so she took all music under her protection—French, German, Italian—and even adopted the "Barber of Seville," although Gluck still continued to enjoy especial favour, had a key to the little apartments at Versailles, and composed his "Armida" in honour of the Queen, who was pleased to behold her own perfections reflected by the genius of her *protegé*.

The "Barber of Seville" was represented. The King was shrewd enough to suspect some political sarcasm in the pieces of Beaumarchais, and winced at them without exactly knowing the reason why; but the Queen applauded Beaumarchais, thus, as she supposed, winning popularity. Malesherbes, philosopher and Secretary of State, had the supreme direction of the Opera. Beaumarchais himself had just been to England, there to negotiate the secret purchase of British timber, wherewith to build French ships.* The French Government had placed itself in the power of Beaumarchais. It would have been impolitic to displease him. The

* The original Memorial concerning that transaction is transcribed in a later chapter of this narrative.

King, therefore, retracted his objections to the "Barber of Seville," which was played on the Paris boards, to the great delight of the people, who were quick to discern in that piece the satire on a demoralized system, and a dissolute society. The Prince de Conti, who was, it is said, especially held up to ridicule by Beaumarchais in one of his characters ("Doctor Bartholo"), expressed his disdain and disgust to the Princesse de Lamballe at the toleration granted to that author. But the young nobility of France, being excluded from Cabinet mysteries, and knowing nothing, therefore, of the reason why Beaumarchais was tolerated, enjoyed the "Barber of Seville," and sang "Figaro," not dreaming that thereby they were inaugurating a revolutionary war-cry against themselves.

Beaumarchais was bold and outspoken. In one of his pamphlets at this time he declares: "Death overthrows the altars of kings, who, living, are worshipped; but Voltaire, though banished from the presence of these temporary idols, is immortal." It was impossible for Government to stifle "Figaro" or to punish Beaumarchais. The people of Paris would have rebelled against any attempt to put down "Figaro," and the Cabinet of Versailles had committed itself to "Figaro's" author.

Any novelty was welcome to the young nobility —those would-be heroes, condemned to inaction— the more so, as the new code of morals lately established by a King and Queen not older than themselves, condemned such intrigues as that by which, in the last reign, the Prince de Conti had, it was said, laid himself open to the lashing wit of Beaumarchais.

But, although immorality was repressed on the surface of society, reverence for religion did not the more abound. The King was scrupulous in all religious observances; but the new philosophy in vogue threw doubt and ridicule upon the ancient usages of the Church. The Queen, with the vivacity of her age and temperament, helped unconsciously to foster this restless longing for excitement and change.

The "Journal d'un Observateur, 1775," records how her Majesty succeeded, against old *régime* prejudice, in having six unmarried ladies introduced at one of the balls at Versailles. This was a great encroachment, considering that, until then, France had, as a general rule, scrupulously immured the daughters of her nobility in the convent until they were presented to the Court and to the world as married women.

The works of Voltaire and Rousseau were eagerly read. Men, incapable of appreciating the fine sarcasm of Voltaire against abuses, thought, by profane scoffs against hallowed uses, to emulate him. Women, incapable of detecting the subtle sophistry of Rousseau, wept over his "Nouvelle Héloise," and began to long for emancipation.

The Queen's brother, the Emperor Joseph II., paid a visit to France in 1777, and, by his conversation there, helped to shake the sands of old feudalism, which were fast running out.

The Emperor Joseph had, nominally, succeeded to his father in 1764; but, in his own empire, he was kept in such strict subjection by his mother, Maria Theresa, "that perceiving," as Lord Brougham says, "he was destined to remain a mere cipher at home while she ruled, he went abroad, and travelled into those dominions of Italy nominally his own, but where he had no more concern with the government than the meanest of his subjects; and from thence he visited the rest of the Italian States.* Upon the plea of his being a mere cipher at home, the "amiable" Joseph may be excused for his share in the partition of Poland, of which the young Count de Ségur has just told us.

Alison gives Joseph credit for philanthropy, philosophy, and an ardent desire for reform ;† but Frederick of Prussia declares of his illustrious contemporary (who was preferred by the Empress Catherine to himself), that "his head was a confused magazine of despatches, decrees, and projects."

The Emperor Joseph called himself a philosopher, and, dressed like a Puritan, arrived at Versailles, under the title of Count Falkenstein.

The Queen was known to be much attached to her family, and so a rumour gained ground that her brother had come to despoil the royal treasury of France, although, as the Abbé Millot affirms, he does not seem to have touched one farthing of it.‡

* See Historical Sketches of Statesmen, &c., first series, vol. ii. (1845.)

† Hist. Europe, vol. ii. chap. 9.

‡ Elémens de l'Histoire de France, par l'Abbé Millot, de l'Académie Française, nouvelle edition, tome iv. p. 126. Paris, 1809.

The affected plainness of dress, demeanour, and equipage, on the part of the German Emperor, was a satire on the splendour and pomp with which the brothers of Louis XVI. were then travelling in the southern provinces of France—a royal raree-show to a starving population.

The young and gay Count d'Artois (afterwards Charles X.), seems to have been especially bent at this time on impressing rural populations with the magnificence of the Court for which the people had the honour of paying taxes. Impossible was it for these young princes, born and bred in the belief of the Divine right of Kings, to foresee the time when the people would make them feel the might of King Mob.

The Emperor Joseph II., although more of a philosopher, was not more of a prophet than these his bespangled French relatives, or he would have restrained his tongue, which, at Versailles, recklessly assailed custom, and talked down dignities—even those of his own family—in the hearing of others.

Madame Campan tells us that the Queen, who had eagerly anticipated her brother's visit, had ordered suitable apartments to be prepared for him, but that he refused to occupy them; and when the

Queen pressed him to do so, assuring him that he would be perfectly free from restraint, and far from noise, he answered that he knew that the Château of Versailles was large enough to lodge so many knaves, that he might well have a place there, but that his *valet de chambre* had already set up his camp-bed at the inn, and that there he would take up his abode. But he dined with the King and Queen, and supped with all the royal family at Versailles.* And then (regardless of any members of the Court who were present, or of the servitors in attendance at the royal table), "the Emperor," says the Princesse de Lamballe, "was strongly inclined to blab; and

* Mémoires, &c., par Madame Campan, vol. i., p. 143. Paris, 1849. Madame du Deffand, the blind clairvoyante, gives a different account of the Emperor Joseph's arrival to that of Madame Campan, above quoted. Madame du Deffand writes to Horace Walpole from Paris:—"The Emperor arrived between five and six o'clock in the evening. He alighted at the Ambassador's. His Excellency was in bed, not in a state to follow his master. . . . . . Yesterday morning he (the Emperor) went to Versailles; he visited all the Princes and all the Ministers; everybody is charmed with his affability. His intention was to lodge at the Bath-house, but he is induced to lie at the Château. . . . . The Marshal de Dures (one of the first gentlemen of the King's Chamber) has lent him his apartment."—Lettres de Madame du Deffand, tome iii., p. 384.

neither men, women, nor children were spared by him.

"He had just visited his relations in Italy, and he had a word for each of those members of his family.

"He began by asking the Queen 'if she punished her husband by imposing as many fasts upon him as her sister Caroline had done during that year on her husband, the King of Naples?'

"The Queen, not knowing what he meant, the Emperor explained himself thus: 'When the King of Naples has been wanting in duty to his Queen, she limits his diet to *soupe maigre* until he has humbly confessed and duly expiated his faults. . . . My sister Caroline,' continued the Emperor, 'is a right regal mistress in the art of training a man; but my other sister, the Duchess of Parma, is not less great in the art of taming horses. She is always in the stables with her grooms, and so contrives every year to jockey a pretty sum, by buying, selling, and training racers; whilst her ninny of a husband tolls the bells with the Brothers of Colorno, to call his good subjects to mass.

"'My brother Leopold, Grand Duke of Tuscany, nourishes his people with plans of economy.

It is a dish that costs nothing. . . . The Grand Duke thus saves himself from outlay for public monuments, national institutions, and such like, and locks up the whole revenues of his state in his coffers. This is, perhaps, the most classical and ingenious system that a sovereign can adopt. . . . I very much praise my brother Leopold for his ability.' *

"'My dear brother, the Archduke of Milan, does not lack cleverness. . . . I am assured that when he escapes from the eyes of his Argus,—the holy Beatrix, his spouse,—he sells his corn to my enemies in time of war, and to my friends in time of peace, so that all his speculations are profitable to him.'

"'As for you, my dear Marie Antoinette,' continued the Emperor, . . . 'I see that you have made great progress in the art of painting. You have put more colour upon one of your cheeks than Rubens would have used for all the drawings of

* The French translator of the Mémoires of the Princesse de Lamballe (which, in the original, are written in Italian) warns the reader that "these jokes of the Emperor Joseph upon his family must not be taken literally; and especially not in the case of Leopold, one of the wisest, the most enlightened, and the most generous princes who ever existed."

his cartoons.' And, perceiving a lady of honour who was still more rouged than the Queen, he added—'I must resemble a death's head upon a sepulchral stone in the midst of all these scarlet furies!'

The Emperor Joseph did not even spare his own mother, who kept him in such subjection at home. The Empress Queen, Maria Theresa, he declared, "was very much astonished, during the seven years' war, to learn from certain papers seized upon various persons arrested as spies of the King of Prussia, that her husband, the Emperor Francis I.,* supplied the enemy's army with all sorts of provisions drawn from her own stores." The king (Louis XVI.) had listened to all this seditious scandal in almost absolute silence, but manifested displeasure when the Emperor ventured the following remark upon the old custom of allowing merchants to exhibit their fancy wares upon the staircases, and in the ante-chambers of the palace of Versailles: "I suppose," observed the Emperor, laughingly, to his sister, the Queen, "that you would not

* Francis of Lorraine, Grand Duke of Tuscany. Was raised to the head of the empire in 1745-6.

suffer the unpleasant odours of merchandise under your nose, were it not neutralised by the sweet perfume of some pretty present!"

"It was then," says the Princesse de Lamballe, "that Louis XVI., in a tone of voice rather differing from that of his habitual gentleness, declared that neither he nor the Queen had ever derived any advantage from this toleration, but that of being able to buy, if they chose, any article which they might need without the trouble of sending outside the palace for it!"

"And that, my dear brother," replied Joseph, "is precisely why I should never allow shops to be in my palace. It tempts an useless outlay of money. Women have not philosophy enough to resist the temptation of procuring what they desire, and even what they do not want, when they can do so without difficulty."

"Custom," replied the King.

"Yes!" cried the Queen, interrupting him; "custom compels us in France to tolerate many things that have long been abolished in Austria; the French must not be treated as Austrians. The Frenchman is the slave of habit; his caprice, even in the change of the fashions, is rather the result of habit than of invention. . . . There is a system even in his levity. . . . One must not deride the old usages and national customs, of an essentially spiritual people. . . . It is easier to kill a Frenchman than to subdue him. . . . Even his follies in general spring from a profound sentiment of honour and national dignity, which demands a stranger's respect."

The Emperor of Austria was thus rebuked by his sister, the Queen of France, but her ladies did not pardon his allusion to their custom of painting their cheeks. * The Queen herself had endeavoured to reform the costume, and some of the customs of France. For this attempt she had

* In opposition to the ladies of the Queen's Court at Versailles, the Countess de Genlis, as governess to the Orléans family at the Palais Royal in Paris, expressed herself much delighted with and honoured by the Emperor Joseph He went to see the pictures at the Palais Royal. Madame de Genlis volunteered to explain them to him. "The Emperor appeared to take the liveliest interest in this conversation; he thanked me every minute; we passed two hours thus; he was truly a *connoisseur* in pictures; he named almost all the great masters without mistake. His countenance was very agreeable. . . . This prince had the politeness to write to me the next day under his *nom de voyageur*."—Mémoires de Madame la Comtesse de Genlis, tome ii., p. 308. Paris et Londres, 1825.

been attacked as an Austrian innovator by the King's aunts, the Noailles family, and others who made a party in favour of old French prejudices, however absurd.

The Queen's toilette was not now made in public, or only partially so. Her predecessors had endured a public toilette as a matter of custom. Even the cold, chaste Marie Lecskinska, the wife of Louis XV., had considered this endurance a part of her daily duty. When Horace Walpole visited Versailles in 1765, he had the honour of being presented, first to the king, just as his majesty had put on his shirt—("the King," says Horace, "dresses and talks good-humouredly to a few, glares at strangers who are present, goes to mass, to dinner, and a-hunting,") and afterwards to the Queen at her toilette; but the gayest of the courtiers were then at Madame du Barry's levee; so that Walpole found Marie Lecskinska "looking like Lady Primrose in the face, and Queen Caroline in the immensity of her cap, at her dressing-table, attended only by two or three old ladies."*

At the toilette of the Duchesse de Choiseul, the

* Walpole's Correspondence, vol. iii., p. 78. Edit. 1820.

first minister's charming wife, Horace Walpole had a better chance of estimating the pomp and luxury of that which, in France in the 18th century, was considered a matter of importance. Let us pause for one moment to consider that picture of the past—the toilette of a French belle—before popular admiration of the republican Rousseau's "Nouvelle Héloise" brought simplicity into fashion, and before Frenchmen migrated to look on the Puritan and Quaker wives of America.

The 18th century French lady of distinction at her toilette is worshipped by man, and crowned by the graces—a goddess. She is enthroned in a mysterious temple, the walls of which are hung with softest satin of cerulean blue; the doors are veiled with the same, so as to exclude all thoughts of the outer world. From the ceiling sportive nymphs—marvellous works of Boucher's art—shower down upon her the emblems of all good gifts of Olympus to woman.

The light is mellow—roseate. The mossy carpet of Ambusson (a tapestry marvel of fruits and flowers) hushes the sound of a footstep. Exotic plants and delicious scents pervade the atmosphere with a sort of incense. Madame is languid; she has only just emerged from her bath, the waters of which, perfumed with essences fetched from the East by the latest charlatan in Paris, are said to be miraculous for perennial youth and beauty.*

Madame, reclining on a couch formed like Venus's shell, is in *néglige*; her form is loosely draperied in muslins newly imported from India, or soft rainbow-hued Persian stuffs, according to the season. Her feet are bare, slipped into slippers with high gilt heels, the form of which heels betoken rank, as do the red heels of the gentlemen worshipping in this temple. (Charles James Fox, when in Paris, 1776, adopted the red heel of the aristocrat; and, at ladies' toilettes and elsewhere, as reports Madame du Deffand to Horace Walpole, '*Le Fox a l'air de se plaire ici.*')

Behind Madame, at her toilette, stand her handmaidens; all coquetterie, prettiness, pleasantness, and ribbons,—such as those from which Watteau

* It was believed that the Count de St. Germain, celebrated for his perpetual youth (war-minister at Versailles in 1775), possessed the elixir of life; and also that Marshal Duc de Richelieu had, at 70 years of age, been made young again by partaking of it. Cagliostro, likewise, was believed to possess the secret which defied both time aud death.

had painted, and from which, since his day, the stage had copied its fascinating soubrettes. It is an important hour, this hour of Madame's court and coiffure.

A crowd of gentlemen attend the former,—heroes of the sword, soon to fight for young democracy in America; or of the pen about to advocate republicanism in France. All these heroes (in velvet coats, silk hose, embroidered vests, lace ruffles, and powdered perruques), are rivals in attempting to beguile the time for Madame whilst her coiffure proceeds. Madame glances at herself, now and then, in the mirror before her, which is supported by carved loves and graces, and is draperied with lace as costly as that which the nuns have worked for the nearest saint's shrine; then, leaning back again, Madame is fanned by her black page, who is arrayed in "barbaric gold," or she sips coffee, handed to her by some gallant, in a cup of Sèvres china.

The heroes of sword and pen emulate each other in trying to provoke a smile, or in winning a glance from Madame. One relates, or invents, the latest news; another originates, or repeats, the best *mot*; the poet steps forward to recite his poem; or the singer to sing his song. The coiffure proceeds: the long hair is duly powdered, perfumed, and puffed up by the abigails, who sustain it *à l'aristocrate* by pearls, jewels, or roses.

An old beau, like Marshal Richelieu, who, for threescore years and ten, has served equally under Mars and Cupid, is privileged to approach close to the throne of beauty, and to guide the abigail's hand where to place the rose, or to drop the jewel, so that the flower may speak its own sentiment, or the gem best accord with the lustre of Madame's eyes. But, now, the supreme moment of interest has arrived! Madame is about to stick on her patches!

Singing, reading, recitation, gossip, are suspended. One handmaiden reverently presents a gold box of black beauty-spots to Madame, the other handmaiden offers her a silver shell, the inner part of which contains carmine, as though dropped there by the fingers of Aurora. Madame leans gracefully forward towards the mirror. With her own dainty hand—the crowd breathlessly looking on—she sticks on her patches, one here, another there; and, by their position, gives a *soupçon* of her sentiments,—a *soupçon* just as delicate as the artificial blush which at this moment suffuses her cheek. Rival heroes who are present look menacingly at each other, and touch their sword-hilts. Many a duel in the Bois de Boulogne at that time had its origin in Madame's toilette. More wounds were inflicted by her mode of placing her patches on her cheeks, than all Madame's court sticking plaister could heal or bind up. No wonder that French heroes began to think it was time to fight for a better cause than this. But Government still, in 1776–7, held French heroes back.

Lafayette, who, by stratagem, had escaped from Old World customs that stifled him, was condemned at Versailles as a rebel, under *Lettre de Cachet.* And yet, at this time, when the cabinet of Versailles was secretly granting assistance to American insurgents, but was afraid of avowing adhesion to their cause, it was said that "Philosophy was seated on the throne of France." Turgot, Comptroller of Finance, had combined with the young King in trying to bring about a gentle, gradual, and salutary reform, which, if fairly carried out, might have saved France from the Revolution that overthrew the throne. "The King was good, but weak; partaking the political sentiments of Turgot, he had not strength to sustain him." * Nevertheless, the unjust persecution of Protestants ceased; state jobbing was fast being destroyed; the revenues of corporations were suppressed. Protestants were not only tolerated now (to the horror of Archbishop Christopher de Beaumont, who was respected by Frederick, the Protestant king, for his consistent intolerance), but philosophers —the Encyclopédistes,—who, until the expulsion of the Jesuists in 1762-4, had been proscribed in France, and were obliged to seek refuge with Frederick of Prussia, talked freely in the gardens of Paris, on liberty of conscience in France, and on the chances of liberty in America. To achieve this freedom of speech Turgot had mainly contributed; thus paving the way for his successor, Necker, the first protestant who found a place in the councils of the King of France, since the days of Henry IV. Who was Turgot? Turgot, Baron de l'Aulne, born in Paris, 1727, was educated for the priesthood, but, although his family and self-interest

* Mémoires de Ségur, vol. i. p. 95. Paris et Londres, 1825.

dictated the fulfilment of the vocation prescribed for him, "I will not be a bad priest, to be a rich man," said he, "nor will I consent to wear a mask all my life, to be dropped before God in eternity."

His mother called Turgot a savage. He was, as a youth, shy, ungraceful, and taciturn, and, accustomed to college life, fled from all his mother's gay guests when at home. Worse still, Turgot was suspected by his family of extravagance, but afterwards it was discovered that—an anchorite in his own habits—he gave all his money to the poor scholars of the college of Louis le Grand, that they might buy books for themselves.

Although he refused to enter the priesthood, Turgot was a great theological scholar. He was elected Prior of the Sorbonne, in 1749, and his first lecture there was upon "the advantages of Christianity to the human race." In his second lecture at the Sorbonne, Turgot predicted that which, as minister at Versailles in after years, he helped to effect, viz., "the separation of the American colonies from the mother country." . . . "The colonies," said he, "are as fruits which cling to the tree only until they are ripe. Ripened, they will suffice to themselves. That which Carthage did, will America do some day."

As Turgot was inflexible in his resolution not to become a priest, his family did what they could to help him in another career. His brother was President of the Paris Parliament. In 1752, Turgot was made Parliament Councillor, and was afterwards appointed *Maître des Requètes.*

In 1753, he was indignant at the mutually unjust animosity prevailing between the Parliament and the Archbishop of Paris (Christopher de Beaumont), concerning the Bull Unigenitus, *i.e.* the refusal of the Sacraments to dying persons suspected of Jansenism, or liberty of conscience, concerning some articles of the Roman Catholic creed. Turgot, therefore, published two pamphlets, one upon "Toleration," and the other called, "The Conciliator." When the Parliament was exiled on account of these miserable quarrels with the Church, Turgot was appointed one of the State Counsellors, substituted in lieu of the Parliament, *pro tem.* By this appointment he was forced to usurp the prerogatives of his own brother, the Parliament President, who shared the fate of the body to which he belonged. This appointment made Parliamentary enemies for Turgot in years to come.

Turgot was an Encyclopédiste, and the intimate friend of d'Alembert, Diderot, Helvetius, Holbach, and Voltaire. Although shy in manner, and slow of speech, as in his earlier years, his society was eagerly sought by these philosophers. He was an eminent classical scholar, and their works were often submitted to his criticism. Turgot was also the disciple of Dr. de Quesnay, the great political economist, who had raised himself from obscurity by his own merits, and to whom most of the political and sanitary reforms of Paris were then due. Even Paris of to-day, one hundred years afterwards, owes many of its improvements to the plans of Dr. de Quesnay, which plans are still preserved in the Bibliothèque Impériale. * De Quesnay died

* Dr. Francis Quesnay, the son of a husbandman, studied medicine through all sorts of difficulties; was Physician to Madame de Pompadour; by her introduced to King Louis XV.; was rewarded for the plans he introduced to his majesty's notice in various ways, and was endowed by that monarch with the well-known heraldic badge of the Heart's-Ease. Louis XV. took

in 1774, just as his pupil in political economy, Turgot, was raised by the new King, Louis XVI., to power.

When Louis XVI. ascended the throne, and Turgot was appointed Comptroller of State Finances, the people were well pleased, and philosophy, which had dreaded the intolerance of a King educated by the exclusive Church party, rejoiced in an unexpected triumph; rejoicing in proportion as the Archbishop of Paris, and other leaders of the Church, were disappointed.

Turgot inaugurated himself into office by a letter addressed to the King: "No bankruptcy!" "No increase of taxes!" "No borrowings!" The King, as before said, declared, "None love the people, but Turgot and myself!" Turgot believed that a central and despotic power is good, if exercised for the benefit of the people. When the ancient Parliaments were recalled (as we have already seen in this narrative), a few months after Turgot's appointment in the King's Cabi-

this flower from a vase in Madame de Pompadour's salon, and, presenting it to De Quesnay, who was present, begged him to consider it as the emblem of the ease his philanthropy had brought to thousands of his people.

net, he could no longer command his majesty's undivided attention.

The Parliament did not forget that Turgot had, as State Councillor, usurped their authority twenty years before. This recall of the Parliaments, advised, as we have seen, by Count de Maurepas, who was jealous of Turgot, created a difference of opinion in the Cabinet of Versailles, and was ominous to the Comptroller of Finance. The people, however, unaccustomed to make nice distinctions, regarded Turgot as their benefactor on the one hand, and the Parliaments as the shield of their rights on the other. The rights of the people and of nature were invariably preferred by Turgot, to the rights of the monarchy, or any other institution; his ministry, therefore, was a great step towards the "Declaration of the rights of man." *

After the Parliaments were recalled, and had put in their claim to be heard by the King, Louis XVI. began to hesitate between their traditional authority, and the plans of reform submitted to him by Turgot, his Finance Comptroller. †

* Biographie Universelle.

† Turgot's system comprised:—

1. The abolition of State jobbing throughout the kingdom.

Old Maurepas, watching like a cunning fox, and envious of Turgot's influence over the young monarch, seized this moment of the King's hesitation between the Parliaments and his Financial minister, to impugn and to controvert Turgot's plans in council. The mischief made by Maure-

2. The suppression of feudal abuses and tyranny.

3. That certain taxes, pressing most heavily upon the people, should be converted into a territorial tax upon the nobility and the clergy.

4. A new and equal distribution of taxation.

5. Liberty of conscience.

6. The recall of Protestants.

7. The suppression of most of the monasteries.

8. The redemption from feudal rents, combined with rights of property.

9. One civil code of law, only, for all the kingdom.

10. The unity of weights and measures.

11. The suppression of wardenships, and of the rights of companies.

12. The suppression of provincial administrations in the defence of municipal interests.

13. The equalization of the temporal wealth of the clergy by the amelioration of the receipts of vicars and curates.

14. That men of letters should be called to the government, so as to enlighten it with their intelligence.

15. That thought should be as free as industry.

16. That a new system of public instruction should be established.

17. That civil authority should be independent of ecclesiastical authority.

—*Vie de Turgot.* Paris, 1862.

pas helped to precipitate the subsequent revolution in France, which might have been averted by a timely reform.

Voltaire called Turgot "the modern Sully." Voltaire declared "that nobody was ever more skilful than Turgot in throwing a dart, whilst hiding his hand;" of which skill Frenchmen had learned the value, when the Encyclopédistes and their writings had been proscribed and suppressed during the past reign. Voltaire had a medal struck of Turgot at Ferney; round the laurel-crowned head of this medal was inscribed, "Regni Tutamen!"

Turgot favoured men of letters, thus giving a new impulse to the public press. He instituted the School of Medicine in Paris. He practically proved the merits of his grand scheme of internal navigation. He improved the moral and physical condition of the common soldier. He refused to accept for himself the 300,000 livres, called the "Pot-de-Vin," an established perquisite of the office of State Finance Comptroller, upon the renewal of government farm leases. He established a school of agriculture in Corsica. Inflexible in his public honesty, irreproachable in his private character, animated by a sincere and single-hearted desire to benefit the human race, Turgot was wanting in patience for the infirmities of others. Those who opposed what he knew to be for the general good, he set down as knaves or fools. His own hand never flinched, even in attacking his own personal interests, if sustained by a sense of right. And so it was said of him, "Turgot acts like a surgeon upon corpses, not remembering that he is operating upon flesh, blood, and nerves."

An honest statesman like this, in France, at that time, was sure of enemies. The Parliament was opposed to Turgot. The Church was opposed to Turgot. The Count de Maurepas was opposed to Turgot. These three—the Parliament, the Church, and De Maurepas—were also opposed to each other; but their common enmity against Turgot united them in procuring his downfall.*

* The Queen was under the influence of the Church, and she did not like Turgot, not esteeming, as the King did, his patriotic measures, which, in the cabinet, outweighed his heresy. One night, the Queen returned to Versailles from the opera at Paris. The King asked her how she had found the opera that night; her only answer was, "cold." The King wished to ascertain

It was Lent, in 1775. The King fasted, and went to mass. Turgot neither fasted nor went to mass. Worse still; he authorised the butchers of Paris to sell meat as at other times, leaving it to the consciences of the people whether they ate it or not. Philosophy applauded this decree. The Church was indignant at it, and accused Turgot of atheism, and of a wish to overthrow all sacred customs.

The people had expected impossibilities from a new reign and a new ministry. They were just now getting impatient, and beginning to doubt whether they were better off than before. The priesthood had still a strong hold on the

whether the Queen had been received with acclamations or not, and pressed for a reply, but could gain none. "Seemingly, Madame," said he, smiling, "you have not worn feathers enough." "Sire," she then said, with mock petulance, "I should like to see how many feathers you would wear there,—you with your Turgot and your St. Germain! I believe that you would be roughly treated at the opera of Paris. . . . ."—Mems. de Bachaumont, year 1775.

The Count de St. Germain, equally celebrated in the annals of Mars and Magic, had lately been appointed Minister of War. He was a notorious reformer. Madame du Deffand, writing to Horace Walpole, in October, 1775, says:—"It is believed that M. de Malesherbes has much influenced this appointment."—Lettres de Madame du Deffand, vol. iii., p. 215. Edit. Paris, 1824.

people, especially on the women, the wives and mothers of families. The priesthood seized this opportunity of making the people believe that nothing was to be hoped for by them from the ministry of Turgot the heretic.

During that Lent of 1775 bread was scarce. It was no hard task to convince a starving people that Turgot, the King's favourite minister, who had sanctioned butchers to sell in Lent meat which they could not afford to buy, and the eating of which would endanger their souls, was responsible for the scarcity and high price of bread.

It therefore came to pass that, in the month of May in 1775, when the young King and Queen, who desired the love of their subjects, were at Versailles, there was an ominous movement amongst the people. Discontent spread contagiously through the length and breadth of France. There was revolt at Dijon, at Lisle, at Amiens, and even in Paris. The people determined on proclaiming their own grievances to the King. The crowd increased as it marched towards Versailles. Peasants, artisans, women with children in their arms, and the mysterious under-current of human life, which, hidden and forgotten in times of peace, only surges up to the surface at times such as this—like the turbid mud which streaks the ocean when the waves are tossed by storms—resolved to seek redress from the King himself. So, one fine May morning, just a year after Louis XV. was dead, a dense mass of human beings thronged and pressed round the palace gates of Versailles, murmuring for bread.

King Louis XVI. faced the mob. He stepped forth, bare-headed, into the balcony, and stood just where his grandfather had stood to witness the festivities in honour of his (Louis XVI.) marriage five years before; the vast cost of which festivities, though remonstrated against by Turgot, had been intended to conciliate the people now clamouring beneath for bread.

Louis XVI. addressed the people. His words of hope, of promise, and mercy, were blown to the winds. His voice was drowned in the clamour of discontent. "Give us bread!" the people cried. The King, believing that the crowd was famishing, that the revolt was simply that of hunger, commanded a placard to be posted up on the walls and gates of the palace, promising that the price of bread should be reduced forthwith to two sous the pound.

This placard was a triumph to the insurgents.

The King was happy in his belief of having done his duty to his people, never thinking how much the enemies of his favourite minister and Finance Comptroller, Turgot, had to do with their mutiny.

The mob was well-pleased with itself; not so much because it had gained cheap bread, as because it had won a victory over the King, the Court, and the Ministry, in the very fastnesses of Versailles. The mob marched off—a vast undisciplined army—half intoxicated with success, to Paris, where a general pillage of the bakers' shops began. Bread was torn from the windows; but many of the insurgents had such little need of it, that, after obtaining it, they flung it aside to those who, attracted by the commotion, stood staring by in stupid wonder, as to what could be the cause of it.

Marshal Biron, in command of the French guards,* came forth with his troops, but the King

* Lettres de la Marquise du Deffand à Horace Walpole, tome iii., p. 181. Edit. Paris, 1824.

sent orders from Versailles that the mob should not be fired upon. The black and grey musketeers also appeared, but under the same restriction. The sight of armed men, however, frightened the insurgents.

The mob, after a few hours, dispersed; but Turgot knew that the late extortion from the King would pave the way for future demands upon his majesy's clemency, with which demands it would be impossible to comply; and he therefore succeeded in getting a *carte blanche* from the King, empowering him to act as he thought best in this emergency.

Turgot then instantly re-established the price of bread, and the next day organized, with Marshal de Biron, encampments to prevent further revolts in the provinces, and to protect the arrival of corn in the capital.

The Parliament sided with the seditious leaders, and issued a violent decree against Turgot and political economists in general; promising, too, although the King's word had been broken, that the price of bread should be reduced. Turgot, supported by Malesherbes, his friend and colleague, resisted this interference of the Parliament between himself and the King. A bed of Justice was summoned at Versailles; but, by the interposition of Maurepas, the bed of Justice limited its authority to ordering the sheriffs to ascertain how far the insurgents had, by their conduct in Paris upon the day of revolt, laid themselves open to the punishment of the law.

The Parliament was satisfied, thus avoiding the odium of punishing the insurgents.

Upon the 17th of May, the sheriffs condemned a grazier and a wig-maker, who had been leaders of the mutiny, to be hanged to a gallows forty-nine feet high.

The economist, Albert, had just been appointed by Turgot lieutenant of police. The whole obloquy of the hanging matter, therefore, fell upon Turgot and his party. It was said of them: "They cannot persuade nor convince; they therefore seek to frighten." Turgot, only lately so popular, now found that the tide was too strong against him, although Voltaire, from his retreat at Ferney, more able to judge of passing events than if blinded by taking an active part in their strife and confusion, declared: "It is unworthy of France to oppose designs great as those of Turgot."

But, in France, money was wanting. Turgot, looking far ahead, revelled in vast schemes for the future; but, as Finance Comptroller, he was cramped by want of means for the present. The people were hoping for and expecting impossibilities. The Parliament was opposed to Turgot, and the King, perplexed by conflicting opinion, wavered whether to adopt his counsels or not. In twenty months, therefore, Turgot's ministry was over. Malesherbes resigned about the same time as did Turgot. Maurepas, who went to show himself at the Opera the night of the mutiny for bread, now went to the Opera again, after writing a mock letter of respect and condolence to Turgot, who haughtily replied to it. Let ministerial changes be what they might, Maurepas, at least, was strong in royal favour.

As said Madame du Deffand, the centre of Paris gossip: "M. de Malesherbes doubts everything; M. Turgot doubts nothing; M. de Maurepas laughs at everything."*

* Chauson, sur M. de Maurepas:—

"Monsieur le Comte, on vous demande,
L'on dit qu'on se révoltera;
Dites au peuple qu'il attende,
Il faut que j'aille à l'Opéra!"

The King began to feel the difficulties of his position. When Malesherbes gave in his resignation, Louis XVI. said to him: "Ah! M. de Malesherbes, how much happier you are than I am! You can abdicate."

The priesthood had disliked the influence of Turgot, the philosopher, in the Cabinet.

Turgot still continued, though out of office, to enforce by his pen the measures which he had advocated as minister. The priesthood had much more reason for alarm, when, after a brief interval, Turgot was succeeded in office by James Necker, the Protestant of Geneva.*

He was the first Protestant who had ever been admitted to the councils of the King of France, since the time of Henri IV.†

* James Necker had married the first love of Gibbon, the historian, and was the father of the future Madame de Stael.

† In the Bibliothèque Impériale there is a MS. in thirteen chapters, "On the Catholic Religion in France," which, upon the 8th of June, 1673, was presented to Colbert by M. l'Abbé de Lezeau. This MS. is believed to be unpublished. "Its end," says the Librarian at the Bibliothèque, "seeming to have been attained when the Government of the King took cognizance of it." The Abbé Lefebore de Lezeau wrote this MS. to arouse the zeal of the King against the Pro-

James Necker, born in 1732, of an Irish family settled at Geneva, was the son of a professor of civil law. At the age of fifteen he was placed in a banking house at Paris; he became the protégé of the rich banker, Vernet, and afterwards partner with Thellusson, at whose death he established a house of his own, in conjunction with his brother and two others. Thellusson had been a great speculator in the corn trade. Vast speculations in

testants. It is a very specious and very strong exhortation to obtain the revocation of the Edict of Nantes. The amount of troubles excited in France by Religionists (Protestants) is, from the Abbé's representations, awful to contemplate. Above all, the reverend author takes care to show that religious persecutions in France had derived their source from a devouring zeal for the honour of God, and for the interests of the King. After painting the inconveniences, miseries, and dangers arising from the system of purification and toleration, the Abbé adds, (folio 51):—"Pope Clement VIII. was marvellously distressed at the contents of that edict, and still more at the authority which had constrained MM. of the Parliaments to register it; . . and (not to speak of the oppositions and lively remonstrances of the clergy of France) M. du Vivier, Chancellor of the University, and Counsellor of the Parliament of Paris, aged sixty-six years, being obliged to vote upon this edict, betook himself to weeping, and to saying that he felt himself very unhappy to have lived until that time to see such an edict published . . . . This edict had been received and established by the authority of the King, to the shame and confusion of this kingdom." It may here be observed, that this quotation is made to corn, of which the commerce had just been declared free, and operations of credit with Government, were the sources of that immense fortune which was the stepping-stone of Necker's political advancement.

James Necker affected the taste of his times for literature, poetry, and philosophy. He was acquainted with the Duc de Choiseul, and was the Administrator of the East Indian Company, of which, by his wealth, he became the centre and the chief director. Elsewhere, we have seen how money

prove by MS. commentation of the text in 1840, that the revocation of the Edict of Nantes was projected long before it was openly decided upon, and that, consequently, those who, only beholding the fatal consequences of it, throw the whole responsibility upon Louis XIV., upon Madame de Maintenon, and Père la Chaise, may be taxed with injustice. In this MS., presented to Colbert in 1673, is to be found the original of the celebrated *mot* of Louis XIV. upon the reformers:—"King Henri IV. sustained and loved them; King Louis XIII. distrusted and feared them; I (Louis XIV.) neither love nor fear them." To this it may be added here, that Louis XVI. did fear, although he did not love them. The admission of Necker to his council for the sake of money was a sore trial to Louis XVI. The "particular orations for the King," by Father Arnould Drion, begin with these words—of which Louis XVI. began now to feel the need—"Send here below the angel Tobias to enlighten me"—MS. Bib. Imp., 7050, Anciens Fonds.

now began to make itself felt in France, as a new power opposed to tradition of class, of creed, of country, and of blood. The government of France was poor. The exchequer had never recovered the exhaustion of the Seven Years' War; the later years of the reign of Louis XV. had not helped to replenish it.

James Necker, at more than forty years of age, had money. He had ambition. He was the friend of the Duc de Choiseul, ex-minister of France, the Queen's friend.

The strife in America was certain to involve France in a war with England. The young King of France wanted strong counsellors, with power both to will and to do. The Cabinet of France wanted fresh blood—or money.

James Necker had won the prize proposed by the Academy of Paris for an essay on Colbert; he had also written a book upon the legislation and commerce of corn, which book had been virulently attacked by economists.

De Maurepas, thinking to patronize James Necker, the son of a Genevese citizen, beckoned him forward. Necker found himself Director of the Royal Treasure of France. He could not fail to be popular with the King, because he refused all emolument for his office.

CHAPTER IV.

Louis XVI. the King, and Louis XVI. the Man—" Reflections" of Louis XVI. upon peace and war—Dr. Benjamin Franklin's arrival in France—Dr. Benjamin Franklin's "Electrical Kite"—Madame la Marquise du Deffand receives Dr. Franklin—Her account of her company—Appearance of Puritan philosophers in France—Dr. Franklin's own idea of his mission in France—His letter to Sir Joseph Bankes upon war—Reception of Dr. Franklin, by Count de Vergennes, Minister of Foreign Affairs—Lord Stormont, English ambassador at Versailles—The Queen at Trianon—Practical joke of the Duc de Chartres—Dr. Franklin's Memorial to the Court of Versailles—The Cabinet of Versailles "declares its intentions"—Public presentation of Dr. Franklin to Louis XVI.—Dr. Franklin applauded at Versailles—Letter of Sir Guy Carleton on Indian affairs (original, unpublished)—Letter of Lord George Germaine to Sir Guy Carleton (original, unpublished)—

Eighteenth century American newspaper advertisements—Original Notes on North American Indians—Montaigne on North American Indians—Dr. Franklin on North American Indians—Original Letter to Lord Dunmore concerning North American Indians—Original Memorial from American Indians—Letter from Lord Weymouth to Sir Guy Carleton, concerning the Count de St. Aulaire—French Canadians tempted by English bounty—Governor Livingstone's speech (American newspaper, 1777)—Extracts from Dr. Franklin's Letters to his Son (original, unpublished)—Letter from General Washington to Ex-Governor Franklin (original, unpublished)—Dr. Franklin crowned at Versailles.

James Necker, the new "Director of the Royal Treasure," had money wherewith to carry his theories into practice. But success at Court begets enemies there: Count Maurepas, Necker's patron, soon became jealous of him, when he found that, his protégé's way being paved with gold, he was soon in a position strong enough to do without help.

It cost Louis XVI. a sharp pang to see James Necker, the Genevese Protestant, installed as his Director of Finance; for, notwithstanding the philosophy of politics, into which Turgot and Malesherbes had, during the last two years, initiated him, the King was still, by habit and education, exclusively attached to the ancient faith of France.

But Louis XVI. was poor in finance, though rich in faith; and he was politically weak. He sacrificed his convictions to necessity, to the love of repose, and to the importunity of others. In his private life, he never flinched from the rules his confessor and his conscience prescribed for and dictated to him. If wanting in the majesty of Louis XIV., in the grace and wit of Louis XV., or in the chivalric greatness of Henry IV., Louis XVI. honoured the throne of France as none of these had done, by exercising as a King the virtues of a man who knew how to resist the temptations of his country, and of his century. *

His passionate love for his Queen, though latent, was faithful to the end. His attachment to his children, when at last they were given to him, made him anxious for their welfare. The devotion of his sister, the Princess Elizabeth, who seemed to have vowed celibacy, that she might dedicate herself to him and to his family, was reciprocated unselfishly by Louis XVI., as

* Réflexions sur mes Entrétiens. Edit. Paris, 1851.

was proved when fear for her safety tormented him more than did alarm for himself, in the perils by which he was surrounded in his later years. *

Louis XVI. was, from the beginning of his reign until its awful end, a martyr to his hereditary rank. His virtues, which would have adorned private life (self-abegnation, and reverence for authority), weakened his hold on the sceptre of France, which needed a tight grasp at this time, when public opinion and society were in a state of transition. His young nobility, the men who had passed their earliest youth with him at Versailles, were, as we have seen in the case of Lafayette and De Ségur, restless for war. They believed in the proverb, "that the sceptre falls when the sword is sheathed;" but they little thought that, in unsheathing their swords in the cause of New World liberty, the sceptre of Old World monarchy would be broken. The war in America inflamed all heads in Paris. The Emperor Joseph II. of Austria, notwithstanding his supposed love for reform, had said, when at Versailles, to his brother-in-law, Louis XVI., "Keep clear of this war, and remember that your rôle is to be aristocrat."

* Thiers' French Revolution, vol. ii., p. 5. Edit.

But public opinion and national excitement were too strong for Louis XVI.; and, by the advice of his Cabinet, he had already too far committed himself to the American cause to recede. In 1777, the Government of France knew that its sham policy of neutrality, between America and England, would not be much longer tenable. The word "Liberty," the war-cry of Boston, electrified Paris.

James Necker "developed" fresh funds for the Cabinet of France. America, as we have seen by her public press at that time, buoyed up the courage of the insurgents by declaring the fact that France favoured them; and by announcing treaties which bound France to America, before those treaties were signed. But Louis XVI personally had a horror of war. "I shall never forget," says he, "that fine speech of the King, my grandfather, to the Dauphin, my father, as they walked together, after the battle of Fontenoy, upon the field which was strewed with the dead and dying: 'See,' said Louis XV., 'what a victory costs! The blood of our enemies is not less the blood of man. True glory, my son, consists not in the shedding, but in the sparing of blood.'"

"And if the true glory of a prince," reflects Louis

XVI., "consists in having such sentiments towards his enemies, what is the affection which he ought to have for his own people? The King, the shepherd, the father, are but one and the same thing. 'God,' said Henry IV., 'has only given me subjects, that I may preserve them as my own children.' *

* At the first Cabinet Council held by Louis XVI. he declared, "In the words and by the spirit of Saint Louis, Injustice shall be with us impossible." As Dauphin he had written :—

1. It is not permitted to take up arms but in defence of the oppressed.

2 War ought not to be determined upon, but after ripe deliberation, and only in a case where it is unavoidable.

3. War ought not to be undertaken but with a view to acquire peace.

4 Arms ought only to be taken up when Right is manifest; it ought not to be regulated by the distrust conceived of neighbouring states, and still less by the motive of self-glory and particular interest.

5. War ought only to be made for causes not only just, but important.

6. The promised advantages of war ought to be compared with the evils which may result from it.

7. It ought always to be remembered, in the midst of hostilities, that amongst the enemy there is a multitude of innocent people—children, women, old men, labourers, ministers of religion, prisoners made in war and hostages—and that it is not against persons powerless to do harm that the soldier should be armed.

8. All violence ought to be abstained from that can only cause

Just at this critical time, when France was balancing between old feudalism and young democracy—when the King of France was distracted by conflicting opinions both in his Cabinet and in his conscience, as to peace or war, Dr. Benjamin Franklin arrived in Paris, as Commissioner from the United States.

Dr. Benjamin Franklin was not a stranger to France. For his scientific discoveries he had already—like Newton and Leibnitz—been enrolled as one of the members of the Academy at Paris.

Turgot, the philosopher, ex-Minister of Finance, respected Dr. Franklin greatly, both as a man of science and a political reformer. Turgot at this time declared that Franklin—

evil and unhappiness, without contributing to the benefit of the enterprise.

9. In the midst even of the horrors of war, morals and modesty ought to be maintained.

10. Moderation ought to be used in conquest, to soften the yoke of a people just conquered; and it ought not to be forgotten that men free until then do not regard themselves as slaves, although they may know that they have been weaker than their enemy. . . . . And to what do not those expose themselves who treat with pride and harshness a people already soured by misfortune?—*Réflexions sur mes Entrétiens.*

"Ravished the thunderbolt from heaven and the sceptre from tyrants." ("Eripuit cœlo fulmen, sceptrumque tyrannis.")*

Paris was much excited by the arrival of Dr.

* Whilst Franklin's discovery (called "the electrical kite") thus brought down the thunders of applause in France, King George III. refused in anger against him to use Franklin's lightning conductors any longer in England. When Franklin heard of this, he wrote the following letter to a friend in England:—

"Passy, Oct. 4th, 1777.

"I have never entered into any controversy in defence of my philosophical opinions; I leave them to take their chance in the world. If they are *right*, truth and experience will support them; if *wrong*, they ought to be refuted and rejected. Disputes are apt to sour one's temper and to disturb one's quiet. I have no private interest in the reception of my inventions by the world, having never made, nor proposed to make, the least profit by them. The King's changing his *pointed* conductors for *blunt* ones is therefore a matter of small importance to me. If I had a wish about it, it would be that he had rejected them altogether as ineffectual. For it is only since he thought himself and his family safe from the thunder of Heaven, that he dared to use his own thunder in destroying his innocent subjects."

The fact of the King of Great Britain having changed his lightning conductors, gave rise in England to the following epigram:—

"While you, great George, for safety hunt,
And sharp conductors change for blunt,
The empire's out of joint.
Franklin a wiser course pursues;
And all your thunder fearless views,
By keeping to the *point*."

London, 1818.

Franklin there. Madame du Deffand writes to Horace Walpole, the 18th of December, 1776: "It is a problem why M. Franklin comes here."

On the 22d of December she reports: "M. Franklin arrived here" (Paris) "yesterday afternoon, at two o'clock: he had slept the night before at Versailles."

On the 31st of the same month she continues: "If you see little Elliot," (afterwards Lord Minto,) "he will tell you of the company which he found in my room yesterday. This is how we were disposed of: I, in my cask" (Madame du Deffand's cask was a basket chair, with a high oval-shaped back, like a cask turned long-way upwards, and nicknamed "Diogenes' Tub"), "Monsieur Franklin by my side, with a fur cap upon his head, and a pair of spectacles upon his nose; then Madame de Luxembourg and M. Silas Deane, a deputy from your colonies. . . . . M. le Duc de Choiseul, the Abbé Barthélemi, and M. de Guignes closed the circle. Little Elliot brought in news from America of the 4th and 6th of December, which news he declared to be true; but nobody wished to believe it, because it was unfavourable to the insurgents, to whose cause all the company I have named are much devoted, except M. de Guignes and myself. . . . M. Elliot did not retail this news until after Messieurs Franklin and Deane had gone out. If Fox and Fitzpatrick had only arrived, my room would have represented Westminster Hall, where, as you see, the royalist party is in the minority."*

We have just read what Louis XVI. wrote, that "Shepherd, Father, and King are one." George III. had scarcely illustrated this view of a sovereign's unity in his treatment of the American Colonies, according to Franklin, who had come to France, there to plead the cause of a people whom he represented as oppressed and outraged by the King of England. Respect due to age and science had been part of the French King's education.†

* Lettres de Madame la Marquise du Deffand à Horace Walpole, tome iii., p. 349.

† The Count de Ségur has already told us how age alone found a place in the Councils of Versailles. Horace Walpole, writing to the Rev. Mr. Cole, in August, 1777, comments: "And though, to be sure, grey hairs are fittest to conduct state affairs, yet as the Rehoboams of the world (Louis XVI. excepted) do not always trust the rudder of government to ancient hands, old gentlemen, methinks, are very ill placed (when not at the Council board) anywhere but in the cloister. As I have no more vocation to the ministry than to carrying on my family, I sigh after a dormitory."—Walpole Correspondence, vol. iv., p. 81. Ed. 1820.

The purity of Dr. Franklin's life was welcome to Louis XVI., who, as we have seen, had been depressed before he came to the throne by the sight of courtly iniquity, and who had inaugurated his own coronation by an allegory in praise of Virtue.

Dr. Benjamin Franklin, in his conversation and habits of life, formed a strange contrast to Frenchmen of his own age and upwards—such as the old Duc de Richelieu, for example, whose gallantries were still notorious, who pawned his most brilliant order—the order of the "Saint Esprit"—to procure him funds for unholy pleasures.* Rather different, too, was this philosopher of Philadelphia, who treated all subjects very sedately, from old Count de Maurepas, whose philosophy it was, as Madame du Deffand has told us, to laugh at everything.

The young Count de Ségur declares: "Nothing was more extraordinary than the contrast of luxury in our capital, of the elegance of our fashions, of all those living traces of the monarchical haughtiness of Louis XIV., of the polished

* Secret History of the Court of France, vol. ii., p. 182. London, 1861.

but superb dignity of our aristocracy, with the almost rustic habiliments, the simple but proud bearing, the plain straightforward language, the unpowdered and unornamented hair, in short, with that antique style which suddenly seemed to introduce within our walls, into the very midst of the effeminate and servile civilization of the eighteenth century, sages, contemporaries of Plato, or republicans of the time of Cato and of Fabius. . . . We were the more enchanted by this spectacle on account of its novelty, and because it happened exactly at the epoch when literature and philosophy spread amongst us a universal desire for reforms, excited an inclination in favour of innovations, and implanted the germs of a lively love for liberty."*

Dr. Franklin seems to have regarded his mission in France as that of Mentor to the King of that country; for in a letter to his friend Dr. Priestley (the same to whom he had vowed, on the threshold of the Privy-Council Chamber, that he would never again put on the clothes he then wore until he had revenged himself and his country for the sentence of the Council against him) he metaphorically

* Mems. par M. le Comte de Ségur, vol. i., p. 101. Ed. 1825.

declares: "A young angel of distinction, having been sent on a mission here below, an aged genius was given to him for a guide."* Although the practical intention of the aged genius was to light up the flame of war in France, he quite agreed, in theory, with the young angel of distinction concerning the advantages of peace. From Passy, that pleasant place in France, not very far from Versailles, where Franklin had settled himself in company with his grandson,† he wrote to Sir Joseph Bankes:

* Mélanges de Morale, d'Economie, et de Politique de Benjamin Franklin. Ed. Paris, 1824.

† A few months after Dr. Franklin had been deprived of his office of Deputy-Postmaster for the Colonies, in 1774, he wrote to his son (the Governor of New Jersey) respecting the grandson who now accompanied him to France:—"Methinks 'tis time to think of a profession for Temple (who is now upwards of 14), that the remainder of his education may have some relation to it. I have thought he may make an expert lawyer, as he has a good memory, quick parts, and ready elocution. . . . . It is indeed my wish that he might learn some art by which he could at any time procure a subsistence; and, after that, if anything better could be done for him, well and good. But Posts and Places are precarious Dependencies. I would have him a Free Man. Upon the whole, in my own opinion, we should turn him to the Law, as a profession respectable in itself, and as the knowledge he may gain in that profession will qualify him for other employments, and be serviceable to him, if he were only to be a mere gentleman."—Autograph, unpublished. Mus. Brit. Ex Dono,

"In my opinion there has never been a good war nor a bad peace. How would the human race be ameliorated, and possessed of the necessities and conveniences of life, if money squandered in war had been expended on works of public utility! How agriculture might have been extended, even to the summit of our mountains! How many rivers rendered navigable or united by canals! What aqueducts, bridges, and new roads! What other public works . . . . which would have made of England a terrestrial Paradise! . . . What might not have been obtained, had national wealth been consecrated for good! . . . If millions of money had been so employed, instead of having been misused in taking away the lives of thousands of human beings, whose labour might have been useful."*

Thus, as far as words and theory go, there was a perfect sympathy between the aged genius at Passy and the young angel of distinction at Versailles, concerning the horrors of war.

Wilmot. Dated from Lord Despencer's, West Wycombe, Aug. 1774.

* Mélanges d'Economie et de Politique de Benjamin Franklin, Ed. Paris, 1824.

Dr. Franklin, on his voyage to France from America, narrowly escaped being captured by British cruisers. The sloop which conveyed him was frequently chased. But his grandson, who accompanied him, declares that, on his arrival in France, Dr. Franklin was privately received with every demonstration of regard and respect by M. le Comte de Vergennes, minister of foreign affairs; which statement coincides with what Madame du Deffand has already affirmed, as to the American Republican having visited Versailles previously to his arrival in Paris. His grandson adds, that "M. le Comte de Vergennes assured Dr. Franklin, and the other American commissioners, that "all safety and convenience which it was possible for strangers to enjoy in France, should be secured to them.*

Soon afterwards the American commissioners began privately to grant letters of marque to a number of French American privateers, which harassed the English coasting trade, intercepted a great number of British merchant-vessels, and took many prisoners. Lord Stormont, his Britannic majesty's ambassador at Versailles, when ap-

* Mems. of the Life of Franklin. Ed. London, 1818.

plied to by the American commissioners respecting an exchange of these prisoners, replied:

"I receive no letters from rebels, unless they are to solicit his majesty's pardon."

Lord Stormont complained to the French ministry of the equipments of American vessels in the ports of France, of the bringing in of their prizes, and of the assistance which, in an underhand manner, France was affording to the insurgents. Lord Stormont insisted that a categorical answer should be made to these complaints.

Count de Vergennes then affected secretly to remonstrate with the American commissioners; and on the 16th July, 1777, wrote to them that they had exceeded the bounds which had been prescribed for them; viz:—"*That American commerce and navigation should experience all the facilities in France which would be compatible with the exact observance of her treaties with England.*"*

The arrival of Dr. Franklin created a great sensation in Paris. The Queen and Court at Versailles were not less interested in that event. Not that the Queen cared much for the theories that formed a bond of union between the King and the

* Ibid.

"aged genius" at Passy, but because, just then, there was a need of excitement at Versailles—of "emotions." Novelties of all sorts were therefore welcome. The idleness of the court was no longer occupied, as in the last reign, by angry feuds between Jansenists and Jesuits; the Bull "Unigenitus" was now only remembered as a bugbear of the past, by all excepting such as Christopher de Beaumont, archbishop of Paris, and his fast decreasing number of disciples. Discussions as to the last new opera by Beaumarchais, or of the latest fashion, had succeeded to that of church controversy; or as to how high the Queen allowed her fine fair hair to be dressed and powdered—so that her coiffeur was obliged to mount a ladder to reach the summit of her majesty's head;—or of the increasing favour of Madame la Princesse de Lamballe, her majesty's newly-appointed superintendent of her household; or of the parties of pleasure at Trianon, where the Queen walked, talked, danced, acted, and treated her court without ceremony—adopting rustic costume, and milking cows whose horns were decked with flowers and ribbons, in pastoral fêtes which were the living reproduction of Watteau's garden scenes; royal but Arcadian delights depicted on fans (costly bagatelles of art) painted by Boucher. Sometimes courtiers at Versailles must have been in great want of amusement about this time, to judge from the following anecdote, for which we are indebted to the contemporary chronicler of small talk, De Bachaumont.*

"Madame the Duchesse de Chartres, and the Princesse de Lamballe, went a few days since to visit Madame the Duchesse de Bourbon, at her retreat at Vauvres. M. the Duc de Chartres wished to be of the party, but the Princesses refused to admit him, upon the pretext that all gentlemen were excluded upon this occasion. M. the Duc de Chartres appeared to submit to this décree, but not without another attempt to get it reversed in his favour. M. the Duc de Chartres then made up his mind for a joke; he took M. de Fitz-James and M. de Thiers into his confidence. The former disguised himself as a bear, the latter as showman, and M. the Duc de Chartres himself was clothed

* Mémoires Secrets, &c., Londres, chez John Adamson, 1777. Madame du Deffand wrote from Paris to Horace Walpole, begging him to send these French Mémoires to her from London. "One cannot get the book here," says she, "but under great difficulties."—Lettres de Madame du Deffand, tome iii., p. 423. Paris, 1824.

in a tiger's skin. In this array they all three went to Vauvres, and the Princesses there, thinking to amuse themselves, desired that the tiger, the bear, and their showman, should be admitted within the grounds, to display their accomplishments before them. The animals appeared remarkably tame, and delighted the princesses, who looked on from the windows, with their performances. But, suddenly, a terrific change took place in the animals' demeanour; the tiger and the bear both broke their chains, and burst away from their keeper, and leaped from the grounds into the château, where dinner was just being served. The Princesses shrieked in terror; the bear and tiger, however, did not touch them, but made an attack on the repast. . . . After some more buffooneries, the animals dropped their skins, and all present laughed at the joke. . . . It would be hard to deny the Duc de Chartres admission to the ladies."

England, in 1777, hoped that the American rebellion would soon be crushed, and that nothing but unconditional submission would remain for the thirteen colonies.

After Dr. Franklin's arrival in France, enthusiasm in Paris for American liberty was impatient of delay, on the part of government, in openly avowing its intentions. Just at this crisis, news arrived in Europe of the surrender of the British army commanded by General Burgoyne to that of the Americans, under General Gates, at Saratoga, on the 17th of October, 1777. This event immediately turned the scale in the cabinet of Versailles. So widely spread was popular sympathy towards America through France, that, upon receiving this news of the defeat of the British army, there was universal joy, as though France herself had achieved a triumph over the traditional enemy who had robbed her of Canada.

Dr. Franklin now struck the iron whilst it was hot. He represented to the French ministry that there was not a moment to be lost if France desired to secure the friendship of America, and to detach her entirely from the mother-country. Dr. Franklin now addressed a *Memorial to the Court of Versailles* (which in time found its way, after it had done its work, into the *Political Magazine* of England, in the same number of which periodical Franklin's character and conduct, both public and private, are much slandered). *

* *Political Magazine*, September, 1781, p. 7; and October,

Dr. Franklin commences this Memorial to the Court of Versailles by complimenting France on her prudence in having hitherto avoided all open interference in the present contest between Great Britain and the Anglo-American colonies, "from a presumption that the former will eventually so far exhaust herself, as to give France an opportunity of more advantageously beginning a war at a later period, when Great Britain has weakened herself in the present contest.

This supposition, however, Dr. Franklin declares, in this Memorial, to be erroneous, as Great Britain, if left at peace with Europe, can always borrow money at pleasure. "In this manner," continues Franklin, "England has become much more powerful than she was the last year, notwithstanding the addition since made to her national debt; and in the same manner she was infinitely more formidable at the close of the last war than at the beginning of it, notwithstanding her debt had increased more thau fifty millions.

"The second supposition is, that the war between

1780, p. 632. "Published London. Printed for J. Bew, Paternoster-row, and sold by every Bookseller and News Carrier in Great Britain."

Great Britain and the United American colonies will certainly continue a considerable time longer, without any open interference on the part of France. But . . . the British Government have everything to lose, and nothing to gain, by continuing this war, . . . and the wants and distresses of the colonists may induce them again to return to a dependence more or less limited on Great Britain. . . . There seems, therefore, no means left to France to prevent the colonists from being shortly reconciled to Great Britain, either as subjects or as allies, but to enter immediately into such engagements with them, as will necessarily preclude all others; such as will permanently bind and secure their commerce and friendship, and enable them, as well to repel the attacks, as to spurn at the offers of their present enemy.

"It must be remembered, that the first resistance of the Colonists was not to obtain independence, but a redress of their grievances . . . . A majority have indeed put in for independence; but they have done it partly in a confidence that France, attentive to her most important interests, would soon give them open and effectual support. But when they find themselves disappointed, when they see some of the powers of Europe furnish troops to assist in their subjugation, another power proscribing their commerce, and the third looking on as an indifferent spectator, it is very probable that, despairing of foreign aid, and severely pressed by their enemies and their own internal wants and distresses, they may be inclined to accept of terms, as it will be the interest and disposition of the British Government to grant them. Lord George Germaine, but a few weeks since, declared in the House of Commons, that his hope of ending the American war this year was principally founded on the disappointment the Colonists would feel when they discover that no assistance is likely to be given them by France. And the British adherents in America will spare no pains to spread and increase that disappointment... They already intimate that France, equally hostile to both parties, foments the present war, only to make them mutual instruments of each other's destruction .....

"The King and Ministry of Great Britain know already that France has encouraged and assisted the Colonists in their present resistance ; and they are already as much incensed against her as they would be were she openly to declare war. In truth,

France has done too much, unless she intends to do more. Without giving the Colonists effectual assistance, it would have been better to leave them wholly unassisted. The British nation, naturally inimical to the French, pants after peace with America, that she may turn her arms against this kingdom, and at once gratify her revenge and her avarice . . . . . Even the temperate Lord Camden, but a few days since, concluded a long and much applauded speech in the House of Peers, by fervently wishing for a peace with America, and a war with all the world." *

* Edward Gibbon, author of the "Decline and Fall of the Roman Empire," was employed to draw up the English manifesto of war with France, which manifesto was the answer to the memorial of Dr. Franklin to the cabinet of Versailles above transcribed. Edward Gibbon, like Mirabeau, was the victim of paternal authority, which tyrannised both over his religion and his love. When a student at Magdalen College, Oxford, in early youth, Gibbon professed himself a convert to Popery; for which profession he was moved off from Oxford to Lausanne, where he was placed under the care of a Calvinist minister. At Lausanne Gibbon fell in love with Mademoiselle Curchod, but the interdict of his father prevented his marrying her. Mademoiselle Curchod became the wife of James Necker, the Comptroller of Finânce in France; and Gibbon became an infidel. The English Government made him Commissioner of the Board of Trade, as a reward for his manifesto against France. He soon lost his place, and died in 1794.—Political Magazine, October, 1780—September, 1781, pp. 7, 632.

Thus urged by Dr. Franklin's Memorial, and fearful lest an accommodation might take place between Great Britain and her Colonies, the Cabinet of France at length resolved instantly to declare its intentions; and, accordingly, on the 6th December, 1777, Monsieur Gérard, Secretary to the Council of State, repaired to the hôtel of the American Commissioners, and informed them, by order of the King, that—"After a long and mature deliberation upon their propositions, his Majesty had resolved to recognise the independence of the United States of America; and that he would not only acknowledge their independence, but support it with all means in his power; that perhaps he was about to engage in an expensive war upon their account, but that he did not expect to be reimbursed by them." In fine, the Americans were not to think that his Majesty Louis XVI. had entered into this resolution solely with a view of serving them; since, independently of his real attachment to them and to their cause, it was evidently the interest of France to diminish the power of England, by severing her Colonies from her.

On the 6th day of February, 1778, a treaty of amity and commerce, and another of alliance, eventual and defensive, between his most Christian Majesty, Louis XVI., and the Thirteen United States of America, were concluded and signed at Paris by the respective plenipotentiaries.

The young Marquis de Lafayette was therefore now no longer regarded by his family as guilty of high treason towards the Crown, in having run away that he might fight for "rebels."

Lord Stormont was withdrawn by the Cabinet of London from the Court of France; and the Marquis de Noailles (who, inadvertently, as we have seen, had assisted Lafayette's flight) was withdrawn from the Court of St. James.

The "aged genius," therefore, had now established his guidance of the "young angel of distinction." In plain language, Dr. Franklin, who had thus determined the counsels of the King of France, was summoned by that monarch to Versailles, there to be presented to him in public. We have seen how, apparently unmoved, Dr. Franklin had, exactly four years since, stood before the Privy-Council table of England, when insulted and disgraced by Wedderburne; we have seen how, with equal outward calmness, he had, in the following year, leaned composedly against the bar of the British

House of Peers, when Lord Sandwich, turning towards him, declared (in reference to Lord Chatham's motion in favour of America), "I think that I have before my eyes at this moment the person who has originated this production—*one of the most bitter and pernicious enemies that this country has ever had!*" Dr. Franklin himself has told us that on that occasion his countenance did not change "any more than though his features had been made of wood." It is not therefore surprising that this son of the American tallow-chandler, this self-taught printer of Philadelphia, who had been openly disgraced without flinching by the Privy-Council of England, should, in this moment of triumph over his personal enemies, appear before the assembled Court of Versailles with equanimity. The young Count de Ségur has already likened Franklin to one of the sages, a contemporary of Plato, or a republican of the time of Cato or of Fabius.* Madame Campan tells us that this philosopher from the New World "appeared at Court in the costume of an American agriculturist. His straight, unpowdered hair, his round hat, his coat

* Mémoires ou Souvenirs; par. M. le Comte de Ségur. Tome i., p. 101. Ed. 1825.

of brown cloth, contrasted with the spangled and embroidered attire, the powdered and perfumed coiffures of the courtiers at Versailles." And that even "the heads of all imaginative Frenchwomen were turned by this novelty." *

Dr. Franklin was presented to his Majesty Louis XVI. in the long gallery of Versailles, by the Count de Vergennes, Minister of Foreign Affairs. "Dr. Franklin was accompanied and followed by a great number of Americans, and individuals of various countries. His age, his venerable appearance, the simplicity of his dress on such an occasion, everything that was singular or respectable in the life of this American, contributed to augment public attention." His Majesty addressed Dr. Franklin as follows:

* Mémoires de Madame Campan. Tome x., p. 177. Edit. 1847.

Madame du Deffand writes to Horace Walpole:—"Sunday, March 22, 1778.—M. Franklin has been presented to the King; he was accompanied by about twenty insurgents, three or four of whom wore an uniform. The Franklin wore a coat of brownish red colour, his hair combed straight, his spectacles on his nose, and a white hat under his arm. Is this white hat a symbol of Liberty? . . . It is not known what title he will have, but he will go to court every Tuesday, as do all the diplomatists."—Lettres de Madame du Deffand. Tome iv., p. 33. Edit. 1824.

"You may assure the United States of America of my friendship. I beg leave also to observe, that I am exceedingly satisfied in particular with your own conduct during your residence in my kingdom."

After this reception, Dr. Franklin, as "new ambassador," repaired to the office of the Minister of Foreign Affairs, in another part of the palace of Versailles. A multitude of people crowded the passages to see him pass. Acclamations greeted him from every side; clapping of hands, and a variety of other joyful demonstrations, announced that warmth of affection of which the French are more susceptible than any other people, and of which their politeness and civility augment the charm to him who is the object of it.*

Dr. Franklin was now beset by applications from Frenchmen for service in the armies of the United States. These applications were more numerous than, as yet, he knew how to comply with. Cau-

* Mems. of the Life of Benjamin Franklin, LL.D., F.R.S., and Minister-Plenipotentiary from the United States of America at the court of France, &c. Written by himself to a late period, and continued by his grandson, William Temple Franklin—(favoured by the description of a Frenchman, M. Hilliard d'Auberteuil). London, 1818.

tion was one of the main features of Dr. Franklin's character; this quality was evinced in the present case by the "model of a letter of recommendation of a person you are unacquainted with," which was found by his grandson among his papers after death, as a draft of his customary negative introduction of a French volunteer into the American service, when he knew nothing against him.*

By the emigration, which quickly followed, of young French nobles to America, the very extremes of human nature were brought face to face with each other, as the following letter may show:—

* *Model of a Letter of Recommendation of a Person you are unacquainted with.*

"Paris, April 2, 1777.

"Sir,—The bearer of this, who is going to America, presses me to give him a letter of recommendation, though I know nothing of him, not even his name. This may seem extraordinary, but I assure you it is not uncommon here. Sometimes, indeed, one unknown person brings another, equally unknown, to recommend him; and sometimes they recommend one another. As to this gentleman, I must refer you to himself for his character and merits, with which he is certainly better acquainted than I can possibly be. I recommend him to those civilities which every stranger of whom one knows no harm has a right to; and I request you will do him all the good offices, and show him all the favour that, on further acquaintance, you shall find him to deserve. I have the honour to be, your obedient servant,—BENJAMIN FRANKLIN."

"*To his Excellency, Sir Guy Carleton, Governor of Quebec, from the superintendent of Indian Affairs in Nova Scotia.*

"July, 1777.

"SIR,

"The Continental Congress having taken, by their emissaries, every method to alienate the affections of the savages of this province from his majesty, have so far prevailed as to induce the tribes of this river, Pasamaquoddia and Penobscoft, to associate last fall with a few banditti from the eastern parts of New England, who, together with some of our provincial rebels, plundered the peaceable inhabitants of the county of Cumberland, seized upon the provision vessels, and even presumed to invest the port, but were finally defeated by his Majesty's troops, under the command of Major Bath, of the R. F. A. Regiment. Since last fall a John Allan, late an inhabitant of this province, has been appointed, by the General Congress, Agent to the Indians, and the beginning of June entered this river with two pieces of cannon, and about 220 rebels, who were to be followed by a more considerable number."*

This letter had been anticipated by the following,

* MSS. unpublished, Haldimand Papers. Mus. Brit.

from which it will be seen that the Government of Great Britain had thought it necessary to conciliate the American Indians, and even to name them by name :—

Letter from Lord George Germaine to General Sir Guy Carleton.

"WHITEHALL, March 26th, 1777.

"Sir,

"In consideration of the measures proper to be pursued in the next campaign, the making a diversion on the frontiers of Virginia and Pennsylvania by parties of Indians, conducted by proper leaders, as proposed by Lieutenant-Governor Hamilton, has been maturely weighed. That officer writes to the Earl of Dartmouth (dated at Detroit, the 2nd September last) that he had then with him deputies from the Ottawas, Chippawas, Wyandotts, Shawanese, Senecas, Delawares, Cherokees, and Ponattonattamus. That their inclination was for war; and that, with much difficulty, he had restrained them from hostilities, which he thought it his duty to do, finding, by a letter from you, dated the 19th July, that you had sent back some Ottawas who had offered their services, desiring them to hold themselves in readiness next spring . . . . It is his Majesty's resolution, that the most vigorous efforts should be made, and every means employed that Providence has put into his Majesty's hands for crushing the rebellion, and restoring the constitution . . . . It is the King's command that you should direct Lieutenant-Governor Hamilton to assemble as many Indians of his district as he conveniently can, and, placing a proper person at their head . . . . employ them in making a diversion and alarm upon the frontiers of Virginia and Pennsylvania. And as there is good ground to believe that there are considerable numbers of loyal subjects in those parts, it is his Majesty's pleasure that you do authorize and direct Lieutenant-Governor Hamilton to invite all such loyal subjects to join him, and to assure them of the same pay and allowances as are given to his Majesty's other corps raised in America, and that such of them as shall continue to serve his Majesty until the rebellion is suppressed, and peace restored, shall each receive his Majesty's bounty of two hundred acres of land . . . . A supply of presents for the Indians and other necessaries will be wanted for this service, and you will of course send Lieutenant-Governor Hamilton what is proper and sufficient. Enclosed is a list of names of several persons living upon the frontiers of Virginia, recommended by Lord Dunmore for their loyalty and attachment to Government, and who his lordship thinks will be able to give great assistance.

"I am, Sir,

"Your most obedient, humble servant,

"GEORGE GERMAINE."

Here follows—"List of persons well disposed towards his Majesty's Government, living on the frontiers of Virginia, with recommendation from Whitehall of Indians, to be heard of at Fort Pitt:

"White Eyes, chief of the Delaware Indians; White Mingo; Corn Stalk, chief of the Shawanese; Kayashuta, chief of the Mingoes; Johnny Mintower, half white, half Indian; Logan, a great warrior of the Mingoes." *

* The following advertisements in the American newspapers of that time show that French nobles from Versailles would find domestic life in America scarcely less strange to them than the "savage tribes," with which they were about to be brought into contact in war:—

"TO BE SOLD.—The time of an English servant girl, who has three years and three months to serve. Inquire of Thomas Aptey, Keeper of the Workhouse, Philadelphia."

"FOUR DOLLARS REWARD.—Run away from the Subscriber,

This offer of bounty-money and of presents to the Indians, on the part of the British Government, was, by the treaty of alliance concluded by Dr. Franklin with France, frustrated in its professed object; for the same letter from Lord George Germaine, above transcribed, declares in another part: "His offer, it is to be hoped, will induce many persons to engage in the King's service, which may enable Lieutenant-Governor Hamilton to extend his operations, so as to divide the attention of the rebels, and oblige them to collect a considerable force to oppose him, *which cannot fail in weakening their main army, and facilitating the operations directed to be carried on against them;* and thus bring the war to a more speedy issue, and restore these deluded people to their former state of happiness and prosperity, which are the

living in East Pennsborough, Cumberland County, the 7th day of March, 1776, a servant boy, named Patrick Kelly."

"RUN AWAY.—A Dutch servant man. . . . Whoever takes up said servant and secures him, so that his master may get him again, shall have thirty shillings reward, paid by William Marshall."

Rather different these fugitive males and this workhouse maid from the confidential valet of M. le Marquis, or from the Abigails whom we have seen in attendance on the toilette of the belle of the 18th century in Paris!

favourite wishes of the Royal breast, and the great object of all his Majesty's measures."

When French armies were being equipped for America, this scheme of weakening the American army was neutralized.

As courtiers from Versailles are about to associate themselves with, or to oppose, these Indian tribes (as Indian appreciation of the presents from the British Government may decide), we may as well listen, as the Court of Versailles did, to what Dr. Franklin has to say concerning the social habits of North American Indians.

By Dr. Franklin's account, American Indians and Versailles courtiers had some few habits of etiquette in common with each other. The young Count de Ségur murmured that "it was essential to have attained a mature age in France before one dared to mix one's self up with politics and legislation;" Dr. Franklin declares, "all with the Indians is regulated by the advice of their sages. When they are young, they are hunters and warriors; old, they fill the office of councillors."

(But now comes a difference, appreciated by young France in 1778.)

"In the *advice* of the elders, consists the whole

of their government: no coercive force; no prisons; no men empowered to constrain other men to obey, or to inflict chastisement upon them.*

"The women amongst these tribes cultivate the earth, prepare the food, nourish and rear their children. The women are the living registrars of the councils of the elders; they record in their memories an exact note of all that passes; and, in time, communicate these oral traditions to their children. They cannot write, but when we consult our written records, we find that their memory is exact, always in precise accordance with our archives. In these public councils, the old men are seated in the first rank, the warriors in the

* Montaigne asserts that three American Indians visited France in the reign of Charles IX., (during his minority,) and that these Indians being at Rouen when the King was there, were asked what they found most remarkable in France? They answered, pointing to the Swiss guards who surrounded the King, that, 1st, They considered it very strange that so many men, strong, armed, and wearing beards, should submit themselves to a child, and that these strong men did not select one from amongst themselves to be their ruler; 2ndly, that having observed in France many men glutted with all sorts of luxuries, whilst their brother men, lean with hunger and poverty, were begging at their doors, they found it strange that the poor man, instead of submitting to such injustice, did not strangle the rich man, or set his house on fire.—Essais de Montaigne. Tome i., livre i., p. 218. Edit. Paris, 1725.

second, and the women and children in the third rank.

"To interrupt anybody whilst speaking, even in ordinary conversation, is regarded as the height of indecency. . . . Compare," continues Dr. Franklin, "this politeness of savages, with that of the House of Commons of England, where scarcely a day passes without a tumult which obliges the Speaker to cry: 'Order! order!'

"Indians listen to preaching with the greatest patience in the world, and even give signs of approbation whilst it is going on. . . . You believe from all this that they are convinced? Not at all, it is only pure civility."

Dr. Franklin then relates, at some length, how once a Swedish missionary called the tribes of Susquehannah together, and preached a long time to them, from the first chapter of Genesis to the end of Revelations. When, at last, the Swedish missionary had done preaching, an Indian orator rose to thank him, and in return to tell him of the religious creed of his own people. The Swedish missionary found this Indian creed absurd; he interrupted him by saying: "I have just proclaimed Sacred Truths, and now you tell me nothing but a fable, a fiction, and a lie!" The Indian, much insulted, answered the Swedish missionary thus: "Brother! it seems to me that your parents have neglected your education; they have not instructed you in the rules of common politeness. You have seen that, faithful to those rules which have been taught to us, we have believed all your histories—why do you refuse to believe ours!"

"In every village there is a vacant cabin, which is called the Stranger's Home." *

Thus accustomed to exercise hospitality towards strangers, the Indians were outraged by the murder of two of their people (of the Cherokee tribe), just as the Government of Great Britain was legislating to conciliate them. Six months after the French treaty of alliance with America had been signed at Versailles, the following letter was addressed to the Earl of Dunmore by the Hon. John Stuart, from Charles Town:—

"28th July, 1778.

"My Lord,

"I was informed by Mr. Cameron of the murder of two young Cherokee Indians, in the back

* Mélanges de Morale d'Economie et de Politique (Observations sur les Sauvages du Nord de l'Amérique). B. Franklin. Edit. Paris, 1824.

parts of Georgia. They went into the house of a back settler, named Hezekiah Collins, without arms, and civilly asked for something to eat, which a woman, the only person then at home, readily gave them. Whilst they were eating, John Collins, son of the master of the house, returned home, and, without the least provocation presented his rifle, and shot them both dead on the spot. The father returned immediately afterwards, and helped his son to sink the bodies in the river. The party of Indians which they belonged to waited for the two young men some days, but at last returned to their towns without them, and, after looking for their return impatiently, concluded that they were killed. In the first transports of rage and resentment, they would have gratified their revenge upon the traders, who, being warned of their danger, escaped. In the meanwhile, the bodies were discovered, and the murderers detected. The old man Collins is in custody, but his son, the young villain, found means to make his escape.

"Mr. Cameron sent a messenger into the nation with messages calculated to calm the Indians' fury, and to prevent their taking revenge upon innocent people. Mr. Cameron also sent proper persons in pursuit of the murderer, and has published a reward of £200 this currency for apprehending him. . . . Sir James Wright has it much at heart, and has offered a reward of £100 sterling for apprehending Collins. . . . The Indians had been to the Congress, and had just finished marking the new boundary line for the new cession. . . . There will be an absolute necessity for giving them some compensation."*

* The infringement of white men upon Indian boundary lines was the original cause of Indian enmity, dreaded at this time by the Government of Great Britain. In 1774 General Haldimand had written to Lord Dartmouth to express his belief, in conjunction with that of the British Superintendents of Indian affairs, that "our constant hemming in the Indians is the cause of the discontent generally prevailing amongst some of the most numerous and powerful tribes." In 1773, General Haldimand had also forewarned Lord Dunmore, in a letter dated from Pittsburgh, that "six Shawanese Indians arrived here, having been sent upon business by their chiefs, and delivered the following speeches:—

"BRETHREN,—We are sent by our chiefs to this place to inquire by what authority a captain from Virginia lately came to our towns upon Scioto, who told us that he had been sent by the governor of that colony and his wise men to . . . survey lands, and to make settlements upon the Ohio, as low down as the Big Bones, which country, he told us, had been sold to the white people by the six nations and Cherokees, and that our several nations had not been considered when these purchases were made . . . but that a large sum of money would be raised by the Virginians for our consent . . . and that the

Thus are the wisdom and forethought of Government sometimes frustrated by the ignorant impatience of the people. At Whitehall it had been decreed, as we have read, that "a supply of presents for the Indians will be necessary," to propitiate the good feeling of the various tribes towards the Crown of England; and here, through the wanton cruelty of John Collins, a back settler, there was

Great Man from Virginia would come there to speak to us in person! . . . But our chiefs would not listen to this Virginian captain, and therefore sent to inquire . . . and to inform you of this, that they might not be blamed hereafter for neglecting anything in their powers for the good of the peace and tranquillity of this country.

Signed—"A STRING," and "A LARGE STRING."

(Which signature seems to have been intended to impress the white people with a sense of Indian number, union, and power). To this address, Alexander McKee, the British agent of Indian affairs, then at Pittsburg, replied, through an interpreter, named Kyashuta, by informing the emissaries that the King's intentions in forming a colony referred to lands his majesty had purchased from the six nations in 1768, and by applauding their wisdom in coming to inquire at this place (Pittsburgh), where they would always hear of their father's, the King of Great Britain's good intentions towards them, and that he hoped they would continue to give every intelligence and assistance in their power to preserve the friendship subsisting between their brethren and the white people! . . . ." — Despatches forwarded by General Haldimand from America to the Ministers of his Britannic Majesty, 1778. Copies. Mus. Brit. MSS. unpublished.

danger of a desperate revolt amongst these powerful tribes against Englishmen, or the necessity of heavy compensation.

Meanwhile, in 1778, Frenchmen were flocking across the Atlantic to fight in America against England—for Liberty. Young French nobles, long held back by the authority of a government which at home was absolute, however weak and inconsistent it had been with regard to its foreign policy, now eagerly followed the example of the Marquis de Lafayette, the fame of whose brilliant deeds in the New World excited their emulation. Was it impatience of forced inaction at home that had caused one of these French nobles, the year before the treaty of Versailles was signed with America, to turn traitor? Of the following letter let the reader judge for himself :—

"St. James, 23rd April, 1777.

"SIR,

"Count de St. Aulaire, who will present this to you, is very strongly recommended to me by Lord Stormont (Ambassador at Versailles), to whom he has been very useful in furnishing very material information upon a particular occasion.

"As this gentleman's services have been the cause of his forfeiting his situation in France, his Majesty commands me to address him to you, recommending that you should find him such employment as you think that he may be qualified for.

"I have the honour to be, sir,

"Your most obedient and most humble servant,

"WEYMOUTH.*

"To General Sir Guy Carleton, K.B. &c."

In the same collection as the foregoing letter from Lord Weymouth to Sir Guy Carleton, are several letters from French Canadians, which show the conflict of self-interest as opposed to their love for their mother country.

In 1778, France was engaged in raising men, money, and ammunition to send out to America (there to avenge upon Great Britain her loss of Canada, twenty years before), just as the King of England had offered (in Lord George Germaine's letter to Sir Guy Carleton) two hundred acres of land to each loyal subject "who shall serve his Majesty until the rebellion is suppressed and peace

* MS. (unpublished). Mus. Brit. among "Original Letters of Major-General Haldimand, Brigadier-General of the Southern Districts of N. America, and afterwards Governor of Canada."

restored." This offer was a trial to French Canadian loyalty towards France, to which country, though under British rule, French Canadians were still linked by faith, blood, and language; but it was a test by which to enable both France and England to distinguish their friends from their enemies in America. As said Governor Livingstone, speaking of the effect of self-interest upon other colonists in comparison with that of pure patriotism:

"It has discriminated the temporizing politician, who, on the first appearance of danger, was determined to rescue his old idol, property, at the hazard of the general weal, from the persevering patriot, who, having embarked his all in the common cause, chooses rather to risk and to lose that all, for the sake of the invaluable treasure—Liberty."*

This discrimination dissevered family ties in America. Brothers, fathers, aud sons took up arms against each other in the civil war, as their separate views of the common cause dictated.

Even Dr. Franklin's family was not exempt from this common curse of a civil war; and to that

* "*Dunlap's, or the General Advertiser,*" March 4th, 1777.

family Governor Livingstone especially alludes in the above quotation.

In 1774, Dr. Franklin, writing from England to his son, William Franklin, the Governor of New Jersey, inveighs against "the Legislature here," for having "extorted many thousand pounds from America unconstitutionally, under colour of Acts of Parliament, and with an armed force. . . . Of this money," Dr. Franklin declares, "they ought to make restitution; but," says he, sarcastically, to his son, "you are a thorough courtier, and see everything with Government eyes."*

Although Dr. Franklin was disgraced by the Privy-Council of England, and deprived of his office as Postmaster-General, his son, the Governor of New Jersey, still clung to his appointment under the Crown, long after his father had arrived in France, there to negotiate the treaties by which France declared war against England. Dr. Franklin, as we have seen, had taken his grandson with him to France, declaring that he desired the lad to be "independent of posts and places, which are precarious things;"—the truth of which say-

* Manuscript original autograph. Mus. Brit. (ex dono, E. Wilmot.)

ing his son experienced; for the Republican party having gained the upper hand, Governor Franklin was displaced by Governor Livingstone, whose speech we have just recorded, and the former—a prisoner—was compelled to throw himself upon the mercy of General George Washington.

To which appeal of Dr. Franklin's son, George Washington replied (in the same bold and clear handwriting in which he formerly wrote his agricultural notes):—

"Head-Quarters, July 25th, 1777.

"SIR,—I have this moment received your letter of the 22nd instant by express.

"I heartily sympathise with you in your distressing situation; but, however strong my inclination to comply with your request, it is by no means in my power to supersede a positive resolution of Congress, under which your present confinement took place.

"I have enclosed your letter to them, and shall be happy if it may be found consistent with propriety to concur with your wishes in a matter of so delicate and interesting a nature. I sincerely hope that a speedy restoration of Mrs. Franklin's health may relieve you from the anxiety her present declining condition must naturally give you. I am, with due respect, sir,

"Your most obedient servant,

"GEORGE WASHINGTON."

"To William Franklin, Esquire, Litchfield."*

Thus did Dr. Franklin's son—with his family—suffer for being "a thorough courtier;" whilst Dr. Franklin himself was loaded with honours at feudal Versailles, for being what England had called "a rank republican."

Madame Campan tells us that "elegant fêtes were given to Dr. Franklin, in whom was united the renown of one of the most learned of men, with the patriotic virtues which had made him an Apostle of Liberty. I assisted at one of these fêtes, where the most beautiful from amongst three hundred ladies were chosen to place a crown of laurel upon the white hair of the American Philosopher, and to kiss him on both cheeks."

* Original MS., ex dono, Wilmot. (Mus. Brit.) endorsed:—"The Congress refused it, and Mrs. Franklin died." Mems. Campan. Tome x., p. 177.

CHAPTER V.

Voltaire's arrival in Paris—Recognition on the road—Voltaire's costume—His Prussian antecedents—His visitors—Kain, the actor—Voltaire's reception of French actors—Madame Necker, Lord Stormont, and Dr. Franklin—Voltaire's benediction of Dr. Franklin's grandson—Madame du Deffand visits Voltaire—Voltaire and Pigalle—Conversation of Voltaire—Voltaire's visit to Madame de Ségur—Portrait of Voltaire by one who knew him—Conversation of Voltaire—Madame du Barry visits Voltaire—Marshal Duc de Richelieu visits Voltaire—The soldier and the sage of the eighteenth century—Voltaire dangerously ill—Dr. Tronchin—The Archbishop of Paris holds a convocation—The Abbé Gauthier visits Voltaire—Voltaire's profession of faith—Rivalry of the Priesthood concerning Voltaire—Correspondence of Voltaire and the Curé de St. Sulpice—Dr. Lorry—Jean Jacques Rousseau—Rousseau's retreat from Paris—Duel between the Count d'Artois and the Duc de Bourbon—"Irène"—The Philosopher revives—Second Academic Deputation to Voltaire—Voltaire enthroned at the Academy—Voltaire crowned—Vive Voltaire! Vive Franklin

—The Princesse de Lamballe and Madame de Genlis—Madame de Genlis visits Voltaire—Voltaire at the Palais Royal—Voltaire and the Orléans family—Madame de Villette—Voltaire's "Brother Cain"—Last moments of Voltaire—Voltaire excommunicated—Signs of the Times—America symbolised in Paris—Dr. Franklin stamps the gift bread with "Liberty"—Voltaire's heart enshrined—Liberty of conscience in the eighteenth century.

Upon the 10th of February, 1778—not a week after the treaty with America was signed—Voltaire, after an absence of more than twenty years, arrived in Paris.

Great changes were taking place in both hemispheres; the pen of Voltaire had done much to provoke those changes.

Louis XVI., even in these early years of his reign, was subservient to the will of his people. His Majesty had just openly subscribed to the popular cause in America, and it was impossible for a monarch who wished to be popular in France to insist that Voltaire should remain in exile. But Louis XVI. did not love Voltaire any more for all that.

Paris eagerly awaited the arrival of Voltaire. The elder members of Paris society desired to renew their personal acquaintance with him, and its younger members (a new generation that had sprung up during the last twenty years), not less familiar with his thoughts, desired to behold the philosopher who had educated them.

The only incident that befell Voltaire on his journey to Paris, in 1778, he himself thus relates :—

"Having stopped in a village to change horses, I alighted from my coach, and perceived a venerable old man standing at some few paces from me; he might have been about my own age, but he certainly was much more active of the two. Upon examining him nearer, I thought I recognized him. 'Sir,' said I to him, 'I ask your pardon, but you much resemble a child whom I saw about seventy years ago!' The old man asked me where I had seen that child; and when I had told him where, 'I was that child!' said he, 'and you are M. de Voltaire!' We then embraced each other."

When Voltaire's carriage was stopped at the barriers of Paris, according to custom, and he was asked if he had anything to declare, "Gentlemen," said he to the commissioners, "there is nothing contraband in this coach but myself."

And a queer spectacle Voltaire must have presented to the astonished eyes of the excise officers when he put his head out of the window; for the public prints of the time inform us, that "his out-door attire is a vast pelisse, which completely envelopes his frail body; a Louis Quatorze wig of wool shades his thin cheeks, and this wig is surmounted by a red cap trimmed with fur."

It was Carnival time when he first re-appeared in the streets of Paris, after more than twenty years' absence; and profane *gamins*, not knowing who he was, hooted at M. de Voltaire, or cheered him, thinking that he was in masquerade for their amusement.

Voltaire, upon his arrival in Paris, alighted at the hôtel of the Marquis de Villette, at the corner of the Rue de Beaume.* He was accompanied by his niece, Madame Denis, who had lived with him long at Ferney. She had joined Voltaire at Frankfort in 1753, when

* Lettres d'un Espion Anglais.—Paris, 1788. (*Passim.*) Bib. Imp.

he fled from King Frederick the Great of Prussia, at Potzdam, because that monarch had hinted to the Marquis d'Argens, their mutual friend, that he, the King, intended to fling M. de Voltaire, his guest and pensioner, aside, like a sucked orange, when he had got all he could out of him.*

Voltaire, whose genius was too universal to be exclusively patriotic, had, a few years before his flight to Frankfort, hired himself out to the King of Prussia for a barony, a pension of 20,000 francs, a chamberlainship, and a silver-gilt key; † and so, writing up Prussian policy, had helpled to foment the war between France (allied with Austria) and England (allied with Prussia), which for seven years deluged Europe with blood.

Voltaire and King Frederick had continued to correspond and to flatter each other from the time of the Seven Years' War until now. It was the policy of both to forget and to forgive injuries.

* Mémoires de Voltaire, écrits par lui-même. De l'Imprimerie de la Société Littéraire Typographique, 1789. Tome i., p. 312-313.

† Ibid., p. 306.

In 1778, when James Necker, the Protestant minister, was about to find funds for the popular war, in which Benjamin Franklin, the American republican, had, by his Memorial, induced the Cabinet of Versailles to engage, King Frederick, the Protestant, hero was worshipped in France. Therefore the past, in which Voltaire had had a share and a shame, was forgotten, or was remembered only to show that philosopher shining with the light of the Prussian King's peculiar favour.

The day after M. de Voltaire's arrival in Paris, a prodigious concourse of all the finest folks of the court and city called to do homage to him.

Only a few of these were admitted, and they found him arrayed in a dressing-gown and night-cap, with loose leaves fresh from the press scattered about him; for Voltaire was correcting his tragedy of "Irène," which he desired should be represented on the stage of Paris during his stay. The Marquise de Villette, his hostess, and Madame Denis, his niece, were deputed to receive most of Voltaire's visitors in the ante-chamber; and there every word was breathlessly listened to and eagerly repeated that in any way concerned him.*

Upon the 13th of February, the choicest company of French actors came to fling themselves at Voltaire's feet. The actors were admitted, but Voltaire missed one from amongst them, and that was the great Tragedian, Kain, for whom he had written a special part in "Irène." Kain died just as his patron, Voltaire, re-entered Paris.†

Kain's reputation as an actor was world-wide; but, though Voltaire had been the first to discover and to develope Kain's genius, he was destined, by the death of his protégé, never to see him act. He tried to make up for the loss by allotting the parts of "Irène" to the most efficient actors that were left.

* L'Espion Anglais. Bib. Imp. *passim.*

† Kain, the celebrated actor, was a goldsmith's son. By Voltaire's advice, he turned from his father's trade to the stage, although it was generally thought that his voice and person were against him. Voltaire had Kain trained at his own expense, and, in 1750, the latter first appeared at the Théâtre Français, in one of his patron's characters. Voltaire was then in Prussia, and being exiled from Paris during intervening years, he never had an opportunity of judging for himself how far Kain realised his predictions.

These declaimed one after another before Voltaire—in Voltaire's praise. The philosopher was well pleased.

"My friends!" said he to them, "henceforth I live but for you, and by you." And all the actors cried, "Vive Voltaire!"

Voltaire bowed; then turning to Madame Vestris, with all the grace and gallantry of his bygone days, "Madame," he declared, "for you I have written all night, as though I were a man only twenty years old, writing his first untiring hymn of love and praise to his mistress."

Night and day Voltaire wrote. He who had filled the world with his thoughts, who ruled its opinions by his pen, was feverish, excited, and anxious as to his Tragedy of "Irène," as though this were his first production.*

The last work is always the best—to its author. Voltaire's proceedings were deemed of sufficient importance to attract the attention of the English

* Madame du Deffand says that the name of this tragedy was originally "Alexis Comnène," but that "Irène" was substituted as more favourable to rhyme. "Voltaire does not cease," she adds, "re-touching, correcting, and altering this work. It occupied his first two nights."—Lettres de Madame du Deffand, tome iv., p. 14.

politician, as of the Paris gossip.* The one records, and the other repeats:

"Monday, February 16. . . M. de Voltaire has had no general reception, because he was indisposed yesterday; but he has received some few personages in private, notwithstanding the precautions exercised by M. de Villette, his host, in watching over the precious health of his guest. Madame Necker, the wife of the Comptroller of Finance, Lord Stormont,† Dr. Franklin, and M. Balbastre the musician have been admitted."

M. de Voltaire varied his conversation to suit each of these guests, and charmed them all by his wit and vivacity; especially did he seek to please the wife of the Finance Comptroller.‡

* L'Espion Anglais. Bib. Imp., Paris, 1788. Mems. de Bachaumont; à Londres, 1778.

† Lord Stormont, after he was withdrawn as English ambassador from Versailles, still lingered in Paris. We shall presently see in the House of Commons, how his lordship was politically employed during that interval in the French capital.

‡ Madame Necker, the first love of Gibbon, and the mother of Madame de Staël, was, says Madame de Genlis, "a philosopher without knowing it!"—Mems. de Genlis, tome v., p. 282.—Madame Necker was at the head of an association for erecting a statue to Voltaire. "But, Madame," remonstrated Voltaire, "the first essential would be to give me a face; the place where

M. de Voltaire had complained of headache, but wishing to flatter the self-love of M. Balbastre, that renowned artist who had come to pay homage to him, he asked him to play a piece on the harpsichord; the musician's skill seemed to charm away the invalid's pain.

Voltaire received Dr. Franklin with evident sentiments of curiosity and admiration. He first addressed Dr. Franklin in English,* but having lost the habit of that language, he resumed the conversation in French, saying, with the tact and grace peculiar to him, "I could not resist the desire of speaking for one moment in the tongue of Dr. Franklin."

Dr. Franklin's grandson was present. The sage

it ought to be can scarcely be guessed; my eyes are sunken by three inches; my cheeks are of old parchment, scarcely drawn over bones which hold to nothing: the few teeth I once had are gone;—surely, no poor man was ever sculptured in such a plight as this!"—Mems. de Genlis. Paris, 1825.

* Voltaire boasted that he had taught his friend (long since dead), Madame du Châtelet, English in three months.—(Mems. de Voltaire, Paris, 1789.) But in 1761 Voltaire wrote a letter to Pitt (Earl of Chatham), requesting that statesman to contribute to the subscription then being raised throughout Europe for the grand-niece of Corneille. The letter is in English, and we can believe, after reading it, that all Voltaire knew of that language, might have been very well imparted in less than three months. —Chatham Correspondence, vol. ii., p. 340.

of Philadelphia presented his grandson to the patriarch of Ferney, and asked him to bless the lad. Voltaire raised his hands, placed them on the youth's head, and said:

"God and Liberty! That is the only benediction suitable to the grandson of Benjamin Franklin."

A deputation of the members of the French Academy, including Dr. Franklin, came to pay respect to Voltaire. This deputation was headed by the Prince de Beauvau.

Voltaire still continued to work at "Irène"—to correct his printer's proofs, and to hear the actors rehearse their parts in his own room; but he knew that the ante-chamber was crowded by people anxious to catch sight of him. The atmosphere he breathed was impregnated with the incense of adulation.

"I am stifled," said he, "but it is beneath roses."

"This new sort of life that the old man from Ferney is leading at Paris, after a long and fatiguing journey in a rigorous season; the continual efforts which he is obliged to make in receiving such visitors as are admitted to him, and, above all, in sustaining his high reputation for wit, by brilliant sallies, as also in maintaining the tone of courtly politeness which he desires may be thought to be still familiar to him—the courtesies and beneficence which he seeks to testify to everybody in proportionate degree; lastly, his temper, to which, for a long time past, he has been accustomed to give free vent, but which he is now obliged to repress,—all this is undermining his health, already too much deranged."

Madame la Marquise du Deffand had written to congratulate Voltaire on his arrival; and he had answered: "I arrive dead; I only wish to revive that I may throw myself at the feet of the Marquise du Deffand."

Afterwards he sent to invite her to witness the rehearsal of "Irène," in his chamber, but the Marquise declared to Horace Walpole, "As this rehearsal takes place between 11 o'clock, A.M. and noon, which is often the time that I begin to sleep, it is doubtful whether I can go, and I fear to encounter all the buffoon fine wits."*

Upon February 21st, 1778, Madame du Deffaud, accompanied by the Prince de Beauvau,

* Lettres de Madame du Deffand. Tome iv., pp. 11-14. Ed. 1824.

went to visit Voltaire. Madame du Deffand and M. de Voltaire had been great friends in their youth, before he was the protégé of Madame de Pompadour, and Court poet of Versailles, and when she was still young and beautiful. Madame du Deffand* was now more than seventy years old, and quite blind; she could not, there fore, see Voltaire, but she could hear him speak, as far at least as the spitting of blood, from which he was suffering, would permit him.

* Madame du Deffand was for a short time mistress of the Regent; she is now old and stone blind, but retains all her vivacity, wit, memory, judgment, passion, and agreeableness. She goes to operas, plays, suppers, and Versailles; gives suppers twice a week; has everything new read to her; makes new songs and epigrams, ay, admirably, and remembers every one that has been made these fourscore years. She corresponds with Voltaire, dictates charming letters to him, contradicts him, is no bigot to him or anybody, and laughs both at the clergy and the philosophers. In a dispute, into which she easily falls, she is very warm, and yet scarce ever in the wrong; her judgment on every subject is as just as possible; on every point of conduct as wrong as possible; for she is all love and hatred—passionate for her friends to enthusiasm, still anxious to be loved (I don't mean by lovers), and a vehement enemy, but openly. As she can have no amusement but conversation, the least solitude and ennui are insupportable to her, and put her into the power of several worthless people, who eat her suppers when they can eat nobody's of higher rank . . . hate her because she has forty times more parts—and venture to hate her because she is not rich.—Walpole's Correspondence, vol. iii., p. 141. London, 1820.

"We were received," says Madame du Deffand, "by niece Denis, who is the best woman and the greatest trollop in the world; by the Marquis de Villette, who is like the dummy in the play; and by his young wife, who is said to be amiable; she is called, by Voltaire and his suite, 'Belle et Bonne.' Having reached the salon (past a whole range of wide-open windows) we found no Voltaire; he was shut up in his chamber with his secretary. We were entreated to wait, but the Prince begged me to let him take his departure. So I remained alone with niece Denis, the dummy Marquis, and Madame 'Belle et Bonne.' They told me Voltaire was dead with fatigue; that, since dinner, he had read the whole of his play to the actors; that he had made them rehearse their parts before him; and that now he was too exhausted to speak. I wished to go, but they made me stay; and, to detain me, Voltaire sent four verses to me, which he had made for Pigalle, who is going to do his bust in marble ....*

* Notwithstanding Voltaire's pretended refusal—already quoted—of Madame Necker's desire to have his face chiselled, it is asserted that Pigalle, the sculptor, had succeeded in making a nude statue of him.

> "Pigalle, au naturel, nous a rendu Voltaire;
> Ce Squelette à la fois offre l'homme et l'Auteur;

"After I had waited a quarter of an hour, Voltaire came in, declaring that he was dead, and could not open his mouth. I wished to leave him. He detained me. He spoke to me of his play. This subject engrosses his whole thoughts; it will be the death of him if not a great success... He has other pretensions—that of going to see the King and Queen at Versailles; but I doubt whether he will obtain permission. He then desired M. le Marquis to tell me of a visit he had had from a priest: but the Marquis began his narration so badly, that Voltaire silenced him, and, taking up the story, related that he had received a letter from an abbé, joyfully greeting his arrival in Paris. 'Grant me,' said this letter, 'permission to come and see you. I have been a priest thirty years: I have been amongst the Jesuits twenty years; I am esteemed and honoured by M. the Archbishop . . . I perform services; I lend my services to divers curés in Paris. I offer to take you under my care. However superior you may be to other men, you are mortal as they are. You are eighty-four years old; hard moments may be in store for you—moments

L'œil qui le voit sans parure étrangère
Est effrayé de sa laideur."

difficult to pass .... I could be useful to you, as I am to M. the Abbé de l'Attaignant, who is older than you are. I go to dine with him to-day. Permit me to come and see you.'

"Voltaire consented: 'That,' said he, 'will save scandal or ridicule.'" *

Madame du Deffand and Voltaire were professed philosophers; but the self-love of the latter was still strong within him; and the former passed her whole life in flying from *ennui*, and in shunning serious reflection. The old age of Madame du Deffand was not pleasant for Voltaire to behold. It was the mirror of himself. The old age of Voltaire was not pleasant for Madame du Deffand to hear. It was her own echo.

The young Count de Ségur, now impatient to fight for liberty in America, contemplated Voltaire by the light of his own enthusiasm. "Never before," says De Ségur of him, "had the chief of any sect combated and conquered so many enemies who thought themselves invincible, so many errors consecrated by time, so many antiquated and deep-rooted customs, and all that without himself appearing in the fight."

* Lettres de Madame du Deffand à Horace Walpole. Year 1778.

One day Voltaire took off his night-cap, put on his Louis Quatorze wig, and went to see young De Ségur's mother, who was confined to her bed by a mortal malady. Madame de Ségur was, like Madame du Deffand, an old friend of Voltaire's, long before his dealings with Frederick of Prussia had exiled him from France. Many years had elapsed since Voltaire and Madame de Ségur had met. The young Count de Ségur was present at this interview between his mother and the philosopher. He declares:

"When I saw Voltaire, he was exactly what my fancy had depicted him to me. In his meagre body I could trace the long and arduous labours of his mind. His antique costume recalled to me the last witness of the time of Louis XIV., the historian of that period, and the immortal painter of Henri IV. In his piercing eye, glittering with genius and malice, I beheld the soul of the tragic poet.... of the profound philosopher, and of the sarcastic observer of the human race. His frail and bent body was but a slight and almost transparent covering to his soul, and to his genius, which seemed to shine through it..... I was all eyes, all ears in approaching Voltaire, as though in momentary expectation of some oracle springing from his mouth. But not even Apollo could have displayed himself at such a time and in such a place; for Voltaire was by the side of a dying woman, whose aspect was only suggestive of melancholy ideas. She seemed no longer susceptible of admiration, or even of consolation.

"Nevertheless, she made a great effort to conquer Nature; her eyes regained some brilliance, her voice some strength. Voltaire sought with delicacy to distract her from the present by exciting her remembrance of the past. He could not cure one sick as she who listened to him, but he reanimated her. She appeared for some moments to feel no longer weak and suffering; she sustained the conversation with some liveliness, and even imparted to me, her son, a last and feeble ray of hope that she might yet live."

A few days afterwards Voltaire went once more to visit Madame de Ségur. A crowd of people gained admission to her salon, that they might behold the philosopher there. Each of these guests was so prepared to accept every word uttered by Voltaire as oracular, that when, during his conversation with Madame de Ségur, he happened to mention that once, being ill, yolks of eggs, meal, and potatoes had been prescribed for him, one of the listeners suddenly embraced young De Ségur in raptures, crying: "Oh! what a man! Yolks of eggs, meal, and potatoes! Oh! what a man! Not a word he utters but has its point!"

Presently, the conversation between Voltaire and the dying lady became more serious; she gently reproached him for his continued attacks on the Church. "Be generous and moderate after victory," said she to him; "what can you fear at present from such adversaries? Fanatics are conquered, their reign is past."

"You are in error there," replied Voltaire with sudden energy, "fanaticism is a fire which is smothered, but not extinct; fanatics are muzzled, but they keep their teeth; they no longer bite, it is true; but, if their teeth be not extracted, the first opportunity will show that they have not forgotten how to use them."

As Voltaire was passing out, he paused to address himself to the young Count de Ségur, who courted the muses. "Strive to deserve the good things that are said of you," said Voltaire to him: "mingle some realities with the lightest images of your poetry, some morality with your sentiment, some grains of philosophy with your gaiety. . . . Go, young man, accept the good wishes of an old man who predicts a happy destiny for you; but remember that poetry, though divine, is a syren."*

Voltaire, becoming daily more anxious as to the success of his "Irène," was, in the midst of the homage paid to him, the victim of a daily disappointment. The King and Queen at Versailles sent no message to him. For this omission on the part of Versailles, not all the worship of Paris could atone. But he still hoped that the Queen would be present at the representation of "Irène;" he seemed to live but for that tragedy.†

* Mems. de Ségur, tome i., pp. 164, 173. *Passim.* Paris, 1825.

† The Emperor Joseph II., during his visit to Versailles, the preceding year, had advised the Queen not to receive Voltaire; the clergy, also, took steps that the King of Philosophers should not appear at Versailles. The Queen hesitated, but having consulted persons in whom she had the greatest confidence, she announced to the Court that Voltaire's writings being full of direct attacks on religion and morals, he would not be received by any member of the royal family. Nevertheless, the Queen added, on her own account, "It is strange that we refuse to admit Voltaire into our presence, as chief of philosophers, when, some years since, Madame Geoffrin, the nursing mother of philosophers, was presented to me by the Maréchale de Mouchy.—(Mems. de Madame Campan. Chapitre viii., tome dixième, p.

The Queen did not acknowledge Voltaire's presence in Paris, but Madame du Barry thrust herself upon him there. He did not wish to receive Madame du Barry, because of the Queen's notorious aversion to the mistress of the late King. Voltaire, in these his last days, desired to conciliate Versailles.

Madame du Barry was not, however, a woman to be refused admittance, even by Voltaire, though the day she called upon him he had so worked

150.) A lady at Versailles had reproached the Emperor Joseph, in 1777, for his want of enthusiasm towards Voltaire; the Emperor answered that, although he should always seek to profit, for the welfare of his people, by the intelligence due to philosophy, his vocation of sovereign prevented his ranging himself among the adepts of that sect. Madame de Genlis affirms that when the Emperor Joseph passed near Ferney, on his journey from France, his attendants inquired of him whether he would not stop to see Voltaire; and that the Emperor answered, that he already knew enough of that philosopher. (Mems. de Genlis, tome ii., p. 269.) The Queen, though submitting herself to her husband's authority, and to the decree of her spiritual advisers, in excluding Voltaire from Versailles, was inclined, for her own part, to look favourably on him, in consideration of the friendship subsisting between the philosopher and the Duc de Choiseul. Voltaire hated the Parliament of Paris, and loved the Duc de Choiseul; he saw in the former a persecutor exasperated and not disarmed by his glory, and in the other a benefactor and a support. The Queen, also, hated the Parliament, and loved the Duc de Choiseul.—Vie de Voltaire. Condorcet. Paris, 1789.

his secretary and himself in the forenoon, that neither of them had found time for the toilette. When Madame du Barry arrived, Voltaire was still in his night-cap; he declined to see or be seen by her. She would take no denial. Neither niece Denis, nor the Marquis de Villette, nor his wife, "Belle et Bonne," could get rid of Madame du Barry. Voltaire yielded at length to her entreaties; and once in her presence, or rather she in his, he became as anxious to please Madame du Barry as he had been to exclude her—"making up, by the graces of his mind, for whatever was wanting in the elegance of his outward appearance."*

Marshal Duc de Richelieu was more readily admitted to Voltaire than was Madame du Barry. The Duc de Richelieu, although one of the greatest sinners in France, was, by reason of his rank and military renown, still received at Versailles, from which Voltaire and Madame du Barry were cast out. The Duc de Richelieu was an old friend of Voltaire's. When the former conquered Minorca in 1756, the latter signed himself the "aged secretary of De Richelieu's glory."†

* Journal d'un Observateur. Year 1778.

† Correspondance Générale de Voltaire. Year 1756.

Both these men were now more than four score years old; they presented a strange contrast to each other.* The hero de Richelieu, with his rouged, wrinkled face, his wig cut, curled, powdered,† and pig-tailed à la mode, his legs plumped out by false calves beneath silk stockings and satin breeches, arched his false eyebrows in surprise at the sight of his friend Voltaire (who was younger than himself) in a cotton night-cap; his frail, bent body lost in the folds of his dressing-gown. The soldier and the sage embraced each other. To get at the French hero, Richelieu, you must "unroll bails of wool and wadding;" to get at Voltaire, it needed but to look at his eyes, which shone with strange lustre, and still seem to shine on men of another century, who declare that neither time nor death can quench the light of Voltaire.

The priests of Paris, in 1778, did their best to quench that light. Outraged by the sight of the people's idolatry of Voltaire, they con-

* "Madame Geoffry called me in joke the *nouveau Richelieu:* I give it under my hand that I resemble him in nothing but wrinkles."—Walpole's Correspondence, vol. iii., p. 104. London, 1820.

† Siècle XVIII., Capefigue. Tome iii., p. 211. Bruxelles, 1844.

sulted the registers of police, those of the department of Paris, and those of foreign affairs, for the last thirty years, hoping (in vain) by so doing to find some charge against him, by which he could be ejected from the capital by the civil authorities, or that would seem to justify the King in sending him a lettre de cachet.* The King would have rejoiced if this search had given him the means of getting rid of Voltaire. For Louis XVI., born and bred in saintly traditions, had a horror of the chief of philosophers. But Louis XVI. was dependent on his Protestant minister, Necker, for supplying him with funds for fighting in behalf of heretics and insurgents, and Necker was the friend, the admirer, and had long been the neighbour of Voltaire.

The people had begun to reign in France, and all that the "most Christian King" of France and the priests could do was to forbid the Queen from joining in the homage then paid by Paris to the patriarch of Ferney.

The excitement of this popular homage, the disappointment that the Queen did not join in it, and

* L'Espion Anglais. Bib. Imp.

extreme anxiety as to the success of "Irène," formed a combination too strong for even the philosophy of Voltaire. He fell sick. He spat blood. Dr. Tronchin was in attendance on him; but Dr. Tronchin tapped his snuff-box significantly, and ordered M. de Voltaire to keep his bed and to take opium.*

The news spread like wild-fire that Voltaire was dying. Even the war for liberty in America was forgotten for the moment by the people of Paris, who dreaded that the Champion of Liberty in France was about to be taken from the midst of them. The street where the Marquis de Villette lived was thronged with people of every rank who came to inquire concerning the health of his guest. Nothing else was talked of, thought of, in churches, at theatres, in the Champs Elysées, or at the corners of streets, but Voltaire's chances of life or death.

The clergy, although from different causes, participated strongly in this popular excitement.

* M. Tronchin, a citizen of Geneva, was physician in chief to the Duc d'Orléans. He was the first to introduce the practice of inoculation into France, and was an associate of the Academy of Science in Paris. He was now about seventy years of age, and died November 30th, 1781.

Priests were upon the watch to pounce down upon the soul of Voltaire. A general assembly of the clergy was convoked at the house of the archbishop of Paris; a consultation was there held as to the best means of gaining admission to the philosopher and of converting him, or at least of extorting from him some outward sign of repentance.

From this assembly stepped forth the Abbé Gauthier. The Abbé Gauthier was the "Chaplain of Incurables," an ex-Jesuit, an ardent enthusiast, and renowned at that moment for having just snatched a notorious Jansenist (the Abbé Villemesens) from the perils into which heresy had ensnared his soul.

In presence of the archbishop of Paris, and the assembled clergy, the Abbé Gauthier declared that he was the instrument appointed by Heaven to convert Voltaire; and, impelled by zeal, he set forth to the house where the philosopher lay.*

* L'Espion Anglais, 1809. ("All Eye.") "Août 1778. Depuis longtems on parloit dans ce pays-ci de deux nouveaux volumes, servant de suite à "l'Observateur Anglois"—"Correspondance Secrète entre Milord All Eye, and Milord All Ear." On n'en pouvoit savoir davantage, parce qu'on assuroit que le Ministère avoit donné les ordres les plus sévères pour empêcher leur introduction. . . ."—Mems. de Bachaumont, 1778. Published 1779, (à Londres.)—"Milord All Eye and Milord All Ear."—Bib. Imp.

The Abbé armed himself with a paper drawn up ready for Voltaire to sign. He entered the hôtel of the Marquis de Villette, and, nobody daring to arrest his progress, crossed the threshold of the chamber where the actors had lately rehearsed their parts, and fell down on his knees by Voltaire's bedside. The Abbé Gauthier declared to Voltaire that he was an envoy of God, and conjured him to profit by the short time that remained to him in repenting of his sins, and in thinking of his eternal salvation. Voltaire's strength had gone out of him; he had been kept on water-gruel, and bled. Dr. Tronchin had warned Voltaire that he was in imminent danger of death; that, "like Damocles, a sword was suspended over his head but by a thread." Thus, threatened by the doctor, and urged by the priest, and fearing, as he afterwards declared, that, if he died unconfessed and unabsolved, his corpse might be thrown into the common sewer, Voltaire made a profession of faith in the following words, as afterwards certified by the Abbé Gauthier *:—

* Vie de Voltaire par le Marquis de Condorcet, 1789. Tome i., p. 156. The Marquis de Condorcet further affirms that Voltaire sent for the Abbé Gauthier to confess him, because, if he lived, he "wished to remain in Paris without being troubled by

"I, the undersigned, declare, that being attacked four days since, by a vomiting of blood, at the age eighty-four years, and not having been able to drag myself to church, M. le Curé de St. Sulpice having added to his good works that of sending to me M. the Abbé Gauthier, priest, I have confessed myself to him; and if God so dispose of me, I die in the holy Catholic religion, in which I was born, hoping that divine mercy will deign to pardon all my faults; and if, having scandalized the Church, I ask pardon for the same of God, and of her. Signed, Voltaire, the second of March, 1778, in the house of M. le Marquis de Villette, in presence of M. l'Abbé Mignot, my nephew, and of M. le Marquis de Villeveille, my friend."*

The "Espion Anglais," in Paris at the time, de-

sacerdotal informers;" and if he died, that "scenes of intolerance might not pursue his last moments." (Ibid., p. 156.) But L'Espion Anglais and the Mémoires de Bachaumont (tome ii.) concur in the statement as above written; it is therefore adopted in preference to that of M. de Condorcet, who is an apologist for Voltaire having made a profession of faith at all, although Bachaumont (tome xii., p. 56) asserts that Gauthier, after Voltaire's death, and for the purpose of getting Christian burial for him, certified (with the above profession of faith) that he went to Voltaire by his own request.

* Mems. de Bachaumont. Year 1779.

clares that "the services volunteered to Voltaire nearly at the same time by the Curé de St. Sulpice and the Abbé Gauthier, had led Voltaire to suppose that they were acting in concert for the good of his soul; which mistake on his part resulted in jealousy between those reverend brethren. This jealousy did not redound to the honour of their profession when it came to the knowledge of Voltaire, who was too much inclined to misjudge religion by the misconduct of its professors. Voltaire in a few days was out of danger; at least the public newspapers announced that fact. The Abbé Gauthier had stolen a march on the Curé de St. Sulpice, but the latter still continued to press his services on Voltaire; therefore Voltaire wrote the following letter, by dictation, to the Curé de St. Sulpice:—

"Monsieur,—M. l'Abbé Gauthier had begun by writing to me on the mere rumour of my illness; * he has since been here . . . and having come from your parish, I supposed that you had sent him. I regard you, monsieur, as a man of the first order in the State; I know that you succour the poor as an Apostle, and that you do your work well as a min-

* Lettres de Madame du Deffand à Horace Walpole. Tome iv., p. 18. Paris, 1824.

ister; but the more I respect your person and office, the more do I fear to abuse your extreme goodness. . . . This letter needs no reply, your time is too precious to waste upon me."

To which the Curé de St. Sulpice answered:—

"All my parishioners, sir, have a right to my care; but such an one as M. de Voltaire demands my especial attention. He, whose celebrity has spread through all Europe, might well demand the aid of a poor curate . . . " *

The Curé de St. Sulpice accused the Abbé Gauthier of having put his scythe into the harvest of another; he drove out the Abbé Gauthier, and

* The time of the Curé de St. Sulpice was much occupied at this date by the Abbé Terray. That Ex-Minister of Finance and protegé of Madame du Barry, who had declared that he did not know where better to put the people's money than in his own pocket, lay dying. The Abbé Terray had promised the Curé de St. Sulpice that he would play his part suitably to time and place. He did so, to all outward appearance, although his bodily sufferings were extreme. He was buried at his estate of La Motte, and Paris sang:—

"Le grand Abbé Terray, le Dieu de la Finance,
L'Etalon des Putains, le Bourreau de la France,
Est donc enfin trépassé;
Ce prêtre à tellement toujours aimé la cotte,
Que pour dernier Asyle il à choisi la Motte.
Requiescat in pace."

usurped his place by Voltaire's side; but the Marquis de Villette, not being able to persuade Dr. Tronchin that the thread by which the "sword of Damocles" was hanging over Voltaire's head was strengthened,—in other words, that his guest, the Doctor's patient, was not in immediate danger of death,—and, wishing to rid his house of rival priests, sent for Dr. Lorry, "a physician who saw things easily (*couleur de rose*) a *petit-maître*, a man of wit," who cheered the philosopher as to his chances of life, and wrote a bulletin by the dictation of the Marquis de Villette, that reassured Paris as to the convalescence of M. de Voltaire.* And when M. de Voltaire himself told Dr. Lorry that he had confessed, that easy physician smiled, more in pity than in approbation. "You think me very impious?" asked the sick man, misinterpreting the smile. To which Dr. Lorry answered, "*Vous craignez qu'on l'ignore, et vous en faites la gloire.*" Then Voltaire excused himself by saying that he did not desire his "body to be cast into the common sewer." †

Voltaire had been brought very low; but he was now permitted to eat an egg; soon he drank a

* Journal de Paris. No. 64.

† Mems. de Bachaumont, tome ii., p. 162.

glass of wine; he began to forget the sword of Damocles, and to remember "Irène." He sent a message to the Duc de Richelieu, to urge on the rehearsals. The priests were discarded; the players were admitted. Voltaire no longer spat blood; and it was announced (March 9th, 1778) that he had sat up to table, and had supped off fried eggs.

The time appointed for the representation of "Irène" drew near. The late illness of "Irène's" author had given a fresh impulse to the excitement with which Paris regarded all concerning him. But, alas! Philosophy! Jean Jacques Rousseau had not courage to stand by and witness the evidences of this enthusiasm in favour of his rival any more than Voltaire had courage to face death. Rousseau had lately thrown himself upon the charity of a clockmaker in Paris, one of his disciples, rather than accept the bounty of the great; but to see the great worshipping at the shrine of Voltaire, was insupportable to him; and he left Paris, to become the guest, or rather the pensioner, of another of his disciples, the Marquis de Girardin, at his estate of Ermenonville. There, a cottage was allotted to Rousseau, close to the château of his patron and pupil, and the republican philosopher taught music to the children of the Marquis de Girardin, especially bestowing his care on one of them, a boy of ten years old. In the training of this child, Rousseau began practically to illustrate his theory of education, as taught in his book of "Emile," of which book he says bitterly, that although it cost him twenty years of meditation and three of work, he received less money for it than for a little opera which he wrote, and sang in six weeks. *

Voltaire was rich ; Rousseau was poor. Voltaire had been a courtier a great part of his life. At Versailles, in 1745–6, he was the poet-laureate of Louis XV., "the hero of Fontenoy." At Potzdam and Berlin, a few years later, he flattered King Frederick by his pen, and wrote the "Pucelle d'Orléans." At Ferney he was the "Suisse Voltaire." For Catherine II. he wrote "Charles XII." and "Pierre I." For the Duchesse de Saxe-Gotha he wrote the "Annals of the Empire." † Voltaire's genius was universal ; his philosophy flexible. He had been all things to all princes.

* Confessions. Tome xxiv. Ed. 1793.

† Période de Triomphe pour l'Ecole du XVIIIe. (Louis XV.) Capefigue. Bruxelles, 1844.

Rousseau had rejected the favours of the great. His friends, therefore, upheld him as a model of noble independence, and his enemies traduced him as an uncouth cynic. Even lately he had thrown himself on the charity of his disciple, the clock-maker, rather than be under obligations to Voltaire's friends, the Academicians and Aristocrats; and now he only condescended to accept the Marquis de Girardin's bounty, because he was regarded as a prophet in the house of that noble, and because he hoped to perfect a paradox—a republican noble —in the Marquis de Girardin's son and heir.

In former years Rousseau had offended Voltaire by rejecting his offers of service. Voltaire did not render justice to the talents of Rousseau. When both these philosophers were cast out of France, Voltaire had written to Madame du Châtelet: "Rousseau has gone back to Brussels to make bad odes." *

Rousseau now, in 1778, turned his back upon

* The Marquis de Condorcet apologises for Voltaire's non-appreciation of Rousseau, thus:—"He had an involuntary repugnance for exaggerated opinions; . . . accustomed to exercise his wit on every object, solemnity in the petty details of the passions, or of human iife, always appeared to him ridiculous." . . .—Vie de Voltaire. Par le Marquis de Condorcet, tome i., p. 164.

Paris and Voltaire, leaving the latter to the worship of the former. One incident, for a moment, shared the attention of Paris with Voltaire and his "Irène;" and this incident was a duel between the Count d'Artois and the Duc de Bourbon. The Duchesse de Bourbon, daughter of the Duc d'Orléans, and sister of the Duc de Chartres, jealous of one of her ladies-in-waiting, named Madame de Canillac, had dismissed that lady. Upon Shrove Tuesday there was a masked ball at the Opera, at which ball was the Duchesse de Bourbon, and also the Count d'Artois. The Count d'Artois danced at that ball with Madame de Canillac. Let Madame du Deffand tell with what results: "The Princess" (Duchesse de Bourbon) "committed the indiscretion of raising the mask of the Count d'Artois, which irritated him to such a point that he broke her mask across her face . . . . . She kept the secret for two days; but not having strength to keep it any longer, she narrated her adventure to her father, her husband, and everybody, and called the Count d'Artois insolent, impertinent, and brutal, &c. . . . . That could not but have consequences: the King desired to prevent these. He commanded the two parties to come to him. The two princes" (the Duc de Bourbon, the husband, and the Duc d'Orléans, the father of the lady) "and the Princess were at Versailles on Sunday morning. They were the first to enter the King's presence: the Count d'Artois came in some minutes afterwards, just at the moment when the king was saying to the Princess that he desired that this adventure might be forgotten; that both she and the Count had been guilty of great giddiness; but that by speaking of it again, they would draw down his displeasure upon themselves. The Count did not say a word, nor did he make any excuse. . . . . One can imagine the despair of the Princess; but nobody thought this affair finished. The Count d'Artois, supping that evening in a large company, said, and repeated, that he should go the next morning, Monday, to walk in the Bois de Boulogne. The Duc de Bourbon, having been informed of this, went there the next morning at eight o'clock, having with him only M. de Vibraye, his captain of the Guards. He awaited the arrival of the Count for about an hour, and, at last, he came with the Chevalier de Crussol, his captain of the Guards. The Count and the Duke confronted each other with great vivacity. The Count said to the Duke,

'You seek me—here I am.' The Duke asked him to consent to his taking off his coat, as it would encumber him; the Count consented, and said that he was going to do the same. They fought very well: the Count with impetuosity, the Duke with much coolness. They made six thrusts, without either wounding the other. When they wished to make another thrust, the Chevalier de Crussot placed himself between them, and told them that there had been enough. The Count said to the Duke, 'Are you satisfied?' 'Perfectly,' replied the Duke. 'If that be the case,' resumed the Count, 'let us embrace each other, make peace, and go and dine together.' The Duke excused himself, saying he must go and cheer up his wife, his father,* and his sister. They separated. The Duke returned home, where, shortly after his arrival, the tramp of horses was heard.... M. le Comte d'Artois entered with the best grace in the world. He kissed the hand of Madame de Bourbon, asked her a thousand pardons, and assured her that he had not recognized her at the masked ball."

* The Duc de Bourbon was the son of the Prince de Condé; but it would seem that he here alludes to his father-in-law, the Duc d'Orléans, and to his sister-in-law, the Duchesse de Chartres, in whom a love of virtue had been cultivated by her father, the Duc de Penthièvre.

Thus did this quarrel end. All the princes went, after dinner, to Voltaire's tragedy, and received extreme applause on entering their boxes."*

Voltaire was not present, as the people had hoped, at the first representation of "Irène." His cough had returned; his health prevented his appearance that night at the Théâtre Francais. But he was continually informed of the progress of the play. During the second act a messenger was despatched to him, who declared that the opening scenes had gained much favour. After the fourth act another flattering emissary arrived. After the fifth Act, M. Dupuis (who had married Mademoiselle Corneille, Voltaire's adopted child), announced to the author that "Irène" was a complete success. Friends then came crowding in, eager to offer their congratulations to Voltaire. They found him sitting up in bed, writing. He was engaged on his play of "Agathocle," and affected indifference concerning "Irène;" anxiety as to the success of which tragedy had nearly killed him. "What you tell me consoles me, but it does not cure me," was all the reply he at first vouchsafed to the flattering assertions that one friend

* Lettres de Madame du Deffand. Tome iv., pp. 26-28; à Paris, 1824.

vied with another in making to him; but, unable long to conceal his interest beneath this phlegmatic exterior, he began, presently, to ask if this speech had had its effect—if that passage had been applauded—if such a dialogue had been well listened to—and, above all, if certain hits at the clergy had excited popular applause (upon the last point he was peculiarly anxious, hoping thereby to regain his character as a consistent philosopher, which character his profession of faith to the Abbé Gauthier, might, he feared, have somewhat damaged.)

These questions on the part of Voltaire must have been trying to the sincerity of his friends; for—as Madame du Deffand wrote to Horace Walpole—"the success of the piece has been very *médiocre*; nevertheless, there was much clapping of hands, but that was for Voltaire, and not for his play."

The illusion of success was, however, kept up by those around Voltaire. Upon the following days more than thirty illustrious individuals, wearing the *cordon bleu*, called to congratulate him; and the Academy sent another deputation to him, to assure him of the interest and sympathy which that learned body had felt in his triumph. It was proposed by this deputation that Voltaire should be crowned in the hall of the theatre, at the Palace of the Tuileries. Voltaire revived.

Neither the King nor Queen had been present at the first representation of his tragedy, but he himself was about to be crowned by the people in Paris. Nay, more; it was told to him that the Queen intended to be present on that occasion, *incognita*. He believed that this was possible, because her majesty, although under the authority of her husband and his priests, had one sympathy in common with Voltaire, and that was her friendship for the Duc de Choiseul, who was Voltaire's friend.*

Upon the 1st of April, 1778, Voltaire, with the black Louis Quatorze wig, and a scarlet cap, upon his head, and enveloped in a large pelisse trimmed with fur, mounted his carriage, which was of sky-blue colour, studded with stars, and drove through the streets of Paris, on his way, first to the French Academy, and afterwards to the theatre. At the Academy

* Vie de Voltaire, par Condorcet. Tome i., p. 130. Paris, 1789.

he was received with all honours by twenty-two of its members, none of the clergy being present. He was conducted to the seat of "Director," and installed there, with his own portrait hanging above him. Flattered by this reception, he was inclined to talk a great deal; but d'Alembert and others restrained him, by declaring that they had too much regard for his health to listen to him. When he re-appeared in the court-yard, a vast crowd had assembled. At the sight of his empty carriage the people had cried: "There IT is!" At sight of its owner they cried: "There HE is!—Vive Voltaire!"

The members of the Academy attended him. "No Prince," as says the Count de Ségur, "had ever been so received as this prince of letters, who presided over the literary Senate of France. Outside, in the streets of Paris, a dense multitude thronged his path. Cries and acclamations rent the air; the pace at which the carriage proceeded was slow, for it was with difficulty that it made its way through the crowd.

At the theatre, "I shall never forget that scene," says de Ségur.

The Count d'Artois was there *incognito*, in the

box facing that prepared for Voltaire, "the saint, or rather the god of the day." The pit was in convulsions of joy. The benches, the boxes, the corridors, were filled to suffocation. The multitude overflowed the enclosure; men, women, and even children, of all ranks and conditions, were there, each full of excitement, and eager to catch a glimpse of Voltaire.

Madame Denis, and the Marquis and Marquise de Villette, awaited his arrival. As he alighted from his carriage at the entrance there was a rush forward. Women, especially, were anxious to touch him, to look at him closely; and some even tried to pluck some hair from the fur of his pelisse, that they might keep it as a charm.

When he appeared in his box, a simultaneous shout was raised of "Vive Voltaire!" and then came another cry of "The crown! the crown!"

The actor Brizard now approached Voltaire, with a crown of laurel in his hand, and placed it on the head of Voltaire, in the midst of the people's acclamations. "Ah!" exclaimed Voltaire, weeping, "you wish me, then, to die of joy!" and he tried to remove the crown from his head; but the people besought him to retain it; the Prince de Beauvau replaced it on Voltaire's head, and then, alternating with rounds of applause, the titles of all Voltaire's works were repeated, and echoed from every part of the theatre. The curtain before the stage now drew up, and the first scene of "Irène" appeared. The play began; but the actors and spectators were so occupied with its author, that they scarcely attended to his work. "Never was a piece so badly played, so much applauded, and so little listened to."

When the play was over, the bust of Voltaire was placed upon a pedestal before the drop-scene. All the actors in the tragedy, who still wore the clothes in which they had played their parts, formed a semi-circle round this bust, palms and garlands in their hands. The sound of sackbuts, trumpets, and drums announced that some grand ceremony was at hand.

A crown of laurel was placed upon the head of the bust of Voltaire; the actor who crowned that bust was dressed in the costume of a monk, he having performed the part of one in the tragedy just represented.

Madame Vestris then stepped forward, and recited a copy of verses; the last of which was:

"Voltaire, reçois la couronne,
Qui l'on vient de te présenter ;
Il est beau de la mériter
Quand c'est la France qui la donne!"

After this, each actor laid the wreath he held round the bust. Mademoiselle Fanier, one of the actresses, kissed the bust, and all the other actors and actresses followed her example. The acclamations were incessant; and these were renewed with fresh force when Dr. Franklin appeared by the side of Voltaire. "Vive Voltaire!" "Vive Franklin!" now resounded from every side. Voltaire and Franklin then embraced each other in the sight of the assembled multitude. In that embrace the people beheld the Old World and the New World united for a great cause, and that cause was Liberty.

Again both King and Queen were absent, but the Duc de Chartres was present. He had lately been unpopular, because he had not vindicated his sister, the Duchesse de Bourbon, in her quarrel with the Count d'Artois. The people were inclined to regard this quarrel as one between Paris and Versailles—between the popular and Parliamentary portion of the royal family who inhabited Paris, and the King and Queen, who, true to old traditions, ruled at Versailles. The Duc de Chartres had excused himself by saying that his sister, the Duchesse de Bourbon, was "neither his wife nor his daughter." The women of Paris had scorned him for this speech; but now, although forbidden by the King to approach Voltaire, and to do homage to him, the Duc de Chartres placed himself in Voltaire's way, so as to attract his attention. This was whispered, and the women of Paris already forgave the Duc de Chartres for his late want of chivalry in not avenging his sister's cause. The King had good reason to dread the consequences of the quarrel between his brother, the Count d'Artois, and any members of the House of Orléans.

When Voltaire was reseated in his sky-blue carriage, studded with stars, to return home from the theatre, the way was so thronged with an adoring multitude that it was impossible for his horses to move on. Young poets and literary aspirants disputed amongst themselves the honour of drawing that carriage from the theatre; the horses were unharnessed; the whole scene was one of triumph and confusion.

Versailles frowned disapprobation, but Voltaire

was crowned king in Paris. He wept again with joy when he reached the hôtel of the Marquis de Villette, and declared that he would buy a house in Paris opposite to that of the Duc de Choiseul.*

The Palais Royal, the abode of the Orléans family, sent its deputy to him. Madame de Genlis, the emissary of the Palais Royal, came to visit Voltaire.† Madame de Genlis, the governess of the children of the Duc de Chartres, was not loved at Versailles. The Princesse de Lamballe shuddered with aversion when she passed her in any public place, and once declared her to have "the face of a lamb, the heart of a wolf, and the cunning of a fox."‡

This portrait of Madame de Genlis, drawn by one generally so meek as the Princesse de Lamballe, shows to what extent the rivalry between the two courts of Paris and Versailles had reached.

* Mems. de M. le Comte de Ségur, tome i., Paris, 1825; Mems. de Bachaumont, year 1778, (à Londres, 1779); L'Espion Anglais, year 1778, (à Paris, 1809.)

† Mems. de Madame de Genlis, tome ii., p. 305, à Paris, 1825.

‡ Mems. de la Princesse de Lamballe. (Introduction). "Colla faccia d'agnello, il cuore d'un lupo, e la drittura della volpe."—Tome i., p. 11, à Paris, 1826.

Madame de Genlis had formerly visited Voltaire at Ferney. Amongst other singular and significant proofs of Voltaire's egotism, she mentions having there seen a fine picture of Correggio banished into an ill-lighted ante-chamber, so as to give place to a wretched daub which represented Voltaire himself with his foot on the neck of his enemy, the critic Fréron. When Madame de Genlis went to see Voltaire in Paris, in 1778, he seems to have been suffering and weakened by all the excitement he had lately gone through. "He received me," she says, "with grace; but I found him so broken and dejected, that I felt certain his end was near."

The Princesse de Lamballe would have been a more welcome guest to Voltaire than was Madame de Genlis. To the last he still clung to the hope of being received at Versailles. With delight he had heard that "Irène" was to be represented there. The Queen herself often acted with the Count d'Artois, the Count de Provence, and such of the royal family who had histrionic talent or tastes, assisted by a selection of the noblesse, male and female. The Duc de Richelieu's son, who was excluded from this number (and therefore jealous at being condemned to be only a spectator), declared that the royal family did not play badly for the puppet-show of Versailles. In former years, when Louis XV. was King (just crowned with laurel as the hero of Fontenoy), and Voltaire was the pet poet of Madame de Pompadour, the King himself had acted in that same theatre of Versailles the part of "Trajan," which Voltaire—sitting looking on in the royal box—had written for his majesty.* Times and rulers had changed. Voltaire was not summoned to Versailles when "Irène" was played there, and, worse still, he was told that, during the representation of that piece, the King, Louis XVI., yawned visibly. No wonder that Madame de Genlis found Voltaire "broken and dejected." He had spitten blood again.

"I do not think he will live," wrote Madame du Deffand to Horace Walpole, "he droops visibly." The popular party in Paris, however, could not afford to lose him yet. Versailles rejected Voltaire, but the Palais Royal invited him, notwithstanding the express desire of the King that none of the royal family should receive him; or, rather, according to the newspapers of the time, "M. de

* Secret Hist. of the Court of France. Vol. i., p. 123, London, 1861.

Voltaire has received the permission he sought from the Duc de Chartres to go and see the young princes dine at the Palais Royal;" it having been previously announced that upon the 13th of April, 1778, "M. de Voltaire was present at the private theatricals of Madame de Montesson" (the wife of the Duc d'Orléans, and aunt of Madame de Genlis), "where he enjoyed almost the same honours as had been rendered to him at the Comédie Française.*

Once again the chief of philosophers put on his Louis XIV. wig, his fur pelisse, mounted his sky-blue carriage, and drove to the Palais Royal. The Duchesse de Chartres was ill, and not out of bed when he arrived there; but when she heard that Voltaire was already in her husband's apartments, she hastily rose, and, having hurried her toilette, went forth to greet the distinguished guest. When she entered, the philosopher was seated by the side of the Duc de Chartres, her husband, and the young princes, her children, were being presented to "le Roy Voltaire." It was by the express desire of the Duc de Chartres that the patriarch of philosophy was thus, as it were, en-

* Journal de Paris.

throned beside him; his royal highness having declared that he was desirous of enjoying his conversation for too long a time to permit him to remain standing.

Now, when Madame la Duchesse de Chartres appeared, Voltaire would fain have knelt before her, but she raised him from the ground, and re-seated him as an equal; and, by the reverence with which she seemed to listen to his discourse, flattered him with the idea that, at the Palais Royal, a philosopher was held in more respect than any prince or other potentate.

Voltaire blessed the children of the Duc de Chartres as he had blessed the grandson of Dr. Franklin, although not in the same words. "He was lavish of compliments upon the children of their highnesses, and declared that the Duc de Valois resembled the late Regent."

The Court at Versailles and the clergy of Paris were wrathful against Voltaire for the favours lavished on him by the Orléans party, and for his sarcasms on the priesthood in the tragedy of "Irène," as performed at Paris. Fear of the people restrained the Church and Court from openly attacking Voltaire at this moment; but, in the Journals "printed by permission of the King," "Irène" was derided. It was unendurable to Voltaire thus to be fought with his own weapon—satire. He fell sick again. He remembered "the sword of Damocles," that Dr. Tronchin had declared was hanging over his head, and trembled.

Once more he dreaded that, if he died in Paris, his body would be cast "into the common sewer." He, therefore, declared his intention of going back to Ferney, that he might "be laid in the tomb he had built for himself" at Gex. His devotees in Paris opposed this intention. They declared it impossible for Voltaire to die. "Le Roy Voltaire," crowned by the people of Paris, was immortal! Voltaire lingered in Paris, glad of any excuse to postpone saying farewell to it for ever. He suffered by night, and longed for Ferney. He was worshipped by day, and still clung to Paris. At this juncture Madame de Villette, in whose house he was still staying, was confined with premature labour.

Madame de Villette was an adopted daughter of Voltaire; he had saved her from being immured in a convent, or, to use his own words, he had "rescued her from the devil," and had educated her as became a philosopher's daughter; he would not desert his dear "*Belle et Bonne*" in her present peril, especially as he had promised to be the godfather of her child.

This was a strange promise for Voltaire to have made, and his disappointment was still more strange that, owing to Madame de Villette's *fausse couche* (caused, probably, by the excitement consequent on his residence in her house) he, with his soul trembling on the brink of eternity, was denied the privilege of dedicating a soul to God.

Voltaire could not sleep at night. He sent to Marshal Richelieu—who, as beforesaid, was the older man of the two—to ask him by what specific he contrived, not only to sleep, but, when awake, to ride on horseback, and to perform various feats of physical strength, for which the philosopher, even in his youth, had no vocation.

The Duc de Richelieu (who was reported to have been initiated into the secret of perpetual strength, and to have drunk of the golden waters of life at the hands of M. le Comte de St. Germain,) sent an opiate to Voltaire, with directions for dividing the dose.* Voltaire, eager for rest and

* Mems. de Richelieu. 1794.

freedom from pain, swallowed the opiate, but forgot the directions; in consequence of which he slept too profoundly for either priest or doctor to rouse him; and, when at last awakened for a moment, he only nicknamed Marshal Richelieu "my brother Cain," and fell asleep again.* This was on the 24th of May, 1778.

The Curé de St. Sulpice was determined this time to be before the Abbé Gauthier. The Curé hastened to the hôtel of the Marquis de Villette, and was admitted into the chamber, where Voltaire lay sleeping, to all appearance dead.

Condorcet does not give a favourable portrait of the Curé de St. Sulpice; † but, from the Curé's own letter to Voltaire, already translated, it may be inferred that in the month of March, 1778, there was wit in the discretion, and charity in the zeal with which he was then inclined to convert Voltaire. In the month of May the Curé's conduct is thus described as that of an "imperious fanatic":—

"He wished absolutely to make Voltaire acknowledge the divinity of Jesus Christ; he roused

* Mems. de Bachaumont.

† Vie de Voltaire, par Condorcet, p. 157. 1789.

him one day from his lethargy by shouting in his ears: 'Do you believe in the divinity of Jesus Christ?' 'In the name of GOD, sir, do not speak to me any more of that man, and leave me to die in peace,' replied Voltaire.*

"Then the priest announced to Voltaire that he could no longer prevent himself from refusing to bury his body."

But, considering that the shadows of death were fast stealing over Voltaire, that his intellect was already so clouded by opium, that he relapsed into the unconsciousness from which he had thus been roughly roused too quickly even to reply to the threat which, until lately, had been his bugbear, who on earth dare to say whether Voltaire did die an unbeliever in that of which, a few weeks before, in possession of consciousness, he had made a solemn and formal profession of faith?

The priests were not likely to give him the benefit of this doubt, having lately been stimulated to fresh indignation against him by the public worship rendered to him, in their defiance. It was time that an example of heresy should be held up as a warn-

* Vie de Voltaire, par Condorcet, p. 157. Ed. 1789.

ing to the people. On every side heresy was gaining ground.

Pigalle, the famous sculptor, had excited the admiration of the world by his statue of Marshal Saxe, the Lutheran hero, who had won the battles of France thirty years before. (This statue had cost Pigalle twenty years to execute, and had lately been set up in the church of St. Thomas).

A Protestant, who presumed to restrict the wealth of the Church, was the director of finance in France.

The Count de St. Germain, as Minister of War, introduced the tactics of Frederick, King of Prussia and Protestants, into the French army. French ports were full of ships, and French arsenals were full of stores, about to be employed in the war that France, allied with heretics and insurgents, was going to fight for the cause of Liberty in America. Dr. Franklin, the Protestant of Philadelphia, as lord of Passy, had, on New-year's eve, 1778, presumed to stamp the bread permitted by the Church to be given away to the poor in that place, with the word "Liberty," and to divide it into thirteen portions, the number of the American colonies. Dr. Franklin and Voltaire had embraced each other in the sight of the people, who had rapturously hailed that embrace; and since then a political engraving was issued in Paris, executed by the King's own engraver, of Dr. Franklin setting America free; America embracing a statue of Liberty, and Minerva protecting Dr. Franklin with her shield. Emigration from France to America increased. In France philosophy and free discussion were openly established.

The King was weak; necessity was strong: but surely the Church was invincible! Voltaire had sown heresy. His recent visit to Paris had caused rank doctrines openly to show themselves—had revealed how widely they had spread. The priests refused to bury Voltaire's body.

Madame du Deffand was curious, like many others, to know what would be done with his corpse. "Will it be sent to Ferney?" writes she to Horace Walpole. "Voltaire was excommunicated by the bishop of that diocese. . . . . He is dead from an excess of opium, and, I should add, from an excess of glory, which has shaken his feeble machine too much." (And yet Voltaire, excommunicated by the hierarchy of the Church, had been "Father of the Capuchins" at Gex!)

Voltaire's family preferred, Condorcet tells us, "to negotiate with the ministry, not daring to wound public opinion by rousing the vengeance of the clergy; nor to displease the priests by forcing them to conform to the laws; nor to defy them by erecting a public monument to the great man whose ashes they were cowardly enough to trouble; nor to compensate to him for the lack of ecclesiastical honours, which he deserved so little, by civic honours, which were due to his genius and to the good he had effected for the nation."

The ministry was, doubtless, well pleased that Voltaire's family were thus willing to show a way of avoiding offence to the clergy on the one hand, or to the people on the other. Consent was therefore given, that the body of Voltaire should be transported to the church of a monastery of which his nephew was abbé; and there (embalmed), that it should await further orders from ecclesiastical authority. The priests did not oppose this project, as it gave them time to deliberate, and for the ardour of the people, so lately excited by Voltaire's living presence among them, to cool down. The corpse was accordingly carried to the Monastery of Scellières, in the diocese of Troyes.

King Frederick of Prussia was in camp, at the head of 50,000 men, when he heard that his old friend and correspondent, Voltaire, was dead. He immediately ordered a special service to be performed for the patriarch of philosophers in the Roman Catholic Church at Berlin, declaring that, had Voltaire been an old Greek, he would have been worshipped as a god! Frederick laid aside his sword for the moment, took up his pen, and wrote his "Eloge de Voltaire."

The Archbishop of Paris forbade the French Academy to perform a funeral service in honour of Voltaire. The French Academy was compelled to submit; but, in revenge, it declared that no further service should be performed for an Academician (at the Grey Friars), until reparation was done to the memory of Voltaire. The Church thus defeated herself in this decree; and King Frederick the heretic gained much popular enthusiasm by his conduct in contrast to it.

The Marquis de Villette had secured Voltaire's heart. At the château of the Marquis, near Ferney, he built a temple for the reception of the urn containing that heart. The inside walls of this temple were hung with portraits of celebrated contemporaries of Voltaire. The Marquis de Villette offered Madame de Genlis to hang her portrait there, saying that he "had reserved a place for her in the heart of Voltaire."* It was now time, however, for Madame de Genlis, who had been accused by the Princesse de Lamballe of having the "heart of a wolf," to show the "face of a lamb." She was shocked that she, the *gouvernante* of young Christian princes, should have such an offer made to her, or that the Marquis de Villette should presume so to address her!

"I made an answer," says she, "full of modesty, in which I acknowledged, *humbly*, that I had no right which could make me pretend to that favour. . . . I have never been able to conceive how M. de Villette could make such a proposal to a person whose principles were already so well known. . . It is true," she adds with characteristic egotism, "that I had not then published my 'Adèle and Théodore;' but the 'Théâtre d'Education,' complete, had made my opinions and religious principles sufficiently known."*

Had not the pen of Voltaire done its work, the Marquis de Villette would not have been able to

* Still in the possession of the heirs of de Villette.

enshrine Voltaire's heart. Until Voltaire wrote, and even long after his name was famous, the people had been restrained in every action by a double bridle. Creed and Corporation had been the great engines of police; the people, now, were prepared to defy doth religious and municipal authority.

In the first half of the 18th century, when Voltaire appeared, there was danger in exposing old abuses. "Where it might entail banishment, worldly ruin, and even death, to speak a free word of criticism upon the doctrines or the hierophants of the dominant church, it was not merely a very excusable but a very necessary and praiseworthy deed to expose the folly and inconsistency of some of the teachers. Gessler may wear his hat any fashion he chooses, and only ill-breeding would laugh at him so long as he does not insist upon any one performing an act of homage to his humour. But when he sets his beaver upon a pole in the centre of the market-place, and orders imprisonment or exile to every subject who will not fall down and worship it, that man does a brave and a wise act who sets the world laughing at the tyrant and his preposterous arrogance."

CHAPTER VI.

Lord North's Budget of February, 1778—Secret Intelligence from France—Lord North confounded—The duke of Grafton and Lord Weymouth—Ministerial evasions—Parliamentary accusations—The royal message—Declaration of France—Proposal to conciliate France—Lord Chatham—Letter of George III. to Lord North—Lord Chatham's last opposition—The Duke of Richmond—The King of Terrors in the House of Lords—Robbing Peter to pay Paul—Lord Chatham's burial—Voltaire's apotheosis—Freemason's fête in Paris—Louis XVI. and Dr. Franklin—Queen Marie Antoinette *enceinte*—The Chevalier d'Éon—Diplomatic Mystery in the Chapel of Versailles—True but strange story of the Chevalier d'Éon—The Chevalier d'Éon's letter to the Ministry—Mutual insults of the French and English press—The "Reverend Mr. Cole"—Politics and Parties at Cambridge—Roman Catholics in England and France change sides—King Frederick of Prussia; neutrality—Voltaire's last Prophecy concerning England and France—The Pope and Voltaire's Bible Commentary—Horace Walpole on Politics Universal—Necker's Reforms in France —*La Reine s'amuse*—Address of the people of Paris to "Our Brothers of Boston"—The Empress Catherine of Russia—French ships manned, and French soldiers armed—Lord Carlisle and M. de Lafayette—Friendship between Lafayette and Washington—Severe Discipline in the American Army—French description of George Washington—Lafayette wounded—Letter of Lafayette to the Duc d'Argens—American impatience—Rumours from the New World in the Old World—George Washington's wife—Letter of Lafayette to George Washington—Letter of Lafayette, from America, to his wife in France.

During all this time (from February to May, 1778), whilst Voltaire was being worshipped, converted, crowned, and excommunicated, and the French Government was silently, but actively, preparing troops, ships, and arms, to send out to America, the course of political events was more strongly marked, outwardly, in England than in France.

The treaties of alliance with America, it will be remembered, had been signed at Versailles on the 3rd and 6th of February, 1778. On the 19th of that month Lord North rose in the House of Commons to move a conciliatory budget.

He proposed: "1st, To repeal the tea duty absolutely. 2nd, To renounce by act of Parliament all right of taxing the Colonies for revenue, and to provide that the produce of any duties imposed for the regulation of trade should be paid over to the Colonies. 3rd, To appoint Commissioners, who should have the power to treat with Congress as such, to put a stop to the war, and to suspend all laws of which the Americans might complain, and which the Commissioners should be willing to revoke."

Considering that this budget was almost identical with Burke's, which had been rejected nearly three years before, and that if the same measures as those now proposed on the part of the Crown had been adopted when rival statesmen in both Houses had then united in pleading in behalf of America, against the obstinacy of the Crown of England, blood and treasure, since irretrievably wasted, might have been spared, it is no wonder that a dead silence fell on the House of Commons at the tardy proposals now made by Lord North, "the ostensible minister."

Those who had supported the Crown were silent from a sense that their support had been given in vain.

Those who had opposed the Crown were silent,

from the conviction that their views, long advocated, were now adopted too late. Those who were in the secret, that the French treaties with America were already signed, were silent, because the moment was not yet ripe for the utterance of that knowledge.

Charles James Fox* was in the secret, although Government did not suspect him of being so. We have heard Madame du Deffand declare that, when at Paris, "*le Fox à l'air de se plaire ici.*" During that visit to Paris, Fox had done something more than amuse himself, having there formed acquaintance politically useful to him; moreover, Fox was in the confidence of the Walpoles. Horace Walpole, as we have seen, was constantly informed

* Charles James Fox, son of Henry Fox (Lord Holland) was born January 13th, 1748. Educated at Eton; distinguished himself there; afterwards went to Hertford College, and then on his travels. In 1768 was returned to Parliament for Midhurst. In 1770 appointed Commissioner of the Admiralty; and afterwards was seated at the Treasury Board; quarrelled with Lord North in 1774; since that time a leader of opposition; had lately been to fetch Burgoyne to London from Dover, that officer having surrendered, to General Gates, at Saratoga, and since returned to England. Burgoyne subsequently refused to return to America, and was elected member for Preston, in Lancashire. He was afterwards dismissed the service, and solaced himself by publishing pamphlets on that subject, and various plays.

of all going on in Paris and at Versailles by Madame du Deffand, in whose company Lord Stormont passed much of his time, after his withdrawal from Versailles, and before his return to England. Besides this, "My cousin, Thomas Walpole," says Horace, "had acquainted me that the treaty with France was signed. We agreed to inform Charles Fox; but as we both distrusted Burke, and feared the childish fluctuations of Lord Rockingham, we determined that Fox should know nothing of the secret till an hour or two before the House met. Accordingly Thomas Walpole communicated the notice of the treaty to the Duke of Grafton on the 16th, and engaged him to acquaint Charles Fox with it just before the House should meet. . . . This was done most exactly."*

Thus primed, Fox rose; and, in the course of his speech in answer to Lord North, asked, "If the concession should be found ample enough, *but should be found to come too late*, what punishment would be sufficient for those who adjourned Parliament in order to make a proposition of concession, *and then had neglected to do it until France had concluded a treaty with the Independent States of*

* Walpole's Journal. Feb. 1778. (Quoted by Earl Russell.)

America?" Fox then hinted that such a treaty had been made at Versailles, and added, "I can answer with truth for the certainty of my information; it is no light matter. I therefore wish that the Ministry would give the House information on this interesting point, and whether they had not been informed, previously to the making of their proposition, of a treaty which would render that proposition as useless as it is humiliating to the dignity of Great Britain?"*

It was now Lord North's turn to be silent, not knowing how to parry this unforeseen question. Fox then asked plainly, "Has not a commercial treaty between France and America been signed within the last ten days?"

(No answer from Lord North.)

"If so," continued Fox, "the Administration is beaten by ten days."

(Still no answer from Lord North. Every eye in the Assembly was upon him.)

"*I myself*," affirmed Fox, "*have been positively informed that a treaty has been signed with the Court of Versailles by the American agents.*" The announcement of Fox electrified the Treasury

* Cavendish, MS. Eg. Coll.

Bench! Burke suddenly rose, claimed the scheme of conciliation as his own three years before, and called on Lord North to give a definite answer with respect to the alleged treaty.*

Afterwards Sir George Savile declared that the Minister's silence was criminal, and a matter of impeachment. "An answer!" demanded Sir George Savile; and, catching up the word, "An answer, an answer!" was echoed from the House.

Lord North could sit silent no longer. He rose; the clamour was hushed into deep silence, so that every word of his reply might be heard distinctly; but the Minister's words came forth falteringly, and their sense was vague, incoherent, unsatisfactory. Lord North owned that "he had heard a report of the treaty, but he could give no answer to the House at that moment. He had had no official intelligence of such a treaty. It might be mere rumour, such as once before was denied by the Ministry of Versailles."†

Everybody present in the House of Commons that night was convinced that the report was true. "The bills were agreed to; but, under the circum-

* Life and Times of Edmund Burke. Thomas McKnight, vol. ii., p. 221.

† Parliamentary History, vol. xix., year 1778.

stances, none could look upon them as the harbingers of peace."

On the 5th of March, the Conciliatory Bills were brought before the House of Lords, and a similar scene ensued there to that which had taken place in the House of Commons. The Duke of Grafton repeated the question (asked in the Lower House by Fox of Lord North) to Lord Weymouth. "If the information be true that this treaty between Versailles and America is signed," said the Duke, "it is absurd to insult Parliament with the appearance of a reconciliation no longer practicable. If Ministers reply in the affirmative, they are guilty in the highest degree in concealing intelligence of so important a nature from Parliament. If they reply in the negative, their conduct is, if possible, still more reprehensible; their incapacity more glaring, in being wanting in that species of information which it is their duty to procure."

Lord Weymouth then declared that, to his knowledge, no such treaty had been signed.

Nevertheless, on the 6th of February, Lord Stormont (who, in Paris, after that date, was in company with Voltaire, Madame Necker, and Dr. Franklin) had written to Lord Weymouth, "I think I am now able to speak to your lordship with some precision, with regard to the treaty between the court and the rebels. My informer assured me, *it is actually signed*; but Dr. Franklin, not thinking himself authorized to grant all the demands made by France, has signed *sub spe. rati.*"

Again, on the 18th February, Lord Stormont again wrote to Lord Weymouth, "Both these treaties were, I am assured, actually signed on Friday, the 6th instant, by M. Gérard." *

Lord Weymouth's denial to the Duke of Grafton, in the House of Peers, is, therefore, as inexplicable by the rules of common sense and honesty, and more so, than had been the evasive answers of Lord North to Mr. Fox in the House of Commons.

As Burke had already said, "American Independence is, in truth, a fact." In the course of this narrative have been transcribed some of the original letters of his Majesty's Ministers to English Governors in America, concerning the military employment of American Indians, and the due rewards for the ser-

* Hist. of England. Lord Mahon. Quoted by Lord John Russell in his Life of C. J. Fox, in which work (vol. i., year 1778), will be found the debates at some length, in confirmation of the brief extracts above from various sources.

vices of these tribes in helping to maintainthe rights of the English Crown in the revolted colonies.

On the 6th of February, 1778, Burke had made a speech of nearly three hours and a half, eloquently remonstrating against the employment of these tribes, and moving that copies of those papers be produced.

No strangers were admitted into the gallery that day. Governor Johnstone congratulated the ministers upon this exclusion, declaring that otherwise "the indignation of the people might have been excited against them to a degree that would have endangered their safety." One member wished to have Burke's speech posted on the church doors.

On the 17th of March, 1778, the royal message was read * in both Houses of Parliament, by which

* *Copy of the original Royal Message to both Houses of Parliament, on Tuesday, the* 17*th of March*, 1778, *inclosing a copy of the French Declaration :—*

"GEORGE R.—His Majesty having been informed, by order of the French King, that a treaty of amity and commerce has been signed between the Court of France, and certain persons employed by his Majesty's revolted subjects in North America, has judged it necessary to direct that a copy of the Declaration, delivered by the French Ambassador to Lord Viscount Weymouth, be laid before the House of Commons; and at the same

King George III. proclaimed that the treaty had been signed on the 6th February between the French King and the rebels in America.

The declaration of France, which was read to the English Parliament at the same time as the royal message, set out by stating, that the United States of North America, *being in full possession of Independence*, as pronounced by them on the 4th of July, 1776, having proposed to the King (Louis XVI.) to consolidate, by a formal convention, the convention to be established between France and

time to acquaint them that his Majesty has thought proper, in consequence of this offensive communication on the part of the Court of France, to send orders to his ambassador to withdraw from that Court. His Majesty is persuaded that the justice and good faith of his conduct towards foreign powers, and the sincerity of his wishes to preserve the tranquillity of Europe, will be acknowledged by all the world; and his Majesty trusts that he shall not stand responsible for the disturbance of that tranquillity if he should find himself called upon to resent so unprovoked and so unjust an aggression on the honour of his Crown, and the essential interests of his kingdoms, contrary to the most solemn assurances, subversive of the law of nations, and injurious to the Rights of every sovereign power in Europe. His Majesty, relying with the firmest confidence on the zealous and affectionate support of his faithful people, is determined to be prepared to exert, if it should become necessary, all the force and resources of his kingdoms, which he trusts will be found adequate to repel every insult and attack, and to maintain and uphold the power and reputation of this country.—G. R."

America, the respective plenipotentiaries have signed a treaty of friendship and commerce, designed to serve as a foundation for their mutual good correspondence. "His Majesty" (Louis XVI.) "being determined to cultivate the good understanding between France and Great Britain, by every means compatible with his dignity, and the good of his subjects, thinks it necessary to make this proceeding known to the court of London." . . . "And" (not not to weary the reader further with this preamble) "his most Christian Majesty, Louis XVI. is firmly persuaded that his Britannic Majesty will find in this communication new proofs of his most Christian Majesty's disposition for peace."* (Thus, in diplomacy, monarchs sometimes mean war when protesting peace.)

The limits of this French declaration left one narrow path still open for the English Ministry to pursue, or rather, to recede upon. Burke, who, three years before, had proposed conciliatory measures towards America, which it was now too late to adopt, now declared, that he and his party did not look upon foreign war as absolutely inevitable.

* Original Declaration of France. Published in the *Political Magazine*, 1780.

"By wisely at once submitting to circumstances, negotiating an advantageous treaty of commerce, and withdrawing promptly the British forces from the United States, the humiliating dictation of foreign powers might yet be avoided, and an European war averted; or, if it should break out, England, by renouncing the impracticable claim of sovereignty in America, might concentrate her forces against France, and recompense herself by conquest for dominions lost by her own folly in North America. Burke moved, therefore, that the independence of the colonies, which was already a fact, should be recognized without delay.

The Rockingham party now assumed a distinct position on the question of American Independence.

Lord Chatham was roused once more.

The last time we saw him in this narrative was on the 1st of February, 1775, in the House of Lords, declaring that he desired nothing better than that the conciliatory measures he had proposed in behalf of America should meet with mature reflection. He had previously implored the Crown to make the first advances towards reconciliation, it being "true dignity to act with prudence and justice." Upon that 1st of February, 1775, Dr. Franklin was at the bar of the House of Lords, having been introduced there by Lord Chatham himself. It was then, as we have seen, that Lord Sandwich openly attacked Dr. Franklin as the instigator of Lord Chatham's speech. It was then, when Dr. Franklin saw "Lord Chatham's production" rejected by 82 to 61, that, he made bitter comments on hereditary legislators, and gave up all hope that the mother country would concede the just claims of the American colonies.

All that Lord Chatham had prophesied in February, 1775, had now, in March, 1778, come to pass. Dr. Franklin had been the main instrument in the fulfilment of Lord Chatham's prophecies. Lord Chatham, in 1775, had declared the cause of Liberty in America to be "the alliance of God and nature—immutable, eternal, fixed as the firmament of heaven." He had then pleaded in favour of that cause with eloquence unrivalled. He had pleaded in vain. Now, in 1778, Lord Chatham would not endure the thought of open recognition of American independence, on the part of the Crown of England, at the dictation of France. He had lately had one of his fits of illness upon him, but the rumour of such a recognition roused him from his lethargy; the mists cleared off from his mind; Lord Chatham looked back into the past. He saw himself in that past—not the old man as now, weak, gouty, irritable, tremulous, and prone to tears—but at the height of his power, wielding the sceptre of England to the terror of France, and by his strong policy winning laurels for Great Britain across the Atlantic. He beheld brave English soldiers toiling up the heights of Quebec, their courage stimulated by the ardour of his own soul; he beheld Wolfe dying from French wounds, and heard him bless God because in his last moments he was told that "the French run." Had he (Lord Chatham) lived in vain? England had refused to concede the just claims of America, and to listen to his own prayers in behalf of liberty in America; was England now to do at the dictation of France far more than that which she had refused to do from a sense of her own justice?

Indignation at the thought of such concession roused Lord Chatham into fresh life, and gave him fresh strength. He had, two years since, proposed conciliation; he would now oppose concession. He declared his resolution of opposing the Duke of Richmond's motion (on the 7th of April) of an address to the King, entreating him "to withdraw his fleets and armies from America, and to make peace with the revolted colonies."

Meanwhile, Lord North had expressed a wish to retire. The King would not permit Lord North to do so. The King declared his wish to keep Lord North at the head of the Treasury, and as his confidential minister also; his Majesty declared his intention to Lord North of never addressing himself to Lord Chatham but through his ostensible minister, adding, "No advantage to the country, nor personal danger to myself, can ever make me address myself to Lord Chatham, or to any other branch of opposition. Honestly, I would rather lose the crown I now wear than bear the ignominy of possessing it under their shackles. . . . You have full power to act, but I do not expect Lord Chatham and his crew will come to your assistance." *

Upon the 7th of April, 1778, Lord Chatham entered the House of Peers, supported on one side by his son, William Pitt, and on the other side by his son-in-law, Lord Mahon. He wore, as was his

* Life of C. J. Fox. Lord John Russell. Vol. i., p. 180.

custom, a rich velvet coat; his legs were swathed in flannel; his wig was so large, and his face so emaciated, that none of his features could be discerned except the high curve of his nose, and his eyes, which still retained a gleam of their old fire. When the Duke of Richmond had spoken, Chatham rose. The stillness was so deep that the dropping of a handkerchief could have been heard.*

"I feel an indignation," said he, in the course of his speech, "at the idea that has gone forth of yielding up the sovereignty of America. I rejoice that the grave has not yet closed upon me, that I am still alive to lift my voice against the dismemberment of this most ancient and noble empire. While I have sense and memory I will never consent to deprive the royal House of Brunswick of its fairest inheritance! Shall a nation that seventeen years ago was the terror of the world now stoop so low as to cry out, 'Take all we have, only give us peace?' It is impossible! I trust the resources of this kingdom are still sufficient to maintain its just rights. But any state is better

* Macaulay's Essays. Life of William Pitt.

than despair. Let us make a vigorous effort, and, if we must fall, let us fall like men."*

The Duke of Richmond replied. (Macaulay bears witness to the Duke's speech being one of great tenderness and courtesy towards Lord Chatham. Lord Camden also attests the "candour, courtesy, and liberal treatment of his Grace towards his illustrious adversary.") In the course of his speech the Duke said: "When Lord Chatham conducted our victorious arms, it was Great Britain and America against France and Spain... It will now be France, Spain, and America, against Great Britain. . . ." During that speech, Lord Chatham was evidently restless and irritable.

The Duke of Richmond sat down. Lord Chat-

* Political Journal, 1780. See Index, under "Chatham." Lord John Russell gives the following different version (in his Life of C. J. Fox) of this part of Lord Chatham's speech to that above rendered:—"My Lords,—His Majesty succeeded to an empire as great in its extent as its reputation was unsullied. . . . Shall we tarnish the lustre of that empire by an ignominious surrender of its rights? Shall we now fall prostrate before the House of Bourbon? . . . Surely, my Lords, this nation is no longer what it was. Shall a people that, seventeen years ago, was the terror of the world, now stoop so low as to tell its ancient inveterate enemy: 'Take all we have, only give us peace!' . . . In God's name, if it be absolutely necessary to declare either for peace or war, and peace cannot be preserved with honour, why is not war commenced without hesitation? . . ."

ham stood up again. He tried to speak, but could not, articulately. He looked round upon the assembly; pressed his hand upon his breast, and fell back upon the seat from which he had just risen, to all appearance in the agonies of death. Three or four lords who were near him caught him in his fall. The whole house was in confusion; peers running hither and thither—friends and foes—to fetch help. Party spirit was forgotten for a moment; rival political chiefs were united by one common sympathy. The House of Lords was awe-stricken by the entrance there of the King of Terrors. The senseless form of William Pitt, Earl of Chatham, was removed from the senate, and from that moment his peers saw him no more. The House broke up in confusion; for the next few hours the American Rebellion, and the question of peace or war with France, yielded in interest to that of the fate of Lord Chatham.

By easy stages he was conveyed back to Hayes, his favourite residence. For a few weeks he lingered there, paralyzed and helpless; his once mighty intellect obscured, or only lighting up from time to time with a flickering consciousness of the affection manifested by his children towards him, and of the devoted attendance of his wife—the wife whom he had always tenderly loved, and whom, in the meridian of his fame, at the height of his glory, he had called his "dearest life." She had devoted the best part of her life to her illustrious husband; and her widowhood and old age were consecrated to his memory.

Lord Chatham died on the 11th May, 1778.

Voltaire died on the 30th May, 1778. The strife in Paris concerning the burial of Voltaire's body was only beginning, when a dispute arose in London as to the most fitting resting-place for the remains of Lord Chatham.

"The City wants to bury Lord Chatham in St. Paul's," wrote Horace Walpole to the Reverend Mr. Cole, "which, as a person said to me this morning, would literally be robbing Peter to pay Paul. I wish it could be so, that there might be some decoration in that nudity, *en attendant* the re-establishment of various altars."†

The King wrote to one of his ministers: "I am rather surprised at the vote of a public funeral and monument for Lord Chatham; but I trust it is

* Chatham Correspondence, year 1760.

† Walpole's Correspondence, vol. iv., p. 101.

worded as a testimony of gratitude for his rousing the nation at the beginning of the last war, and his conduct as secretary of state; or this compliment, if paid to his general conduct, is rather an offence to me, personally. As to adding a life to the pension, I have no objection."*

The Common Council of the City had petitioned the House of Commons that the corpse of Lord Chatham might be interred at St. Paul's, and Burke supported the petition, on the plea that "St. Paul's was a mere desert, while Westminster Abbey was overstocked." The House of Commons unanimously moved an address to the throne that the body should be buried at the public expense. Even some of the King's courtiers, who were present in the House of Commons, dared not

* This life clause was in fulfilment of a promise made by the King in 1775. When Lord Chatham, having offended the King by his views on the American question (which views were expressed by him, in his speech partly instigated by Dr. Franklin)—the King had said:—"As to any gratitude to be expected from him or his family, the whole tenor of their lives has shown them void of that honourable sentiment. *But when decrepitude or death puts an end to him as a trumpet of sedition, I shall make no difficulty in placing the second son's name, instead of the father's, and making up the pension* £3,000."—Letters of George III. (Lord Brougham). Quoted by Lord John Russell, in Life of C. J. Fox. Vol. i., p. 190.

oppose this motion. "The gracious consent of his royal master to the request of the Commons," was announced to that assembly by Lord North.

Lord Chatham was buried in Westminster Abbey. Upon the day of his burial political rancour was subdued. The civil strife of opinion, then rife, was hushed at sight of his funeral. Those who had differed with Lord Chatham in life were proud to bear his pall. In the Northern transept of Westminster Abbey, Lord Chatham was laid in his tomb.

The Marquis de Villette had enshrined an urn containing Voltaire's heart. The widow of Lord Chatham erected an urn to the memory of her husband.* The memory of Lord Chatham was a

* In the *Political Magazine*, of 1781, it is stated:—"A beautiful marble urn has lately been erected at Burton Pynsent, in memory of the late illustrious Earl of Chatham, executed by Mr. Bacon, of Newman Street, who is now preparing the statue of his lordship for Westminster Abbey, at the expense of Lady Chatham, by whom the following inscription, engraven on the urn, has been written:

Sacred to pure affection,
This simple urn stands a witness of unceasing grief, for him who,
Excelling in whatever is most admirable,
And adding to the exercise of the sublimest virtues
The sweet charms of refined sentiments and polished wit,
By social commerce rendered beyond comparison happy the course of

bond of sympathy amongst Englishmen. The memory of Voltaire was a brand of discord amongst Frenchmen. The Church had excommunicated Voltaire's dead body. The Government of France now forbade his plays to be acted. The people of France revolted against these decrees of Church and State. We have already heard how the lay members of the French Academy declared that, until justice should be rendered by the Church to the memory of Voltaire, not another ecclesiastical service should be performed by the Grey Friars for the repose of the soul of any French Academician. Not content with this decree, the Academicians and others now resolved to deify Voltaire, in the midst of Paris, where he had lately been crowned by the people; and thus to defy both Church and State.

Almost all men of letters on the Continent, in the

Domestic life, and bestowed a
Felicity inexpressible on her whose faithful
Love was blessed in a pure return that raised her
Above every other joy but the paternal one, and that
Still shared with him.
His generous country, with public monuments,
Has eternised his fame.
This humble tribute is to soothe the sorrowing
Breast of private woe.
To the dear memory of William Pitt, Earl of Chatham,
This marble is inscribed by Hester, his
Beloved wife, 1781.

eighteenth century, were Freemasons. Freemasonry had been the bond of union among them, and had afforded them means of communication, as also of giving publicity to their opinions, when men of letters ("philosophers") were exiled from France, because suspected of heresy to the Church, before the expulsion of the Jesuits, in the reign of Louis XV.

Frederick of Prussia was a Freemason; his court had formerly (when intolerance reigned supreme in France) been the refuge for proscribed philosophers, whose pens and animosity against their mother country (which had cast them out), the protestant King used to his own political advantage. The late Pope, "Benedict the accomplished," had tried to suppress Freemasonry, but in vain. It flourished in exact proportion to the bigotry of an exclusive creed, which permitted no teaching but its own, and which condemned any other communion than its own.

The Freemasons' lodge most in favour with men of letters in Paris, in 1778, was the "*Lodge of the Nine Sisters.*" At this lodge, therefore, it was decided, that the apotheosis of Voltaire should be celebrated. Freemason brethren assembled there on the 28th November. Each brother, upon his arrival, was arrayed in his scarf, and invested with his order, according to the degree he held in Freemasonry; and then entered a large enclosure which the lodge contained, this enclosure being in the form of a circular temple. ("Brother Franklin" was conspicuous upon this occasion.) One hundred and fifty brothers (visitors) were now ushered in with great solemnity; and when these one hundred and fifty brothers entered the enclosure, around which those arrived before formed a circle—a circle of men illustrious in literature, in art, in politics, and in science—an invisible orchestra played a slow march.

When all were seated in deep silence, and no sound was heard but that of solemn music, Brother Cordier de St. Firmin, an Abbé, advanced into the centre of the building, and announced that Voltaire's niece, Madame Denis, and Voltaire's late hostess, the Marquise de Villette, desired admittance. Permission being granted, these ladies entered; one conducted by the Marquis de Villette, who had enshrined Voltaire's heart, and the other by the Marquis de Villeveille, who had signed his name as witness to Voltaire's profession of faith. The ladies were attired in deep mourning; they stood, mournfully, before the assembled brethren, who all rose to receive them. (These brethren presented a brilliant spectacle, what with their cordons of every colour, their diamond stars, and their orders of merit, which were all worn in honour of Voltaire.) The whole assembly, accompanied by Mesdames Denis and de Villette, then filed off through a narrow passage, like the entrance of a tomb, into a vast hall, which was hung all round with black, and lighted only by lamps so arranged and shaded as to produce a sort of twilight, thus increasing the lugubrious effect of the scene. All round the black walls were transparencies containing sentences from the works of Voltaire, in prose and verse: his Thoughts, which seemed here to flame forth in letters of fire. Beyond this vast hall was Voltaire's cenotaph, upon one side of which Madame Denis was seated, and the Marquise de Villette (Voltaire's "Belle et Bonne") upon the other side.

The "Venerable" Brother la Lande, who was a member of the French Academy, now stood forth and read aloud an eloquent discourse in praise of Voltaire. After this discourse was over, another Academician stepped forward and moved all hearts present by a lamentation for the loss of Voltaire;

but, after a moment's pause, the tone of this lamentation changed; from mournful pathos, the speaker suddenly burst into an eloquent declamation, or rather fierce vituperation against the enemies of Voltaire; and when, in the course of this, the orator declared, "If Voltaire's death reduce not his enemies to silence, I do not believe that even a thunderbolt could crush them to it," the unseen music of the orchestra, reverberating on all sides, resembled peals of thunder. During this crash of instruments, the cenotaph disappeared, and in the place where it had been, a large picture uprose, representing the apotheosis, or deification, of Voltaire. This picture did more credit to the enthusiasm of Voltaire's disciples than to their taste for fine art. The matter of it, however, and not its manner, inflamed the minds of all its beholders. Brother Boucher recited a poem which he had composed for the occasion, and which was highly seasoned with aspersions against the clergy. The refusal of the priesthood to bury the body of Voltaire was fiercely satirized, and harshly contrasted with the toleration lately evinced by the priesthood towards the remains of the defunct Cardinal de la Roche Aymon, and the deceased

Abbé Terray (late finance comptroller and favourite of Madame du Barry), the former of whom was designated a "hypocrite," and the latter a "concussionist minister."*

The excitement of the assembly reached to a point of frenzy when, after having roused intense indignation by these odious comparisons, Brother Boncher declared, in solemn tones, that, whether consecrated by the Church or not, "any ground wherein rest the ashes of Voltaire, must be sacred ground," and that "a god might dwell on the earth wherein a great man reposes."†

After the apotheosis of Voltaire, "Brother Franklin" was more popular than ever in Paris, and with him the cause that he represented. His share in the honours rendered to Voltaire was not likely to advance Dr. Franklin in the favour of Louis XVI. (Madame Campan declares that the King even delighted in treating a portrait of Franklin with indignity); but the King was already subservient to the will of the people, and it was only at the instigation of his priests that

* L'Espion Anglais, tome i. Ed. 1809. (Declared contraband in Paris, 1778.) Londres. Also, Mems. de Bachaumont. 1779.

† Appendix I.

he dared to offend his subjects, as in the case of Voltaire's exclusion from Versailles during the last few weeks of his life, and the excommunication of Voltaire in Paris after his death.

But the love of the people for the royal race was not yet dead; a feeling of joy had passed through France when it was announced that the Queen was *enceinte*. She had been reproached for being childless by the fishwomen of Paris when the Comtesse d'Artois gave birth to the Duc d'Angoulême.

According to old custom, these *poissardes* (whose shrill voice was the voice of the people at large) were admitted within the palace upon such occasions; and when another than the Queen brought forth an heir to the throne of France, they murmured loudly against her Majesty, although never had the amiability of Marie Antoinette been more manifest than on that day when she constituted herself the nurse of her sister-in-law, who had thus supplanted her.*

The Queen in her heart had passionately longed for children, as was revealed when her hope, so

* Mems. de la Princesse de Lamballe. Tome i., page 225.

long deferred, was first declared likely to be realized. The Princesse de Lamballe asserts that the joy of the Queen in this hope amounted to ecstasy. "I shall be a mother!" she exclaimed; and then, as if to re-assure herself, the Queen repeated over and over again, in a low soft tone of delight, "I shall be a mother!" Then, unable to contain her joy, her Majesty despatched couriers to her own mother, and to her relatives, and caused the news to be proclaimed throughout France, and announced to the various courts of Europe. At the Queen's happiness the King's aunts (who, in their hearts—if they had any—had hoped that their niece, the Austrian, would have no children) declared themselves much shocked; protesting against such openly-expressed joy, as indecent in a woman, and unbecoming the dignity of a Queen of France.

To Maria Theresa the intelligence was politically welcome. The Queen Empress, who kept her son Joseph II. in strict subjection, regarded all her children, more or less, as her own political tools; and her daughter, the Queen of France, had not yet fulfilled her expectations.

Marie Antoinette was not born to be a politician;

in her friendships, her enmities, her joys, hopes, and fears, she was more woman than Queen. For example: politically and traditionally, as an Austrian princess, she disliked the alliance of France with America; and yet, as a novelty, she had welcomed Dr. Franklin, and had inaugurated the fêtes by which he had been welcomed at Versailles.

Again: the Chevalier d'Éon, who was a thorn in the side of French diplomacy, was to the Queen merely a matter of much amusement. Prodigy and paradox quickly succeeded each other in France in the year of wonders, 1778. The Chevalier d'Éon was both a paradox and a prodigy,* and, therefore, a singular type of his time. In his early youth he had been employed in diplomacy by Louis XV., and, owing to his remarkably effeminate appearance, was enabled to pass, unsuspected, in woman's clothing, whenever and wherever it suited the purpose of his mission. In this disguise the Chevalier d'Éon had acted as reader and *dame de compagnie* to the late Empress of Russia, Elizabeth Petrowna, and thus helped to knit the

* Mémoires du Chevalier d'Éon . . . d'après les Matériaux Authentiques déposés aux Archives des Affaires Etrangères. Bruxelles. 1837.

interests of France and Russia together, while defeating the diplomacy of Sir Hanbury Williams, the English ambassador at St. Petersburg, in the middle of the eighteenth century.

At a subsequent period, the Chevalier d'Éon was sent by Versailles to the Court of London; not as a woman, but as a Frenchman of high rank, who had distinguished himself in various courts of Europe for his diplomacy, and who was also famous for the zeal with which he had defended the honour of his country by his sword. George III. did not like the Chevalier d'Éon, but he was favourably regarded by Queen Charlotte, she having known him in Germany before her marriage with his Britannic Majesty. George III. worked himself up to a paroxysm of displeasure against the Chevalier, which compelled the cabinet of France to recall its envoy. This was in 1773, the year before Louis XV. died. Whatever was the cause of offence, whether personal or political, which the French envoy had given to the King of England, France just then desired peace with England; and, therefore, to soothe his Britannic Majesty, Louis XV. decreed that the Chevalier d'Éon should be condemned to wear woman's clothing for the remainder of his (the Chevalier's) life. The decree was irrevocable, so that the accession of Louis XVI. did not mitigate the fate of the unfortunate diplomatist.

Marie Antoinette, not privy to this state secret, and believing the *Chevalière* d'Éon to be a marvel of woman's wit in diplomacy, expressed a wish that *she* should be presented to her; but M. le Comte de Vergennes, Minister of Foreign Affairs, hearing that her Majesty had expressed such a wish, requested her to grant him a private audience, during which he told the Queen that the wonderful Mademoiselle d'Éon was nothing but a disgraced diplomatist; the Queen, therefore, came out of her cabinet smiling, and declaring that her curiosity was cured for ever.*

At a later date, however, the Queen's curiosity revived. All Paris was talking of the mystery of the Chevalier d'Éon's fate; and even at Versailles, where he was only spoken of as "Mademoiselle d'Éon," wonder and whispers could not be stifled. The Queen confessed to the Princesse de Lamballe, her confidante, how curious she was to see this prodigy. The Princesse de Lamballe declared

* Mems. Campan. Chapitre viii., p. 152.

that she herself was not less curious than her Majesty, and devised the means by which the Queen might catch a glimpse of the Chevalier, "without compromising the royal dignity, or trespassing on the ministerial authority which had forbidden the Chevalier to present himself before her Majesty." (The King's Cabinet had forbidden d'Éon a public reception on the part of the Queen, but the interdict did not extend to the *chance* appearance of the Chevalier before her Majesty.) The doomed diplomatist was, therefore, favoured from an unknown hand with a passport to the chapel of Versailles on the Sunday following this conversation between the Queen and the Princesse de Lamballe.

The Chevalier d'Éon was no longer young. His effeminate exterior had, years since, given place to a more manly aspect; his appearance, therefore, in woman's clothing, was both absurd and horrible. To be admitted to the Chapel Royal of Versailles he was compelled to be in full dress.

"The Sunday following, the Chevalier arrayed himself *en costume*: large hoop; long train; vast robes; sleeves with five rows of lace; immense woman's wig, with powder; very fine lappets;

white gloves; a pretty fan in hand; perfectly shaven; diamond ear-rings and necklace; and giving himself all the coquettish airs of a pretty woman.

"When the Queen appeared he unfortunately was in such haste to see her Majesty, that, in precipitately thrusting himself forward, his wig and head-dress fell off. Much confused, he tried to replace these; which he did hind-side before, and his appearance was so ridiculous that the King, the Queen, and all their suite, had much difficulty in refraining from laughter as they passed him. . . 'As to myself,' says the Princesse de Lamballe, 'I was a long time before I could recover my gravity, and even to-day, as I write, I laugh at the recollection.' . . . What added to the absurdity of the circumstance was, that in the midst of mass some charitable person having drawn the Chevalier aside and re-adjusted his wig, he re-appeared in the chapel as though nothing had happened, carrying the train of his dress over his arm; and, having seated himself in front of the altar, fanned himself *a la coquette*, with imperturbable *sang-froid*.

"The Bishop, who officiated, esteemed himself fortunate in not having a sernon to preach that day, declaring that he would not have been able to have done so with becoming seriousness; and that even as it was, he was only able to go through the service by keeping his eyes constantly fixed upon his mass-book.

"This adventure caused the Chevalier's company to be more eagerly sought than ever, . . but nobody ever knew, except the Queen and myself, that we had been the innocent cause of this comical adventure." *

Although the laughing-stock of others, the Chevalier d'Éon describes his punishment of wearing woman's clothing as the most horrible that could be inflicted on man. He had confidently hoped that, when Louis XV. died, this punishment would be remitted; but the Countess de Guerchy (widow of the French ambassador in London) implored Louis XVI. that such should not be the case. The Chevalier d'Éon and the late Count de

* Mems. de Lamballe. Tome i., p. 244. Ed. Paris, 1826. In the Journal de Paris, March 13, 1778:—" Mademoiselle la Chevalière d'Éon went yesterday to see M. de Voltaire at the house of the Marquis de Villette. Everybody in the house flocked to the passage through which the visitor had to pass, so as to catch a glimpse of this celebrity. Mademoiselle d'Éon, who came by invitation of the philosopher, seemed very bashful: keeping her muff up to her nose, and her eyes cast down to the ground."—Quoted in Mems. Bachaumont.

Guerchy had been bitter enemies; owing to accusations made by the former against the latter, the Count de Guerchy had been disgraced in London, and compelled to resign his post as ambassador. The Count de Guerchy had died in 1767, and his son, then a child, was now a man, thirsting to avenge the wrongs of his father. The Countess de Guerchy dreaded a meeting between her son and the Chevalier d'Éon, the latter being famed for his skill as a duellist; she, therefore, prostrated herself before Louis XVI., and implored him not to revoke the sentence which, compelling the Chevalier to dress as a woman, also forbade him, on penalty of death, from duelling, or in any way proclaiming his real sex. Louis XVI., always undecided, did not know what means to devise that might reconcile the safety of young de Guerchy with the pardon of the Chevalier d'Éon, and, as usual, applied to old Count de Maurepas for advice. Maurepas did not hesitate a moment. "But in truth, sire," said he, "the young Count de Guerchy, the heir of a noble house, and a French gentleman, would incur the charge of infamy in drawing his sword against a woman; and . . . the *Chevalière* d'Éon. . ."

"*Is* a woman," pronounced the King, eagerly seizing the hint; and from that day forth the Countess de Guerchy was satisfied as to her son's safety, and the Chevalier d'Éon was irrevocably doomed.*

Thus condemned, the Chevalier wrote to the Count de Vergennes, in September, 1774, to this effect: ". . . If I must retain a woman's garb, I would desire that such of the public as are not known to me should believe that I am really a woman. . . . Never did man upon this earth make such a sacrifice to the will of his King and country! I do not wish that that which to me is the loss of my whole existence should be considered as a puerile joke for the world to laugh at; that what to me is a horrible tragedy, should be an amusing comedy to my fellow-men; that they should laugh at a harlequin, when they ought to weep over a martyr. . . . How great the physical and moral miseries in which I am clothed with this robe! . . It will be my winding sheet. . . To me it is a habit of everlasting mourning. . . . Let my disguise be honoured as such. . . Were

* Mems. du Chevalier d'Éon. Tome ii., p. 291. Ed. Bruxelles, 1837.

the public once convinced of the fact that I am a disguised man, I am degraded into a popular punchinello, an ambulating masquerader; . . the very children in the streets would hoot at me as the mummer. . . . Were it so to be, not the salvation of any one in this world—not even of my mother—nor the orders of any sovereign, not even the commands of God himself, would make me submit to such humiliation. . . . I prefer, a a hundred times over, death to dishonour, and I would rather go and precipitate myself into some American gulf, there to bury both my sex and my shame, than I would endure such a fate as this."*

In 1778, when the Government of France sanctioned and facilitated the departure of Frenchmen for America, the Chevalier d'Éon implored the King and his ministers to permit him to go to the New World, there to fight against England, the king of which country he regarded as the origin of all his misery.

The French Government, however, did not desire that, by the Chevalier's re-appearance in his own sex and character, a slur should be cast upon

* Ibid, p. 295. Tome ii.

the justice and humanity of Versailles just at this time, when the people began loudly to criticize the conduct of their rulers; neither was it deemed wise that the Cabinet of France should lay itself open just then to the imputation of having broken faith with the Cabinet of London in the matter of the Chevalier d'Éon.

The Chevalier wrote a most pathetic appeal to the Count de Maurepas on the 8th of February, 1778, again imploring permission to resume his military career in the New World.*

This permission not being granted, and his last hope thus giving way under him, the Chevalier became desperate and litigious. He instituted a lawsuit to recover a sum of money owing to him by Beaumarchais (the author of "Figaro," and the agent of the French Government in American affairs); and he wrote to several ladies of the court various letters, which revealed how the family of the Count de Guerchy had been preferred to himself, "a faithful subject, who for many years had served the interests of France well in camp and cabinet." It was in March, 1779, that d'Éon wrote these letters, and the consequence was, that

* Mems. de Bachaumont. Ed. 1788.

he was exiled to Tonnerre, where he had an estate, which henceforth became his prison.

Prince Henry, the brother of Frederick of Prussia, went to visit him there.*

It was impossible for the Government of France to prevent the truth concerning the Chevalier d'Éon from oozing out, and this truth distilled bitterness in Paris against the supposed tyranny of Versailles, andg ave rise to scandalous stories and gross caricatures of monarchy in England.

But even the reputed cause of the jealousy of the King of England against the Chevalier, gross as these caricatures assumed it to be, and striking at the roots of royal domestic happiness at St. James's, was, in its irreverence and assumption, equalled by the scandalous tales which England now fostered against France and Frenchmen. War between the two countries had already roused the passions and blinded the judgment of men on both sides of the Channel.

In the *Political Magazine* of 1780, an awful account of French morals and manners is published, the author of which shrinks not even to attack the memory of the late Cardinal de Fleury, who was re-

* The Chevalier d'Éon died in London, in 1810, aged 83.

garded by the pious in France as a departed saint.

The "Rev. Mr. Cole," also, (Horace Walpole's correspondent) seems to have made it his especial business to rake together every book and paper that could make the cause and character of England and Englishmen good, by proving the cause and character of France and Frenchmen bad.*

(To that time of war and bloodshed in both hemispheres the words of the present Emperor of the French seem peculiarly applicable: "If the two people—French and English—misunderstand each other so much, it is because they know each other so little.")†

The Rev. Mr. Cole was a curious correspondent for Horace Walpole; that Cambridge divine being hardly less of a bigot to his idea of Church and State in England than Archbishop Beaumont of Paris was to Church and State in France.

The philosopher of Strawberry Hill declares (to Mr. Cole), "As to orthodoxy, excuse me if I think it means nothing at all but every man's own opinion."‡

Gout, and a *gout* for old MSS., were the common

* Cole MSS. Mus. Brit.

† Idées Napoléoniennes. Tome i., p. 123. Ed. 1834.

‡ Walpole Correspondence, vol. iv., p. 267. Ed. 1820.

sympathies between Horace Walpole and the Rev. Mr. Cole. "Whatever MSS. you lend me," writes Walpole to Cole, "I shall be very grateful for; they entertain me exceedingly, and I promise you we will not have a shadow of an argument about them. I do not love disputation even with those most indifferent to me. I know the sincerity and disinterested goodness of your heart. . . . Nevertheless, the destruction that violent arbitrary principles have drawn on this blinded country has moved my indignation."

The Rev. Mr. Cole had done much to foment these principles. He had been wrathful because "the University of Cambridge had long been divided into parties on account of the articles of Religion;" and now ("a scandal to be spoken") he declares, "All the Regius Professors, and He of Modern History (though lately preferred by the King and the Bishop of Peterborough), Masters of Peter house, Beret, Pembroke, Magdalen, and Sidney, with the Chancellor at their Head, are against any loyal Address to the King to enforce the Laws against the Rebels in America. Fanaticism and Faction were always steady Friends."†

* Ibid. Vol. iv., p. 96.

† Cole MSS., Mus. Brit.

In 1775, the Rev. Mr. Cole had corroborated, in a memorial (on the address of the University and petition of the town of Cambridge) that—

"The Duke of Grafton's behaviour, in turning now the second time against an indulgent master, in his utmost distress, must in time make his character pretty well known, before detested by all sober men. . . . When the bedel went to him, to wait on him with the address, and to beg his presenting it, he told him, 'He wondered the University could expect it at his hands, and informed him, that he had no accommodation for him at his house.' His friends say, in excuse for his brutality, that his (the bedel's) coming late on a Sunday night, when the Duke was ill, and had taken physic, was a reason of his peevishness. . . ' " (The address was presented by six bishops.) . . . "The Riffe Raffe," continues his reverence, "of the town of Cambridge had been long infatuated with republican principles, therefore no address was likely to come from that quarter; so that the Mayor and Alderman Turnell easily collected a number of hands to favour rebellion; and though only two of the aldermen signed the paper, yet I can easily account for no address from the ten aldermen, &c. . . . .

when two of them, Purchas and Finch, never come to church, but always from the Cradle were Presbyterians."

The Rev. Mr. Cole then separately names each individual in Cambridge who refused to sign against the rebellion in America, or who was suspected of signing reluctantly. Amongst these, "Dr. Cooke, *Provost of King's*, would naturally have been against it, but, with his twenty-one children, and lately disappointed of the Deanery of Rochester, yet, in hope of some other soon, dared not show his disaffection, till he is well seated in some good preferment, and then he will show his ingratitude, as more agreeable to his natural disposition." *

* The Reverend Mr. Cole, hoping to warn his royal master against seditious subjects at home, takes the pains of affixing to 160 signatures of self-called "Rational Burgesses, Bailiffs, and principal inhabitants of the town of Cambridge," who, in their address, presumed, "whilst pitying the infatuation of our brethren in your Majesty's American Colonies, to rely that every method would be pursued, consistent with the dignity of government and the preservation of the constitution, to prevent as much as possible the effusion of blood"—a MS. note which shows up, more or less, each of these "Rational Burgesses" to be of a bad, seditious, unorthodox, or unfortunate character. For example:—

"John Jebb, M.A., is a violent man against the 39 articles; Francis Turnell, Alderman, is a peevish, discontented man, a cook of Christ's College, and a Raw Timber-Merchant. R. Edwards,

The Rev. Mr. Cole was a scholar of repute, and a sensible man, yet party spirit blinded him to the absurdity of these statements against his own countrymen who differed with him in political opinion. From these absurdities, the animadversions of the Rev. Mr. Cole may be guessed, as regarded the French, whom he now virulently regarded as the "enemies of the human race."

The Roman Catholics in England were favourably regarded by Mr. Cole and his school, inasmuch as they had expressed their sympathy with the Crown of Great Britain upon the American question, as opposed to France, in an address to the King, which was signed by all the first names of the Roman Catholic nobility in England. This address declares, "In a time of public danger, when your Majesty's subjects can have but one interest, and ought to have but one wish and one sentiment, we humbly hope it will not be deemed improper to assure your Majesty of our unreserved affection to your government, or of our unalterable attachment to the cause and welfare of this, our common country, and of our utter detestation of the designs and

(common-councilman), a Butcher, Broker. John Anderson is a Miller, Baker, and Warm Republican. And (worst of all), William Hollick is—a 'Dissenter.'"

views of any foreign power against the dignity of your Majesty's crown, and the safety and tranquillity of your Majesty's subjects. *

Both in France and England it was a time of change and turmoil. In either country old links were being broken, and new ones formed. Roman Catholics in France were yearning with sympathy towards heretics and insurgents in America; Roman Catholics in England, although excluded by English law from many of the benefits of the English constitution, were giving in their adhesion to the head of the Protestant faith in England.

Frederick of Prussia, though naturally allied by blood, Protestantism, and treaties with England, viewed the movement of France in favour of America with more favour than he regarded the hostile attitude of England against America.

There was no longer any question between peace and war. In May 1778, just before Voltaire's death, Madame la Maréchale de Luxembourg had deplored to that philosopher, that England and France, misunderstanding each other and their own relative interests, should thus once more fill the world with fire and blood. "Is there no way,"

* Appendix K.

Madame de Luxembourg asked Voltaire, "of stopping this? Is the time gone by for a good, sound treaty of peace between France and England?"

Marshal Broglio was present at this conversation. Voltaire answered the lady's question by laying his hand on Marshal Broglio's sword, while he said, "That, Madame, is the only pen with which a treaty between France and England can now be signed. . . *In another century these two great nations may write treaties with ink, and not with blood.*" *

The alliance of Spain was now confidently spoken of in France and America—thus verifying the Duke of Richmond's prediction, that, contrary to what it was in the last war, when England and America fought against France, England would now have to defend herself against France, Spain, and America united. Frederick of Prussia, although he did not take an active part with France and Spain against England, acceded to the maritime treaty of neutrality which was concluded between Russia and other neutral powers, to insure the protection of their flags and merchant ships by the belligerents. † By this means, it was declared,

* Mems. Contemporains, 1778. Tome xi., p. 65. Ed. 1780.

† Les Conseils du Trone. Tome ii., p. 151. Paris, 1828.

King Frederick gave a new and very just sanction to a principle of the rights of the people, forbidding, in consequence, all hostility against merchant ships, &c., by limiting it strictly to armed men.

Frederick resisted all overtures of England, possibly because "he had not a high idea of a King who has not the twentieth part of his subjects under arms;"* and certainly because he was just then (1778,) engaged in that which was likely to light up the fierce flame of war throughout Germany. His movements puzzled politicians of more than one country.

The Count de Salgas wrote from Switzerland to General Haldimand, the Governor of Canada: "If the news retailed at Geneva concerning the movements of the King of Prussia be true, I do not understand his designs; for upon what ground can he begin a war with the Emperor of Austria, whereby to sustain the pretensions of Bavaria, which do not concern him?"†

The people of France, however, gave credit to the King of Prussia for vindicating the rights of the people in Europe, of which rights the people

* Ibid. Tome i., p. 312.

† MS., Mus. Brit., Haldimand Papers.

of France had traditionally regarded Austria as the oppressor. Frederick had warned the Emperor Joseph II., brother of the Queen of France, that if ever he attempted to gain the upper hand over the princes of Germany, he might expect a vigorous resistance."

Thus, even though the King of France had signed an alliance with America, and the King of Prussia had not, the latter was still regarded as the more liberal monarch of the two; especially by Frenchmen, who could not forgive either the King of France, or the priests of France, for their aversion to Voltaire, for the memory of whom the Protestant king professed to share the French people's idolatry.

The Pope's nunzio in France had offered an immense sum of money in behalf of his Holiness, to buy up Voltaire's commentary on the Bible. But it was too late to stifle Voltaire's heresies. The voice of the people was already declared, in France, to be the voice of God. In June, 1778, Horace Walpole again wrote to his intolerant correspondent, the Reverend Mr. Cole: "I will not dispute with you, dear sir, on patriots and politics. One point is past controversy—that the ministers have ruined this country; and if the Church of England's satisfied with being reconciled to the Church of Rome, and thinks it a compensation for the loss of America, and all credit in Europe, she is as silly an old woman as any granny in an alm's-house. France is very glad that we are grown such fools, and soon saw that the Presbyterian Dr. Franklin had more sense than all our ministers together. She has got over all her prejudices, has expelled the Jesuits, and made the Protestant Swiss, Necker, her Comptroller-General. It is a little woeful that we are relapsing into the nonsense the rest of Europe is shaking off."*

Necker was at this time popular in France. He compelled certain rich benefices to defray the charge of certain public institutions, according to ancient law, which the Church had infringed upon at the cost of the State. Necker's own wealth, backed up by State power, had ameliorated the condition of public hospitals, and provided fitting

* The Bull for the general suppression of the Jesuits is dated 1773 (France having taken the initiative in the expulsion of the Jesuits years previously, under the administration of the Duc de Choiseul).—Lettres du Pape Clement XIV. (Ganganelli). Tome ii., p. 182 to p. 212. Amsterdam, 1776.

shelters for the sick and poor. By restricting the infringements of the Church upon the State, he had developed resources for the latter to the amount of 300,000 livres a year, which might now be used in aid of the cause of liberty in America.*

It was humiliating enough for Louis XVI., the "eldest son" of the Church of Rome, thus to submit to the dictation of his Protestant minister; and

* Liberty and America were synonymous to Frenchmen in 1778 — witness the following ironical "Address to our Brothers of Boston," which went the round of Paris at that time:—

"Parlez donc, Messieurs de Boston,
Se peut-il qu'an siecle où nous sommes,
Du monde troublant l'unisson,
Vous vous donniez les airs d'être hommes.

Raissonnons un peu, je vous prie;
Quel droit avez-vous, plus que nous,
A cette liberté chérie
Dont vous paroissez si jaloux?

D'un pied léger la Tyrannie
Vole, parcourant l'univers;
Ce monstre, sous des noms divers,
Ecrase l'Europe asservie.

Et vous, peuple injuste et mutin,
Sans Pape, sans Rois, sans Reines,
Vous danseriez au bruit des chaines
Qui pesent sur le genre humain.

Et vous, d'un si bel équilibre
Dérangeant le plan régulier,
Seuls auriez le front d'être libre
A la barbe du monde entier."

scarcely less so for the Austrian Queen of France to have her expenditure limited by the Swiss Comptroller.

But the Queen did not pause to philosophize upon the stern law of necessity. Happy in her hopes of becoming a mother, and forbidden, in consequence of those hopes, to amuse herself out-of-doors, her Majesty beguiled the time by play. She soon lost such heaps of Louis-d'or at games of chance, that his financial advisers presumed to remonstrate with the King, although his Majesty, as a husband about to become a father, feared to interfere with the Queen's pleasures. Louis XVI. rightly conjectured that this passion for gambling was but temporary, on the part of Marie Antoinette, although the rumour of it gave offence in Paris, where it lately had become known that Louis XV. had anticipated the resources of his kingdom by 180 millions, great part of which treasure had been squandered on his own pleasures.*

The Empress of Russia, when she bid for French popularity, knew better how to employ her wealth than did the Queen of France, who desired the love of her subjects beyond everything, save an heir to the throne of France.

* Notes des Reçeveurs Généraux. MSS. Bib. Imp., and Mus. Brit.

The Empress Catharine, declared by Frederick of Prussia to be greater than Semiramis, sent to Madame Denis, Voltaire's niece and his universal legatee, 150,000 pounds, wherewith to purchase Voltaire's library of 6,210 volumes, her Imperial Majesty voluntarily allowing Madame Denis to retain copies of any works or MSS. that she pleased. The Empress Catharine, moreover, sent a magnificent present of furs to Madame Denis, and a letter full of devotion to the memory of Voltaire. Not content with this, the Russian potentate caused an exact plan of the château of Ferney to be taken, so that she might have an abode erected in her own dominions on the same model; while she ordered a monument to the memory of Voltaire in Russia, to which all her subjects might make a pilgrimage.

In comparison with these decrees of a Russian *autocrate*, those of the King of France appeared tyrannical; as in France Voltaire's plays were forbidden to be acted, or his works to be sold, his body to be buried, or his heart (possessed by M. de Villette) to be consecrated.*

* Afterwards was published in Paris the following extract from the Burial Register of the Royal Abbey of Our Lady of Scellières, in the diocese of Troyes:—"Upon this day, the

These prohibitions of Versailles caused Paris to murmur against tyranny at home, although Government was making active preparations for co-operation in the war for liberty in America.

French soldiers were now armed. French ships were now manned. The provinces, the cities, the ports of France were alive with preparations. French ships had already sailed across the Atlantic, carrying men, and arms, and treasure.

As Lord Carlisle wrote to M. de Lafayette, in October, 1778: "Now, I think that all national disputes will be best decided when Admiral Byron and the Count d'Estaing encounter each other."*

2nd of June, 1778, has been buried in this church, Messire François Marie Arouet de Voltaire, gentleman-in-ordinary of the late King's Chamber; one of the 40 members of the Academy; aged about eighty-four years; deceased in Paris the 30th of May last, presented to our church yesterday, where he is consigned until, conformably with his last wish, he may be transferred to Ferney, to the place which he selected for his burial." (It is observable, as a matter of retribution, that these honours of Gentleman of the King's Chamber, &c., &c., were originally bestowed on Voltaire through the patronage of Madame de Pompadour, to whom he was afterwards treacherous. He himself tells us in his Mémoires that he owed these things to her dishonour, from which "I concluded that to make the least fortune, four words to the King's mistress were more profitable than writing a hundred volumes."

* Correspondance de M. de Lafayette, tome i., p. 169.

The most lively friendship had grown up between General Washington and the young Marquis de Lafayette. The enthusiastic Frenchman, who had left his country, his friends, his bride, and the most brilliant court in Europe, to fight for liberty, declares that the first moment when he saw Washington he knew, and felt, that he was the man of whom he had dreamed, whose cause was henceforth to be his own—the hero of his imagination in flesh and blood before him.

It was at a public dinner, where a number of members of Congress were present, that Lafayette first saw Washington. He immediately singled him out, he said, from the officers who surrounded him, by his commanding air and person. When the party was breaking up, Washington took Lafayette aside, complimented him, in a gracious manner, on his disinterested zeal and the generosity of his conduct, and invited him to make his head-quarters his home. "I cannot promise you the luxuries of a court," said he; "but as you have become an American soldier, you will, doubtless, accommodate yourself to the fare of an American army."*

* Washington Irving's Life of Washington, vol. iii., p. 816.

And hard fare that was, to judge from the account of a French priest (who went out to administer to the sick and wounded), who thus describes the appearance of the American troops :*

"The American troops have no regular uniform, with the exception of the officers and the artillery corps. Several of the regiments have white overcoats trimmed with fringe, and linen trousers, which are large and easy, so as not to incommode them, nor to chafe their limbs in the long marches under the burning heats. Their nourishment is less substantial than ours, and they have less vigorous constitutions; but, thanks to their clothing, they bear the fatigue of marching better. In France" (and here the Abbé's observations may be worthy of English attention)—"In France, too much is sacrificed in our armies to the *coup d'œil. It has been forgotten that troops are made to fight, and not for show.* In some of the American regiments are negroes, but these black men are always commanded by whites. The discipline is very severe; the power of the officers

* Nouveau Voyage dans l'Amérique Septentrionale. Par M. l'Abbé Robin. Imprimé par Moulard, Imprimeur Libraire de la Reine, de Madame, et de Madame la Comtesse d'Artois, 1782. Copy preserved in the library of Sir Joseph Bankes.

over the soldiers is very extended. Castigation is inflicted for light faults. I myself, in company with some French officers, have been witness of rigorous punishment incurred by an American soldier for a slight breach of discipline. The culprit was bound to a cannon wheel; his shoulders were naked; his arms were extended in front of him, so as to give tight tension to the muscles. Each soldier in the company was, one after another, compelled to strike the culprit with a huge stick. The culprit was soon streaming with blood—inundated. But not a shiver of his frame, not a sigh, not the slightest sign of suffering, did he manifest. (This was not a peculiar instance. I have noticed it in other cases.) Is it courage? Is it that the bodily frame is less sensitive in men braced by the air of forests?

"The use of tea and milk," declares the reverend Abbé, "prodigiously enervates the fibres."

The Roman Catholic priest, from whom the above is quoted, is as enthusiastic as the young Marquis de Lafayette, in favour of George Washington.

"I have seen Washington!" cries the Romish priest. "I have seen that man, the soul, the support of one of the greatest revolutions which ever happened. I have observed him with that attention which the sight of great men inspires: it seems as though one believes that in their features mnst be seen traces of the genius which distinguishes them above their fellow-men. Washington, more than any man I ever saw, is made to encourage this opinion; tall in stature, noble, well-proportioned, of an open countenance, gentle, tranquil, of a simple and modest exterior, he attracts and interests Frenchmen, Americans, and even his enemies. Placed at the head of a nation where the climate and habits of life give little energy, Washington has, like Peter the Great, led his troops to victory through defeats; like Fabius, but with fewer resources, and greater obstacles, he has conquered without fighting, and saved his country. Old men, women, and children flock upon his path with equal alacrity, and congratulate themselves for having seen him; he is followed in the cities with torches; his arrival from place to place is celebrated by public illuminations. Americans, that cold people, who, in the midst of their troubles, have never followed but the impulse of methodical reasoning, are animated, inflamed, for him, and the first songs which sentiment has dictated to them have been to celebrate George Washington."

Nevertheless, when, in September, 1777, Washington had lost the battle of Brandywine, and Philadelphia was conquered by the English, the Congress was cold towards him, his troops were depressed, and his enemies decried him. This battle of Brandywine was the first affair in which Lafayette took an active part.

We have elsewhere seen how, when Lafayette arrived in America, he had sent this message to the Assembly: "After my sacrifices, I have the right to demand two favours: the one is to serve at my own expense, the other is to begin my service in America as a volunteer." We have also seen how the Assembly unanimously conferred upon Lafayette a command in the American army.

At Brandywine, Lafayette was shot in the leg by a ball, whilst rallying his troops.

During six weeks of intense suffering, he dreamed only of diversions against England, in Canada, in the Floridas, the Antilles, and the East Indies. Lafayette corresponded with French Ministers on these schemes. In December, 1777, he wrote the following letter to the Duc d'Ayen, one of his relatives (of the family of de Noailles):

"At the camp of Golphe, in Pennsylvania.

". . . .When I joined the army in the month of August, I was astonished not to find enemies. After some marches in Jersey, where nothing occurred, we heard that General Howe had embarked at New York. . . . General Washington went before them, and after having taken several positions, he determined to await the English at the stream of Brandywine, upon some very good heights. On the 11th of September the English came to attack us; and whilst they amused us by their cannon, and many movements in face of us, they caused the greater part of their forces, with all the picked troops of the army, to file off, and all the grenadiers commanded by General Howe himself and Lord Cornwallis, to pass a ford four miles upon our right. As soon as General Washington observed this movement, he detached the whole of his right wing to go before them. Some cursed advices, which had all the appearance of truth, and which contradicted the first reports, caused Washington's detachment to stop a long time in its march, and when it arrived the enemy had passed. Then it was necessary to combat in open plain against troops superior in number. After having sustained for some time a very lively fire, and killed many English, the Americans yielded. A part was rallied and brought back; it was then that I was wounded. To cut the matter short, all went badly on all sides, and General Washington was beaten. . . . When my wound, after six weeks, permitted me to join the army, I found it fifteen miles off from Philadelphia; reinforcements from the North had arrived; General Howe's communications were interrupted by two forts, one on the side of Jersey, the other on the little Isle of Mud. . . . These two forts sustained for a long time all the efforts of the English by land and by sea. . . . Two young Frenchmen, who served as engineers, acquired much glory—these were MM. de Ferney, of the regiment of Rouergue, and Manduit-Duplessis, who commanded the artillery there; the latter is an officer of French artillery. Some Hessians, commanded by Count Donop, attacked the fort where Manduit was, and were repulsed with considerable loss. Count Donop was taken mortally wounded. These forts, after making a vigorous resistance, were evacuated. Lord Cornwallis then passed into Jersey with 5,000 men. . . . An equal number of our troops were there, under one of our majors-general.

"Being still but a volunteer, I wandered there, and finding myself by chance with a detachment which was near the enemy, the good conduct of my soldiers justified an imprudent attack. We were told that *Milord* Cornwallis was wounded there. He then repassed the river, and we did so likewise."

"America," declares Lafayette in 1777, "awaits with impatience that we declare ourselves for her, and one day I hope France will determine to humiliate proud England. This consideration, and the steps that America seems to me decided on taking, give me great hopes of the glorious establishment of independence. I do not see ourselves so strong as I had expected, but we are able to fight; we shall do so, I hope, with some success; and with the help of France, we shall gain, with cost, the cause that I cherish, because it is just, because it honours humanity, because it interests my country, and because my American friends and myself are strongly engaged in it in advance.

. . . It is said that England sends us Hanoverians. Some time ago (much worse) Russians were announced to us! A little threat of France will diminish the number of these supplies. The nearer I see the English, the more I perceive that it is essential to speak to them loudly."

To his wife Lafayette wrote on the 6th of January, 1778:*

"At the Camp, near Valley Forge.

"What a date, my dear heart, and what a country to write in, the month of January! It is in a Camp; it is in the midst of woods. It is at 1500 leagues from thee that I find myself enchained in the midst of winter! . . . . . . Thou wilt have received the letter which I sent to thee when I heard of thy *accouchement*. Dear heart! how happy that event has made me! . . . What pleasure shall I have in embracing my two poor little girls, and in asking pardon of their mother! Thou wilt learn by the bearer of this letter that my health is very good, that my wound is cured, and that the change of country does not affect me. Dost thou not think

* Correspondance et MSS. du Général Lafayette. Publiés par sa famille, Bruxelles, 1837.

that after my return we shall be great enough to establish ourselves in our own house, to live there happily together, to receive our friends there, to establish there a sweet liberty, and to read in the newspapers there of foreign countries, without having the curiosity to go and see what passes in those countries? I love to build castles in France of happiness . . . ."*

At the beginning of 1778, Lafayette was sent into Canada with the title of "General of the Northern Army," but his operation there failed for want of men, time, and money. The news of that failure stung France anew to revenge her past Canadian losses. On the 1st of September, 1778, Lafayette wrote to Washington a letter, from which the following extracts are taken, as showing how France at last had begun to manifest herself openly for America:—

* It is possible that the expected arrival of Mrs. Washington at the camp stimulated Lafayette's new year's remembrance of his own wife. "In the month of February, 1778, Mrs. Washington rejoined the General at Valley Forge, and took up her residence at head-quarters. The arrangements consequent to her arrival bespeak the simplicity of style in this rude encampment. 'The General's apartment is very small,' writes she to a friend; 'he has a log cabin built to dine in, which has made our quarters more tolerable than they were at first.'"

"Tyvertown.

"Sea-sick Frenchmen have arrived at Boston. .... All will go well now, provided the Count d'Estaing be promptly in a condition to spread sail. All the resources which the Continent supplies ought, I think, to be employed for the acceleration of that moment. Sails, masts, biscuit, water, and provisions are necessary.... I am eager to regain superiority, or at least equality with the English upon the American seas.... I sigh for the moment when I shall find myself again with you; and the pleasure of acting under your immediate orders, with the French fleet, will be the greatest that I could possibly experience. All will then go well. The Count d'Estaing, if Rhode Island is yet to be taken, which I ardently hope, would be glad to secure that prize in concert with General Washington, and that will cut short all difficulties.

"Congratulate me, my dear General, I shall have your portrait; Mr. Hancock has promised me a copy of that he has at Boston. He has given one to the Count d'Estaing; and I never saw a man more pleased in possessing the portrait of his mistress than the Admiral appeared on receiving yours, "LAFAYETTE."

Let us now see what were the antecedents of this Count d'Estaing, concerning whom Lord Carlisle had written, "Now I think all national disputes will be best decided when Admiral Byron and the Count d Estaing encounter each other."

END OF VOL. I.

CPSIA information can be obtained
at www.ICGtesting.com
Printed in the USA
LVHW100435110522
718424LV00003B/132

9 783375 007157